The Author's

Carrie Duggan

To the lovely Antelope
peeps!

" Reading gives us a place
to go when you have to stay
where you are!"

Love you all!

Love

Duggan

For Pam-Gran

1924 - 2020

A Labyrinth of Stories

Penny Figment floats aimlessly into the depths of
The Author's Library. She walks very closely to the
bookshelves, running her fingers across the spines of
all the books that have been chaotically organised
and stacked haphazardly. With a cup of tea in one
hand, she follows the direction of the bookshelves,
wherever they may lead.

Penny has no idea where she's going. She's always
getting lost in her own bookshop and she's lived
above it, all her life. However, she loves the way the
bookcases are so tall that they loom over and protect
her, like ancient trees in a forest. There are endless
journeys, that can take you anywhere; it's a labyrinth
made up of books and curiosity. With long
passageways that seem never-ending and books to
your left and right. Armchairs are scattered
throughout and usually next to the windows that
show the rolling hills and forest for miles beyond.

The moment Penny takes a book off the shelf and
opens it to the front page, she's engulfed in the story.
She's suddenly transported from the simple life she
lives to an entire new world, free for her to explore.
Some stories are brand new and then there are the
old favourites. There are tales of romance and
adventure, of mystery and obscurity. Penny knows
that she can leave the world behind just by turning
the page and reading the words that someone else

3

has written. The Author's Library is a bookshop that has sold thousands of books in its lifetime. No two tales are the same.

This morning, Penny decides to read *The Princess Bride,* an hour before opening up the bookshop. She sits cross-legged on the floor, places a cup of tea beside her and adjusts her glasses. Even though she owns hundreds of books in her flat above the bookshop, there are still so many stories for her to discover.

But an hour and a half later, she's completely lost in the book. When Penny looks up at the time, she shrieks and scrambles onto her feet.

'Shit!' she thinks, as she quickly hides *The Princess Bride* behind a stack of hardbacks. 'I'm late.'

While accidentally spilling her tea which has gone cold, and tripping over her own feet, Penny sprints to the front of the shop. When she unlocks for the day ahead, she breathes a sigh of relief and slowly wanders back into its depths.

No one comes for the first hour, but that doesn't bother Penny. Usually, she wishes she could hide in the pages of her favourite books and stay there, for as long as possible. Besides, Penny has gotten used to being alone in her bookshop, for almost two years.

She decides to organise the fantasy books on the top shelf. Penny, a short and nimble young woman, begins to climb up the bookshelves.

'If I could fly…' Penny begins to think, as she

scuttles across the bookcase, 'I would love to have a pair of phoenix wings and soar over my bookshop. Then, I could reach the top shelves, much easier…'

'What a peculiar place to find you, Miss Figment,' a familiar voice calls out.

'Huh?' Almost letting go of the bookcase in shock, Penny clings on for dear life. She breathes a sigh of relief, when she looks down and sees Mr. Marblelight, a regular customer. He's smiling up at her and Penny smiles back at him, as she slowly descends to the floor.

Mr. Marblelight always comes to The Author's Library and Penny's known him all her life. His beard, eyebrows and eyelashes are the colour of snow and they stand out against the brightly coloured suits he wears. His blue eyes twinkle behind hexagon-shaped glasses.

'How do you manage to climb up your bookshelves?' he asks her, brushing the dust of his violet suit and his eyes widening in wonderment.

'How else am I meant to reach the top shelf?'

He chuckles. 'Good point. At times like this, you always remind me of Emily.'

'Yeah, she always had the answer…'

'You broke another one!?' Penny cried, when she saw her mum holding two ends of a broken ladder.

'It was an accident,' Emily replied, as she quickly hid it behind the bookcase as if it never existed. 'How was I supposed to know that a ladder doesn't make a good set of

stilts? Shit, I can't get these splinters out. They bloody hurt, could you help me?'

'Fine...' Penny grumbled. She walked over, held her mum's fingers up close and yanked the splinters out.

'Ow!' Emily shrieked.

'It serves you right. This is the second ladder we've broken, this month. We can't afford another. How are we going to reach the top shelves?'

'We'll figure something out,' Emily said, softly. 'There's always an answer to our problems...'

'Excuse me?' said an old woman who was looking up at the top shelves. 'I want to buy that copy of Homer's Odyssey. I just can't seem to reach it...'

Emily looked up at the looming bookshelves, then back at her daughter with a wicked grin on her face.

'What are you thinking?' Penny asked.

'Climb onto my shoulders.'

'Why?'

'Don't question it. Just do it'

Emily crouched down and tentatively, Penny climbed on her shoulders. Her heart almost jumped out of her chest, when Emily leapt back onto her feet and lifted Penny into the air.

'Can you reach the top shelves now?' Emily asked.

'I can!' The two of them burst into triumphant laughter.

'I told you, Penny,' Emily said, triumphantly. 'You can find the answer to any problem, if you use your imagination...'

Penny quickly shakes herself back to reality and looks back at Mr. Marblelight.

'Can I help you with anything, today?' she asks.

'I just want to buy this.' He holds up an old copy of *The Lion, The Witch and The Wardrobe* and hands her the exact amount of change. 'I loved reading this series when I was a boy. I remember hiding it in my desk and only reading at night, because my parents never approved. But I'll certainly enjoy it, tonight.'

Mr. Marblelight bows slightly to Penny and she watches him leave.

'He really does remind me of a wizard,' Penny thinks. 'Maybe he was, in a past life...'

Throughout the day, Penny serves a few happy customers and is mostly left alone with her imagination, until she eventually closes up the bookshop. Then, she rushes upstairs to her flat and quickly returns, wearing her pyjamas and wrapped up in a duvet. She sits by her favourite window, which is the largest and amongst the fantasy books. She snuggles into her duvet and watches the sunset, before finishing *The Princess Bride*.

As night-time begins to fall, Penny's eyes start to droop, even though she wants to keep reading. Eventually, her head rolls forward, her nose is buried deep in the pages and then she's gently snoring. The rain falls heavier and the wind crashes against the window. Thunder gently rumbles in the distance and lightning illuminates the bookshop, just for a brief second.

At 11:58pm, the doorbell rings.

Penny jerks awake. She doesn't know if it's her snoring that has woken her up; it wouldn't be the first time. Then she hears the doorbell again, echoing throughout. She tucks her knees underneath her chin, too frightened to move as if any sudden action could result in her tragic death.

'Is there someone at my door, at this time of night?' Penny thinks. 'What if it's a ghost? That wouldn't be surprising; I'm sure my ancestors like to haunt me. Sometimes, I can feel their presence, drifting in-between the bookcases. Who knows…'

When the doorbell rings for a third time, she shrieks with fear.

'Would a… Would a monster… a monster ring the doorbell? Maybe it's a very polite serial killer. Or a scary clown, who's haunted me since birth.'

The doorbell rings for a fourth time. Penny slowly stands up and clutches the duvet around her, as a protective shield. She also grabs *The Princess Bride*, which has now turned into a weapon.

'I'm sure everything's fine. Nothing to worry about,' Penny reminds herself, as she turns left towards the romance novels, before back-tracking to the books that she's pretended to have read. She stops to a dreaded halt when she faces the spooky novels and physiological thrillers.

'They're just spooky stories,' Penny thinks. 'I just have to keep walking. Nothing is out to get me. Everything is fine.'

Even so, she quickly paces in-between the bookcases; she can feel a slight chill creep up on her which makes her shudder and constantly look behind. Hardly anyone buys books from the horror genre and she's been too scared to change anything in case some unknown spirit curses her for life. Even Emily refused to go there and almost convinced Penny that there were monsters hiding under the bookcases.

When Penny is a few feet away from the scary stories, she breathes a sigh of relief. Then, a flash of lightning and thunder makes her jump a foot into the air. She throws her duvet off her shoulders and begins to run aimlessly throughout her bookshop, forgetting why she was wandering around at night in the first place.

She stops when she reaches the front door and then remembers. There's a silhouette of a human figure standing on the other side.

'You're such a fool,' Penny thinks sternly. She marches towards the door but stops as she places her hand on the door-handle.

'There's no serial killer that would want to kill me,' Penny reminds herself. 'No scary clowns and no tormented schoolgirls with telekinetic powers... Yaaahh!'

Penny throws the door open and is hit with the cold wind that smacks her across the face. *The Princess Bride* is raised and ready to attack.

But standing on the other side of the door is a very handsome stranger. He's completely soaked through, shivering and tall enough that he can rest his hands on top of the door frame.

'Can I come in and use your phone?' he asks her.

'Say something,' Penny thinks, her book still raised in her hand. She opens her mouth to speak but she doesn't know what to say. 'For the love of the Gods, say something!'

'Can you help me?'

'Why aren't you saying anything?' she thinks. 'At least lower the paperback.'

'Are you going to help me, or not?'

Penny continues to gawk at him, completely silent.

'Fine.' He slowly turns around and starts to walk back out into the pouring rain.

'How do I know if I can trust you?' Penny blurts out.

'What do you mean?' he asks, slowly turning back.

'Well, I don't know who you are.'

'You can trust me. I promise.'

'That's what they all say. You could be a very polite serial killer. Or an evil-yet-misunderstood octopus…'

'I'm definitely not an octopus,' he replies, tentatively. 'Please, let me come in from the storm? I just need to call my sister and then I'll go.'

'Are you sure I can trust you?' Penny asks. 'Are you sure you're not an evil time-traveller…'

'I'm prepared to trust the woman who's threatening me with a paperback,' he says.

Horrified, Penny quickly shoves *The Princess Bride* onto the nearest shelf and stands to the side to let him in.

'Good point,' Penny replies, reluctantly. As he slowly walks inside, she darts into the depths of The Author's Library, humiliated.

'I'm Christopher, by the way.' he calls out after her.

'That's nice.'

He tries to follow her but he completely loses his way. Instead, he begins to wander around.

*

Christopher has always wanted to visit the bookshop, but he never thought it would be in the middle of the night. He also never thought he would be threatened by the bookseller in her pyjamas. He doesn't even know her name. Whenever he walks past during the day, he spots her through the window. She's always recognisable: auburn hair, tied up into two buns on the top of her head; green eyes that twinkle and appear bigger behind her glasses. She also has a round face with constantly rosy cheeks and a fashion sense that consists of rainbow colours, retro t-shirts and double denim. A small tattoo of a jigsaw puzzle is inked on her collarbone.

Tonight, after a pretty lousy evening, he only rang

the doorbell when he saw the lights still on. As he steps further into the bookshop, it's a strange sensation; Christopher hasn't bought any books or even read anything for fun, in years. There was a part of him that missed the experience. Besides, he knew that if he walked all the way back to his sister's in the freezing cold, Millie would only cause a fuss.

*

'There's a handsome man in my bookshop…' Penny thinks. Meanwhile, she paces back and forth, recounting what's just happened. 'I threatened him with a paperback book and then I ran away from him… There's a handsome man in my bookshop and I threatened him with a paperback… There is a handsome man in my bookshop!' Penny peers around the corner but she can't see him. She slowly turns back, sinks down to the floor and leans against the bookcase.

'What do I do? Obviously, I have to help him. I didn't just let him in because he's the tall and handsome stranger that I've dreamt of. And you can't shut the door in people's faces… especially when they're beautiful. People as attractive as him should come with a warning sign. Either that, or he doesn't exist. Does he exist? Or am I imagining people, again?'

When she peers back around the bookcases, she finally sees Christopher looking at the nineteenth century literature. When he turns slightly in her direction, she hides again.

'He definitely exists,' Penny mutters, to herself. 'But what do you do when there's a handsome man in your bookshop, during the middle of a storm? I was not prepared for this…'

'Who are you talking to?'

Penny yelps and looks at Christopher, who's standing over her, completely baffled.

'Nothing!' she says, stumbling onto her feet and then standing rigidly still. 'I'm Penny Figment.'

There's an awkward moment when Penny thrusts her hand forward for Christopher to shake.

'Err… Hi? Could I borrow your phone, to call my sister? Then I'll be gone and I won't disrupt you, anymore.'

'Of course.' She gives him her mobile and a wide smile, which Christopher acknowledges but doesn't respond. Instead, he disappears behind the bookcase and makes his call.

Penny stands on her tiptoes and peers through the cracks in-between the books to get a better look at him. He's incredibly tall with a slim body and muscular limbs; his eyes are as dark as a void and he has a long face and crooked nose. His hair and beard are long, dark brown and slightly scruffy.

'He looks like a rebellious heartthrob in a period novel. He's gorgeous…' Penny thinks. 'But he looks really moody. Beautiful but tragic. He never found his true love, even when he's adored by all the women in the land. Instead, he falls in love with a humble bookseller…'

'My sister's not picking up the phone. Neither is my brother-in-law.' Christopher admits, walking back to Penny and handing her the phone.

'That's fine. Stay as long as you want,' Penny replies, dreamily. She's so lost in her own thoughts, that she's staring blankly into space.

'Are you ok?'

'Yes!' She's suddenly awoken, as if someone had set off an alarm off in her head.

Startled, Christopher takes a step away from her. 'You've been staring at the same set of books for several minutes.'

'Well, yeah? Who doesn't? I was… I was just looking… looking at… books?' Penny quickly realises that she's staring straight ahead at a collection of books she's never read before. She blushes, profusely.

'Have you read any books by Daphne Du Maurier?'

'Err… Yeah,' she lies, as convincingly as possible, crossing her arms and avoiding eye contact. 'Pfft. Of course I have.'

'Which one is your favourite?'

'That's a good question.' Penny looks at Christopher and then back at the books by Du Maurier; she repeats this several times and then points at the first book she sees.

'That one,' she lies.

'My Cousin Rachel?'

'Yeah.'

'What's it about?'

'A cousin? A cousin called Rachel?'

There's another awkward silence, where Christopher stares at her and furrows his brow. Even though Penny wants to run away into the depths of her bookshop, she stays put.

'You haven't read anything by Du Maurier, have you?' Christopher asks her.

'Err… No, I haven't.' she admits, reluctantly. 'Shit.' She thinks.

'I thought so.'

The two of them blankly stare at the books in front of them. Neither of them say anything for several moments.

'I'm Penny Figment.'

'I know.'

After her awkward and embarrassing interaction with Christopher, Penny manages to save her dignity by making them both a cup of tea. The two of them sit in two worn armchairs, trying to make polite, yet awkward conversation:

'So, do you live here?' he asks, nervously.

'Yeah, I live upstairs,' she tells him. 'This bookshop is my home.'

'Cool.'

There's an awkward silence, between them. Penny makes them another cup of tea and drinks hers very quickly. She notices him looking up at all the surrounding books, completely lost in his thoughts, and decides to copy him.

'What's your favourite book?' she asks, when she looks back at Christopher.

'What?' Christopher asks, startled.

'What's your favourite book?'

'I don't know. I don't have one.'

'Of course you do. Everyone does.'

'Not me.'

'What do you do for a living?'

'I'm an academic that specialises in English literature...'

'Wait? You study books but you don't have a favourite?'

'I guess not.'

There's another awkward silence, between them. Just as Penny is about to make a third cup of tea (to try and diffuse the boredom), she stops herself. Instead, she leans forward and looks intently at Christopher.

'What are you looking at me like that, for?' he asks.

Behind his dark eyes, Penny can see a strong sense of sadness. She couldn't find the twinkle, where the passion would usually be. It was almost as if being so expressionless was all Christopher could handle. It just happened to be a feeling that Penny knew all-too well. That feeling of unhappiness and unfulfillment that dominates your entire soul.

'I don't believe you're as boring as I think you are,' she announces.

'Excuse me?'

'Have you ever had fun in your life? When was the last time you read a book for pleasure?'

'None of your business,' Christopher replies, quickly and defensively. 'Anyway, why are you asking me all of this? I hardly know you.'

'I can sense it within you, you know,' Penny tells him calmly, although her heart is racing beneath her pyjamas. 'I can tell that you're unhappy and you've felt that way for a long time.'

'I'm fine…'

'That's what they all say.'

Christopher stands up, about to walk away. Then, he sits back down again and looks directly at Penny. 'What about you?'

'I'm definitely not boring.'

'You got that right. You act like you just came back from Wonderland and never fully recovered.'

'Funnily enough, I like it that way,' Penny tells him, with her arms crossed.

'You're a weirdo.'

'Cheers,' Penny says, casually. Although it reminds her horribly of when she was back in secondary school and being called that was the worst insult of all time. When she wanted to blend in with everyone else, it was Emily who told her to embrace who she was because life became more enjoyable. Penny had tried to do that, ever since.

Christopher swiftly stands up and walks away, leaving Penny on her own.

'They always run away.' Penny thinks. She sighs and sinks into her armchair. 'Remember: it's better to be on my own, so no one can hurt me…'

*

But Christopher stops in his tracks when he's on the other side of the bookcase. For the first time in years, he looks up at all the surrounding books; he doesn't recognise half of the titles, but he still closes his eyes and absorbs it all. He suddenly feels the urge to buy a lot of books and read them all in one night, just like he used to. Even though he doesn't want to admit it, maybe Penny's right. He's not entirely happy and has known this for a long time; Christopher just always knows how to cover it up.

*

When Christopher swiftly emerges back from behind the bookcase, all Penny can do is gawk at him. She stays frozen in her armchair and watches him walk towards her. For a moment, she can't quite believe it.

'He came back,' She thinks. 'They never come back.'

'I don't quite understand what's happened

tonight...' Christopher says, as if he's thinking aloud. He slowly begins to stroke his beard with gentle fingers.

'To be honest, neither do I...' Penny thinks.

'You seem like the sort of person who loses herself in every book she opens.'

'I'm a bookseller. I've been doing it for years.'

'How do you do it?'

'We've only just met.' Penny reminds him.

'Exactly!' he cries. 'But maybe I was meant to come to your bookshop tonight...'

'That's mad...'

'I want to forget everything, tonight.' he tells her. It's almost as if he can't believe it himself. 'How do I do that?'

Penny ponders this, for a while. Then, a wicked grin begins to grow on her face.

'Come with me.'

She grabs him by the hand, drags him out of the armchairs and swiftly into the depths of The Author's Library.

Between the Bookcases

When Christopher eventually leaves and promises to come back, the storm-clouds disappear. Penny watches him walk away and then slowly stumbles back, an exhausted mess. But she stops when she reaches the largest window and takes a few moments to watch the sunrise, it's something she's never done before but it's still just as beautiful as the sunset. A warm fuzzy feeling begins to bubble in her tummy when she thinks about her new friend, Christopher.

'Tonight was fun,' she mutters, before collapsing onto the floor and falling fast asleep.

Penny sleeps for a couple of hours, before having only ten minutes to get ready and open up her bookshop for another day ahead. Her clothes are mismatched, her hair resembles a bird's nest and she trips over her shoelaces. It's a good thing her glasses can cover the dark circles underneath her eyes.

Even though it's a successful day all Penny wants to do is crawl upstairs and hibernate under her duvet. Instead, she spends her day dealing with customers and lugging stacks of heavy books onto shelves. All while waiting for Christopher to come back, even though there's a part of her that thinks he won't. Penny has fallen for these promises before and, eventually, her high hopes had plummeted into despair.

At the end of the day, there's been no sign of him.

She watches the sunset and tries to read *Dracula* but her mind feels foggy. As she slowly goes up to bed, she can't help but feel disappointed.

The next day is the same, with no visit from Christopher. The day after that, is fairly uneventful. There are a few customers buying books and some mundane but polite conversation.

'I wish you were here. You always made life fun.' Penny thinks, as she sinks into an armchair that used to be Emily's favourite. She would always read dystopia with her legs dangling over the arm, while muttering to herself with a black coffee by her side. It's lonely times like this when Penny misses her mum, the most.

For almost two years, Penny's been working in the bookshop on her own. She told herself that it was better for her to be alone and occasionally see her grandma, than to put her trust in anyone else. How could she ever be lonely, when she was surrounded by hundreds of stories?

Yet, Penny had forgotten everything, when she met Christopher. For the rest of that night, they'd taken a slow stroll throughout The Author's Library. They looked up at all the surrounding books and spoke about their favourite ones. It was almost as if they both had problems to ignore and completely lost track of time.

It's suddenly become quiet in the bookshop, when Penny slides off the chair and onto the floor. She tucks her knees underneath her chin and lowers her head, letting her hair fall forward.

'Why do I do this to myself? Not again,' Penny thinks, harshly. 'Christopher's not coming back but I believed him. I've scared him away, like I've done before. Just don't even bother anymore. Besides, I'm only protecting myself if I don't trust anyone else…'

She doesn't bother to stand up and continue with her day. She doesn't care if customers notice her and Penny won't even look up when she can sense someone sitting next to her.

'Go away,' she mutters.

'I need to talk to you.'

The voice is familiar but uncommon. When Penny looks up and sees Christopher, her eyes widen in shock and her arms become as heavy as lead. She doesn't know what to say, as if her mouth has been glued shut, so instead Penny stares at him, dumbfounded.

'He's back,' Penny thinks. 'They never come back…'

'I wanted to see you,' Christopher begins to tell her, 'but I became swamped with work and then… shit happens…'

'He's back…' Penny thinks.

'I haven't been able to think about anything else, since that night. My sister thinks I've gone mad and my brother-in-law said that I'm finally developing a personality…'

'Your brother-in-law's not wrong…'

*

Until he met Penny, Christopher had forgotten all about the power of escapism in books. He thought stories were just words on the page and he couldn't emotionally connect them.

'*The War of the Worlds,*' Christopher announces.

'Huh?'

'My favourite book. When you asked me, I didn't have an answer. But since then, I rediscovered it and it's always been my favourite. I couldn't stop reading it and I guess I'd forgotten all about it.'

'Why are you telling me this?'

'Only because it took one night with you and I feel alive again! How did you do it?'

It was as if he had forgotten how to have fun. The fun that Christopher used to have once led him into a lot of trouble and it took a long time to build himself back up. Since then, he's strived for an ordinary life but there was something missing. It was almost as if he had a grey cloud over his head and then Penny came along.

'You came back,' Penny says, in a monotone voice with her mouth hanging open.

'We've already established that…'

'Why have you come back?'

'Well, I said I would,' he replies. 'But that night felt

so surreal I wanted to make sure it had really happened. That I wasn't just imagining things.'

'It is real,' Penny reassures him. 'I can promise you that.'

Christopher sighs and leans his head back against the bookcases. 'It's been a long time since I've had any kind of fun and forgotten about everything else.'

'Me too,' Penny mutters, just loud enough for him to hear.

'I guess I just want to completely let go and enjoy my life, even for a little bit.'

'Maybe I could help you with that.'

'How?'

Penny gets onto her feet and drags Christopher up with her. Then, she casually links arms with him and they slowly walk past the customers with their heads held high.

'What are we doing?' he asks.

'Don't question it. Just go with it.'

Soon enough, when the customers are behind them, Penny sprints into the depths of The Author's Library and drags Christopher behind her.

'Why are we running?'

'Does it matter?' She sprints ahead of him. All the books to their left and right fly past in a colourful flurry.

When they begin to slow down, Christopher takes her by the hand and spins her around, like a doll on top of a music box. Penny, who isn't elegant at all, trips over her own two feet and would have fallen face first, if Christopher hadn't caught her. She then leads him by the hand, further into the unknown, with a skip in their step; either twirling each other or spinning themselves, until they become dizzy.

Whenever they see a customer, they immediately link arms and slowly walk as if everything were normal. Then, they'd break away and start following the directions of the bookshop, flailing their limbs and dancing to the sound of their own laughter.

Eventually, the two of them stop running and finally catch their breath. The remaining customers disappear and the sun begins to set. Once more, they're the only two people left.

'I'm exhausted,' Christopher admits, falling to the floor and wiping the sweat from his brow. 'But that was the most fun I've had, in so long.'

Penny blushes. 'There's one more thing I want to show you. Come on.'

She drags him onto his feet and takes him once more, into the bookshop. They stop when they reach the largest window amongst the fantasy books; it looks out at the world beyond The Author's Library.

'This is one of my favourite things to do,' Penny tells him, as the two of them sit on opposite ends of the window sill.

'I can't remember the last time I watched the sunset,' Christopher says.

'I've started doing this, every day. It soothes me,

when life gets too hectic. Even I need to calm down, sometimes…'

They say nothing else but comfortably sit in silence, watching the sun disappear into nightfall.

*

'I'm glad he came back,' Penny thinks, as she watches Christopher. They've only met twice, but she already knows that she can trust him, like a friend. Penny hasn't felt that way, since her mum died.

'Hey, Christopher?'

'Yeah?'

'Do you wanna hear a mystery?'

'Go on, then.'

Penny takes a deep breath and watches the last moments of the sun disappear. Then, she exhales and looks back at Christopher. 'It all started about two and a half years ago…'

They zoomed throughout The Author's Library, on their book trolley. Penny sat on top, laughing like a mad woman, while Emily steered it from the back with one foot on the ground and built up speed. The bookcases flying past them, became a blur and both of them grinned like Cheshire Cats.

Simultaneously they felt the adrenaline pulsating through their body and the wind ran through their hair. Emily glided them in-between the bookcases and they soared at a rapid pace.

'We're going really fast!' Penny cried, as Emily narrowly dodged another bookcase.

'We're fine, Penny.' Emily cackled. 'We're absolutely... Oh, shit.'

Before Emily could say anything else, she turned a sharp left; she didn't see the dead-end, covered by a maroon velvet curtain, in front of them and slammed her foot on the ground, coming to a sudden stop. Although they didn't crash the trolley, Penny was swiftly thrown off. She hit the wall and dragged the curtain down with her.

'Penny,' Emily cried, as she rolled the trolley away and rushed over to her daughter. 'Shit, I'm so sorry. Are you ok?'

'I'm fine,' Penny told her, wearily. She tried to heave the heavy curtain off herself.

'Next time, I won't steer so fast...'

Emily's voice trailed away, when the two of them looked up at the large door that was covered by the curtain.

'Bloody hell,' Emily whispered. 'Mum's going to kill me...'

'So, you had a secret door in your bookshop, which you never knew about?' Christopher asks.

'Grandma told my mum, when she was a little girl, to never look behind the curtain. She said it was there for decoration and nothing more. No further questions. Then, I was told the same thing, too.'

'You never had a curious urge to look any further?'

'My grandma's a ferocious woman. I'm sure she was a dragon in a past life,' Penny tells him. 'Also, it was a really boring answer. So we always found our fun elsewhere…'

'Grandma always told us to never look behind the curtain.' Penny reminded her. 'We should put it back.'

'She can't tell us what to do anymore.'

'That woman will tell us what to do, until the day she dies.'

Emily grabbed hold of the oversized door handle and tried to twist it. At first, the door didn't budge.

'It's locked, mum. You're gonna be able to open it.'

'At least… let me try,' Emily grumbled. Her face began to turn red and beads of sweat ran down her forehead. Eventually, after one last pull, the door became unstuck and it slowly creaked open.

'Eureka!' Emily cried, as she stood at the entrance to a staircase that led down into darkness before completely disappearing. 'We have to know what's down there.'

Penny looked at her mum, baffled. 'Are you mad?'

'We both are.'

'Don't try that with me. Even I know that this is a bad idea.'

'Why?'

'You don't know what's down there.'

'So, let's go and find out.'

'Grandma would hate this…'

'It's the start of a new adventure.' As she ignored her daughter's concerns, she began the descent.

'Oh, for God's sake…' Penny grumbled, before chasing after her.

'You don't have to come with me,' Emily told her.

'Someone has to look after you.'

'I can look after myself. Don't forget that I am still your mother…'

'So, what did you find down there?' Christopher asks, his eyes widening in excitement.

'I counted one hundred and twelve steps, until we reached the bottom.'

'What happened then?'

Eventually, Penny and Emily stood at the entrance of a basement. It was a fraction of the size of the bookshop and didn't have the bookcases that twist and turn. It was lined with a midnight-blue wallpaper and had a dark wooden floor. Remainders of melted candles in their candelabras were dotted around the room, hanging on the wall and presented in the middle of a table; even when Emily lit them all, there was barely any light. Two bookcases lurked at the backed, camouflaged by the darkness.

'What the hell is all of this?' Penny whispered, as she began to wander around the room.

'Aren't you glad we found out?'

'I'm not going to tell you that you're right. But this is amazing. How did we never know about this?

'Look.'

Emily pointed at the ceiling and Penny looked up and gasped. It was covered in an incredibly detailed mural, that seemed to be hand-painted.

'Holy-moly-guacamole…' Emily mumbled.

She slowly circled a large, round table which sat in the centre of room; three abandoned chairs lay around it. There was crystal ash tray in the middle, which still held stale ash and cigar butts. An old bottle of dark rum was sat next to it and three glasses of different sizes were gathered round. Across the table were Greek tragedies, philosophies and epic poetry all left open, with handwritten notes around the text.

'What else did you discover?' Christopher asks, hanging off the edge of his seat.

'Not much, after that.' Penny admits. 'We were just too excited about what we'd discovered. We knew it was the start of something.'

'Did you ever go back, after that?'

'We went back once more and asked each other questions but never knew the answers. But then... shit happens, you know? Now, I haven't been back since.'

'Do you think you'll ever go back?'

Penny opens her mouth but she doesn't know what to say next. It used to be a secret but now that Emily was gone, Penny had no one to share it with. So instead, she forgot all about it. Until now.

'Maybe sooner than I thought.'

A Brief History

The following evening, Penny finds herself standing in front of the door to the basement, which is still hidden behind the velvet curtain. Ever since she told that story to Christopher, she couldn't get it out of her head. Every time she reaches out to open the door, she quickly retracts her hand. The last time she went down there, Emily was still alive and it became their little secret; they came up with all sorts of answers, as to what happened beneath the bookshop and each one was crazier than the last. Going back down there now, wouldn't be the same without her.

'Do I even want to know? Penny thinks. 'What if the basement was a place I never should've uncovered? Maybe I should leave it all alone and never look back. Maybe there are some mysteries that will never be solved.'

Stroking the tattoo on her collarbone, Penny looks up at all the old adventure tales; they're stacked high and mighty on sturdy bookshelves that were made from the wood of an old ship. It gives Penny a sense of comfort, as it's the oldest part of her bookshop.

Books are always moved about, to make way for the new and upcoming ones. Yet, the adventure books have always had their specific spot and it's been that way, since 1911. It was created by Ruth Figment, Penny's great-great-grandma and the first female owner of the bookshop.

Penny's ancestors have been selling books since 1678 but the shop's original name was Fowler & Sons. Until Ruth took on the responsibility, all her predecessors had been male. Even though she had four older brothers, it was her father's dying wish for his only daughter to become the next bookseller. The first thing she did, was change the name and she called it The Author's Library.

'This could be the start of my own adventure,' Penny mutters, gearing herself up. 'Mum would never give up and neither would Ruth Figment. So, I have to know.'

Before she can change her mind, Penny pushes the curtain to one side, flings open the door and marches down the steps. Her heart pounds with excitement and she immediately runs into the middle of the room, giddy with glee.

'Where should I go first?' She wonders. Penny almost didn't see the bookshelves at the back of the room because they were hidden in the dimmed light, as if they blend into the surroundings, and the books are covered in dust from years of abandonment.

'Why are you all hiding down here?' Penny asks, as she edges closer and adjusts her glasses to get a better look.

The shelves are filled with several heavy, old atlases that need two hands to handle. Penny unravels one of the maps, the paper is aged, slightly torn but also covered in handwritten notes and directions around every country and across every ocean. Everything is signed by Ruth Fowler.

'Why is all of this hidden away… But what about you?' She gasps.

Wedged in-between a large atlas and an old copy of *Sherlock Holmes* is a small, leather-bound notebook. Cautiously, Penny takes it off the shelf. It's overfilled with loose pages of notes and old photographs. She holds her breath as she carefully brushes off the dust and opens the front cover. The journal is dated back to 1900 and once again signed by Ruth Fowler.

'It's her travel journal…' Penny gasps, in awe. 'I can't believe it's here! But why was it hidden down here?'

While carefully clutching onto the notebook, Penny slowly heads back upstairs. She sinks into the nearest armchair and begins to read her great-great-grandma's journal, until well into the night. She looks closely at every photograph, trying to find Ruth; Penny guesses it's the woman in the admiral's uniform, standing tall and proud. She reads through every story and letter, forgetting about everything else and keeps her focus on the first owner of The Author's Library.

The Author's Library
1913 - 1916

I

12ᵗʰ October 1913

It's just an ordinary day in The Author's Library, when Ruth Fowler meets her future husband. The usual commotion of customers, has left her dashing and disappearing into the depths of her bookshop, like a madwoman; carrying high stacks of books, while Max happily trots by her side (an eleven year-old English Sheepdog with the attitude of a puppy). She's nimble enough to dash from one end to the other, with her hair tucked messily underneath her hat that she never bothers to pin in back into place.

When customers walk past her, sometimes they stare at Ruth for wearing a navy admiral's uniform, which is tailored to her slender, muscular body. Yet, Ruth continues to organise the mystery books, without caring what people think of her; it's the way she's always been.

A decade beforehand, Ruth and Max had sailed on their own adventures, on a boat she called *The Wanderer*. They navigated across the oceans, on an expedition for adventure. Ruth planned every route herself and scribbled on every map she used and studied her atlas' when the seas were calm. They were caught in countless storms, sometimes lost at sea for days, with no direction and barely any nourishment to survive on. But Ruth never gave up. She always adored her life as an explorer.

Customers were already astonished by Ruth's expeditions; everyone was even more shocked when she became the next bookseller and was surprisingly good at her job.

When Ruth carries yet another high stack of books, she quickly walks past Robert Figment. He's a quiet man, who she often sees in her bookshop but has never spoken to. He's slightly shorter than all the other gentlemen, but his voice is as calm as the ocean after a storm and his eyes are as bright as the sea in the sunlight. He carries a satchel which ends up being full of books that he buys from the bookshop. He twiddles his thick but tameable moustache while he browses.

From the other side of the bookcase, Ruth can feel her heart pounding beneath her shirt and her cheeks begin to flush crimson. She quickly drags Max by his collar and hides amongst the adventure tales. Utterly bamboozled, Max totters around the corner to see who his owner is hiding from; then walks back, sits in front of Ruth, and cocks his head to the side.

'No, I can't talk to him.' Ruth says to her faithful companion, who raises his eyebrows in judgement.

'I've never spoken to him before. Do you remember what happened, last week? When I crashed into him and dropped an entire stack of Shakespearean literature, on his foot? It was humiliating.'

Max smiles, barks and rolls onto his back with his paws in the air.

'Don't you laugh at me,' Ruth says, crouching down and giving Max a belly rub. 'He seems like such a wonderful man, but nobody knows anything about him. I'd never know what to say.'

Max barks loudly.

'Sshh! Yes, I know we've dealt with worse situations, than this. When we had to use the stars and moon when we were lost. We've fought off invading ships and we both remember when I almost married that Norwegian aristocrat…'

Max barks, again.

'You're right,' Ruth admits, slowly walking backwards. 'I shouldn't be afraid of him. He's just another human… Oof!'

Without realising, Ruth crashes into Robert and the two of them collapse to the floor. Then, Max sprints over and starts to lick Robert's face.

'I'm so sorry. Maximillian! Get off him.' Ruth cries, as Max is still giving him wet kisses. She stumbles onto her feet and helps Robert up, before dragging her dog away by the collar. The dog scowls at Ruth and tootles off.

'It's nothing to worry about. These things happen,'

Robert reassures her. 'But isn't it funny that we're always bumping into each other, like this.'

'It certainly is,' Ruth mutters, shuffling from one foot to the other. 'Maybe the universe is trying to indicate something?'

'Or, maybe we should just become acquainted with each other.' Robert says, offering Ruth the crook of his elbow.

'I'd like that.'

Arm-in-arm, the two of them take a slow walk into the depths of the bookshop. Max soon comes back and trots alongside them, smiling along the way.

After an hour of wandering and polite conversation, Ruth sits in her armchair amongst the adventure books and Robert takes a seat in the one opposite. Max curls up at Ruth's feet.

'What's your favourite book?' Robert asks.

Ruth takes a copy of *Treasure Island* off the shelf and happily flicks through the pages. 'This was my favourite book when I was a child. My father would sit in this chair and read it to me. I loved this story and absorbed every word. He even told me stories of his own adventures, inspiring me to have my own.'

'I hear you were an explorer?'

Ruth brushes her fingers against the bookcases, beside her. 'These bookcases were once my ship that sailed across the seas. My father wanted all his children to have their own adventures but I was the only one insane enough to do it. No one believed I could, until I did.'

Robert leans forward and looks at Ruth with intrigue, while twiddling his moustache. 'Tell me more.'

Ruth reaches inside into her blazer pocket and takes out a leather notebook.

'This was my travel journal,' she says. 'All my adventures are written down here because I didn't want to forget any of it: the spectacular people I met, the glorious sights I saw and the trouble I got into. I learnt more about myself on my travels than in any other part of my life. I'm confident in who I am because I chose to see the world; I trusted my intuition and it gave me the courage to see what's out there. I'm empowered because I relied on myself to follow my own adventure.'

'Can you tell me a tale of one of your adventures?'

'I'd love too.'

Ruth puts on her glasses and flicks through the pages of her journal until she reaches a specific page. Then, she clears her throat and the reads tale, aloud:

3rd September 1906

I encountered the worst storm, last night! Max was nearly thrown off *The Wanderer* and almost drowned a watery death. I would've lost him forever, if I hadn't grabbed him by the collar, just in time! The ocean is a temperamental mistress; I always pay her waters the upmost respect and she still shows me no mercy! Thankfully, I managed to lock away my most vital possessions, just before she hit us. I only lost one atlas and a few pages of notes...

When Ruth finishes one tale, Robert begs her to read another. He hangs onto every word she says, until they're the only two left and the evening has fallen. When Robert leaves that evening, he promises to come back.

II

10th August 1914

'What's your favourite book?' Ruth asks Robert. It's a quiet day and the two of them walk arm-in-arm, whilst Max plods alongside.

'Have I not told you, already?'

'You haven't.'

Robert takes a copy of *The Adventures of Sherlock Holmes* out of his satchel and shows it to her. 'You sold me this book, a few weeks ago and I read it in one evening. It's now become my favourite book.'

'You like mystery novels?' Ruth asks.

'I love them. I wish I'd read *Sherlock Holmes*, sooner, but I never would have thought to. But now I must read more of it. I love reading a book filled with ambiguity, where you try to guess what happens at the end.'

'You're religious, also?'

'How did you know?' Robert asks, as he tucks the copy of *Sherlock Holmes* back into his satchel.

'Sometimes, I'd see you looking at a copy of *The*

Bible, with such intent,' Ruth replies.

Robert reaches into his satchel again and takes a copy of the *Holy Bible*. The black leather and gold lettering has faded, but the pages are still secure inside.

'I've had this copy for many years,' he tells her. 'It's not just a book I read but it's the scripture I follow. I read this every night and it stays with me always.'

'How admirable of you.'

The two of them smile at each other and continue to slowly walk into the depths of The Author's Library. While neither of them say anything, they enjoy being in each other's company. Ruth can't keep her eyes off Robert Figment. Such a handsome man yet he's still kind enough to always listen to her.

'I would love to kiss you,' Ruth says, not realising that she didn't think it to herself.

'Pardon me?'

Ruth snatches her arm from Robert and covers her face from embarrassment. 'I didn't… I thought I… I didn't say anything.'

Robert stops Ruth in her paces and takes both of her hands in his own.

'Allow me to kiss you, Ruth?'

Slowly, Robert draws her in for a kiss and the two of them are transfixed in a perfect moment. Robert gently places one hand on Ruth's waist while she places both hands on either side of his face.

'I love you,' Ruth whispers, as they break apart.

'I love you, too,' Robert whispers back. They don't say anything else, but they rest their foreheads against one another.

Suddenly, they can hear music playing outside. Ruth and Robert listen to the melody from a quartet of folk musicians, who play the accordion, guitar, banjo and drum. The song is lively, the lyrics are catchy and Robert begins to tap his foot to the beat of the song. Ruth gives him a wicked grin throws off her hat, letting her short curls fly free from its updo.

'Shall we?' Robert asks, offering her his hand.

'We shall.'

She takes his hand and Robert directs her a few paces, before leading her into a dance. He places one hand on her waist and the other interlocks with her fingers. They continue to skip and gallop while staying close to each other. Neither of them is very elegant, as they try and dance to the same rhythm. They keep stepping on each other toes and soon become increasingly sweaty while Max weaves in-between them with a goofy smile on his face. Robert spins Ruth around when the music becomes faster, making her throw her head back and laughs uncontrollably. He holds her close when the song begins to slow down.

Customers stare at this oddity but Ruth and Robert are only preoccupied with each other. They can't stop staring at one another and grin until their cheeks ache. The world beyond the bookshop doesn't interfere with them falling in love.

Ruth and Robert become wrapped up in their own perfect world, dancing into the night and they never want to stop. The two of them are so fixated on each other, that they didn't notice the music coming to an end. They didn't see the soldiers beginning to march through the town, past The Author's Library and off to fight in the Great War.

III

24th January, 1916

Instead of working in the bookshop, Robert Figment sits in his armchair, looking closely at today's newspaper. Every so often, he looks up, leans back and stares into the distance; then he reads the newspaper again. He's been coming back to the same spot, all week. Customers that walk by glare at him. Although hardly anyone comes into the shop and Robert's used to this level of distaste by now.

For over a year, The Author's Library has been getting quieter and fewer customers were buying books. People couldn't afford the luxury while a war was going on and no one wanted to buy books from the man who chose not to fight for his country. People frequently accused Robert of cowardice and they thought his reason for not doing so was lame. So the Figments were earning less money day-by-day and they had to cut back on food and heating.

Ruth tried not to worry about their predicament. She stood by his side when he told her that he didn't want to fight in a war which went against what he believed in. She defended him against anyone who hurled abuse at him and even threw out the customers who turned aggressive. As she walks in-between the bookcases and carries their son, Patrick, she sees her husband and sits in the armchair opposite.

'God, please show me what to do.' Robert prays, bowing his head and clutching his *Bible* to his chest.

'Robert, please be kind to yourself,' Ruth says, with Patrick on her lap. 'This isn't healthy.'

'There are rumours that they're going to call up every man to fight,' Robert says, running his fingers through his hair. 'What to do…'

'They're just rumours, they're not necessarily true.'

'But if conscription becomes law, then I'll have to fight. I won't do it.'

'But what if you must?'

Robert looks at his wife with tears in his eyes. 'Ruth, I'm a Christian and I don't believe in violence nor do I believe in murder. This war goes against everything I believe in. I'll never forgive myself if I was involved in an act so unforgivable.'

'I know.'

'I'm sorry for grief I've caused you. But I won't betray my faith in God.'

When Ruth places a gentle hand on Robert's cheek, he finds it reassuring. 'I will always stand by your side, no matter what. We'll get through this, together.'

'What shall we do, if this becomes mandatory?' Robert asks, as tears begin to roll down his face.

Ruth wraps her arms around him and he cries on her shoulder. She holds on tightly, to her husband and son.

'We'll just live in the moment, for now,' she finally says. 'Let's face that problem when it arrives and hope that the future won't be as terrible as we think.'

IV

2nd March 1917

Once again, Ruth finds Robert sitting in his armchair. But when she sits next to him, he doesn't look up to acknowledge her. He keeps his gaze on the letter he's holding in one hand and aggressively twiddles his moustache with the other.

'What is it, Robert?'

He still doesn't look up but hands her the letter. As she reads it, Robert leans back in his chair and runs his fingers through his hair. In just a few seconds, Ruth has to fight the urge to burst into tears but she knows that she needs to be strong, for the both of them.

'It's an ultimatum,' Robert says, keeping his gaze

ahead. 'I either become a soldier or be arrested and branded a coward.'

'I won't let anything like that happen to you.' Ruth tells him. She holds his hand in her lap. Then, she re-reads the letter.

'There must be a way to get you out of this,' she mutters.

'Ruth, I'm not an exception to the law.' Robert looks sternly at his wife. 'I must enlist to fight.'

'But if you don't believe in this…'

'They only see me as a man healthy enough to be a soldier. They won't care about what I value.'

'Robert, let me help you…'

'There is nothing you can do.' Robert quickly stands up and begins pacing back and forth. 'This isn't one of your adventures, where there's a solution to every problem at sea. This is what I'm facing.'

We're facing this together, Robert. No matter what.'

'Either way, I'll have to leave you.'

'If you go out to fight, then you could be killed.'

'If I go out to fight, there's a chance I might come back, one day.'

'But it's not what you want.'

'Is this what anyone wants?'

'I don't care about anyone else. I care about you.'

Robert walks over to his wife and kisses her on the forehead. Then, he sits back down in his armchair, stares straight ahead of him. Ruth slides her hand into his.

'If only I could hide you away, until the end of the war.' Ruth says. 'I'd keep you safe, until all is calm again…'

'I wouldn't want to put you or Patrick at risk.' Robert sighs and then looks at her. 'I know what I must do.'

'Tell me.'

'If they want me to fight in the Great War, then I will…'

'What about your faith…?'

Robert turns to face her and Ruth stops talking. 'I can go off to war and help our soldiers without killing another human being. I won't even pick up a weapon.'

'How can you become a soldier, if you refuse to fight?'

'I'll become a stretcher-bearer and help injured men off the battlefield.'

Ruth blinks furiously and fights the tears back. 'You could still be killed…'

'That's a chance I'll have to take. This is the only way I can honour my faith in God and obey the law.'

'The world is so dangerous, right now,' Ruth whispers, lowering her head.

'What other choice, is there?' Robert replies gently, quickly wiping away the tears from his eyes. 'I don't want to leave my family, but it's what I must do. I'll try and keep myself alive, so I can come back to you, one day.'

'How will I live my life without you?'

Robert chuckles and cups his wife's cheek. 'You've been living a wonderful life, long before you ever knew me. I know you'll be strong, throughout this.'

'I'm just a bookseller,' Ruth admits.

Robert lifts Ruth's head with his fingertips and then holds her firmly by the shoulders, looking her in the eye. 'Yes. You are a bookseller. Keep selling stories and give hope to those who need it.'

'You're a part of my story,' Ruth says. 'How will I know that you're safe?'

Robert sighs. 'I don't have the answer for that. So you'll just have to trust me.'

'Of course.'

Robert draws Ruth back into an embrace and gently kisses the top of her head. 'Just promise me you'll look after yourself and raise our Patrick to love stories as much as we do.'

The two of them gently kiss and they linger in the intimacy, for as long as they can. They close their eyes and hold onto each other, feeling the warmth of each other's breath.

'I don't think this leaves us with much time left.' Ruth admits.

'Then, let's not waste another second.'

V

3rd March 1916

Robert-Johnathan Figment slowly wanders in-
between the bookcases, just as the dawn begins to
break. He holds his *Bible*, which has a photograph of
his family, tucked inside. For a few minutes, he
watches the sunrise, enjoying the silence that
encompasses him. The bookshop has always made
Robert feel safe and he hopes that one day, he will
return to it.

Overwhelmed with realisation, he suddenly falls
to his knees and drops everything. He takes a
handkerchief out of his pocket and begins to silently
sob into it.

'Please keep me alive, so I can come back to my
family?' he prays. 'Protect my Ruth and Patrick…'

When he looks up, he sees Ruth, holding onto
Patrick with Max by her side. Robert stumbles to his
feet and rushes towards him. He crouches down and
wraps his arms around his son, holding him close.

'Take care of your mother, Patrick,' he says, when
they break away. 'Can you do that for me, while I'm
gone?'

Patrick nods, with tears beginning to roll down his
soft cheeks. Robert holds onto his son, for one last
time.

'You are such a brave boy,' he whispers. When he
starts to cry, Patrick tries to wipe away his tears with
his little hands. Then, Robert stands up to face his
wife.

'I promise you…' he says, before Ruth can interrupt him with a kiss. The two of them embrace each other, both wanting to forget the grim reality that surrounds them. When they break apart, Ruth clings onto her husband, resting her forehead against his.

'Tell me this is the right thing to do.' she whispers.

'It's the right decision.' he reassures her.

'I'll do all that I can, so that I can one day return to you. I must go, but never forget how much I love you.'

'I'll wait for you to come home,' Ruth tells him. They kiss for one final time, lingering on each other's lips for as long as possible.

'Goodbye,' Robert whispers. He turns away and slowly walks out of The Author's Library. Ruth waves him goodbye and Patrick blows him kisses.

When Patrick begins to cry again, she kneels down and dries his tears with the sleeve of her shirt and kisses the top of his head.

'Your father is a very brave man.' she says, holding Patrick close to her bosom. 'We must always be as brave as he is.'

Ruth takes Patrick by the hand and leads him to the children's books. She gives him a stack of stories to read and leaves Max to watch over him. Then, she begins to walk further into the depths of her bookshop. As she winds her way around every bookcase, she knows exactly where to go.

She finds herself amongst the adventure books and sinks to the floor with her back against the bookshelves. Ruth hides her head in her hands and begins to cry, running her fingers through her hair. This morning, the bookshop has never felt emptier. She slowly begins to lie down onto her side, cradling her knees to her chest and gently shutting her eyes.

Whenever *The Wanderer* was at rough seas, Ruth always had the confidence in herself, to get through it. She always knew which sails to pull and her timings were immaculate. She was never afraid of the storm; in fact, she always embraced it. But now, Ruth couldn't be more afraid. She gracefully accepts the heartache and continues to silently sob.

After some time, Ruth opens her eyes and the first thing she focuses on is a worn copy of *Treasure Island* next to *The Adventures of Sherlock Holmes.* Ruth crawls over and takes *Sherlock Holmes* off the shelf; she doesn't remember misplacing this book with the adventure tales. Not thinking twice about it, Ruth begins to flick through the pages. On the back page is message in Robert's handwriting:

Ruth,

I thought that if I purposefully misplaced this book amongst some of your favourite stories, you would be inquisitive enough to notice. If you are reading this, then I am correct. My favourite book, next to yours. We are but two individuals with different stories to tell. Yet, our stories are still connected. You've lived the life of adventure, on the high seas you once sailed. Keep living your own adventure, Ruth. Keep sharing your stories. Keep going.

All my love,
Robert.

Ruth re-reads the message, once more. Then, she reads it again and again until the tears start flowing down her cheeks. She grabs her travel journal, finds a spare page lurking at the very back. She then finds a pen and ink and begins to write:

My Robert. You wonderful man.

I have faith in that wherever you go, you will bring some hope to this tragic war. No matter what, just remember that you will always have a home with me and Patrick, in The Author's Library. I promise to wait for you, every day. I will read the books you love and imagine you by my side, always. I will tell Patrick that his father is a wonderful and courageous man.

When you return, we shall continue to live the rest of our lives together and entwined.

Thinking of you, always,
Ruth.

Ruth writes so quickly that she can barely read her own handwriting and her tears have smudged the ink. Nevertheless, she closes the book and then goes down into the basement. It's the first time she's stood underneath her bookshop. The room is bare, apart from an empty bookshelf. Ruth clutches her travel journal and *Sherlock Holmes.* She walks over to the lone bookcase and places both books on the shelf; keeping her prized possessions safe, until the day she reunites with her husband. Ruth then swiftly turns away and emerges back into The Author's Library.

Ruth closes the basement door and then turns to see Patrick, who is looking up at her and clinging onto Max. She smiles at the two of them, takes Patrick's hand and Max follows at her side. The three of them wander into the depths of the shop.

Friendship Around the Corner

Ivy Thistlethwaite, Penny's godmother, always comes to The Author's Library. While they don't talk as much as they used to, Penny usually finds her amongst the feminist books. Ivy is recognised by her striking purple eyes that stand out against her dark skin and pitch-black curls that float around her shoulders, entwined with colourful flowers; her clothes are equally as bright and float graciously with every move. Today, she stands on her tiptoes and runs her delicate fingers across the bookshelves, tickling the spines.

Ivy's been coming since 1971: she escaped to the bookshop when she had nothing else; Emily and Nora took her into their home and soon saw her as part of the family. Ever since then, Ivy's been eternally grateful for their kindness and especially her sisterhood with Emily.

On the night before Emily died, Ivy promised her that she would watch over Penny and she always stood true to her word. Even if Penny doesn't always see her, Ivy's watching over her. Whenever Penny finds a flower petal on the ground, like a footprint in the sand, she knows that Ivy's been.

She looks at Penny but there are tears in her eyes. It had been almost two years since Emily died, and Penny hasn't been the same since. She had slowly become quieter over time, as if all her thoughts were hidden inside her head, desperate to come out. Once Emily died, Penny had no one to share the fun with.

When Penny and Ivy look at each other, they're comforted by the other's presence but their hearts ache at the reminder of Emily Figment: the woman who would skip throughout The Author's Library and brought so much joy to their lives.

'Hiya, Penny.'

'What's the matter?' Penny slowly walks towards her and slips her hand into her godmother's.

Ivy smiles and wipes her tears away with her other hand. 'This is one of my favourite places to be. Your mum and me used to hang out here, when we were your age.'

Ivy takes an old copy of *Frankenstein* off the shelf and shows it to Penny.

'Do you remember?'

'Mum loved that book.' She used to read to me before I went to bed when I was little, and you would do all the voices.'

'I remember Emily telling me that she would only ever read a book if it contained at least one of three things.' Ivy giggles like a schoolgirl and counts them off, on her fingers. 'It had to feature some kind of monster, it had to be written by a female author or it had to have a worthy point to prove.'

'She always used to tell me that a book wasn't worth reading unless it had something important to say.' Penny remembers. 'When you helped Mum to raise me, I used to think I had two mum's…'

'You were such a beautiful child, growing up.' Ivy

remembers. 'We would take you for walks, throughout the bookshop, when you became restless. Emily and I would hold your hand and swing you off your feet. I was the one who had to tell her to be careful with you.'

'Do you remember Tiny-Dancer?'

'Emily bloody loved that cat. He hated everyone else but tolerated her when she fed him treats and sang him songs from the 80s. It was such a shit cat...'

'I never saw Tiny-Dancer, after Mum died.' Penny admits. 'It's odd. Sometimes, I miss him...'

On a busy day in The Author's Library, Emily sat cross-legged in the middle of the bookshop. A stray, black cat with white paws lay asleep in her lap.

'He's so cute,' Emily cried, as she scratched the cat behind his ears and watched him purr.

'Seriously, Emily?' Ivy said, as she stood over her old friend. 'I nearly tripped over that damn cat, on my way in and he hissed at me.'

Emily ignored her best friend and began to sing Elton John's Your Song *to the cat. When he stretched out his paws, Emily squealed in delight.*

'For God's sake...' Ivy grumbled with an irritable sigh.

'Mum, there are customers that need serving,' Penny reminded her, when she walked past carrying a large stack of books and a line of customer following behind.

'I'm serving him,' Emily replied, as she rubbed the cat's belly and made kissing-noises at him.

'I'll give you a hand,' Ivy said to Penny. She took a stacks of books from her goddaughter and began to carefully organise them onto the shelf.

'Thanks, Ivy.' Then Penny stood over her mum, with

her hands on her hips and a frown on her face.

'Is he going to buy anything?' Penny asked her,
sarcastically.

'He's adorable, though.'

'How did he get in?'

'It doesn't matter. He's my favourite customer.'

'He's a cat.'

'I'm going to call him Tiny-Dancer.'

'Really?' Penny tried to give Emily a convincing smile
through gritted teeth.

'You don't like the name?' Emily said, sharply. Her
head immediately snapped up and glared at her daughter.

'No,' Penny quickly replied, as she shoved the
remaining books onto the nearest shelf. 'It's your cat, after
all.'

Since that day, Tiny-Dancer always came back. He
snuck through the front door and strolled in-between the
bookcases with his tail in the air; always looking for Emily
and the box of treats she kept behind the till. Sometimes,
Emily would carry him in her arms as she worked in the
bookshop and valued his opinions just as much as the next
customer. But both Penny and Ivy knew that the love was
never reciprocated; Tiny-Dancer just wanted the treats…

The giggles slowly trail off, when Penny sinks to
the floor with her back against the bookcases. When
Ivy sits down to join her, Penny quickly wipes the
tears from her eyes and hopes that she didn't see.

'It's difficult to think back on all those happy
moments,' Ivy says, placing a daisy behind Penny's
ear. 'Sometimes, it's hard for me to look at you,
without being reminded of Emily. But I'll always be
watching over you and your family is always closer

than you think.'

'Ivy? What can you tell me about my dad?' Penny asks.

'I thought you knew a lot about him, already,' she replies. 'I remember Emily telling you stories about him all the time.'

'Yeah, I remember. It was almost as if I knew him. But I haven't heard those stories in so long. Could you tell me, again?'

'Of course.'

Ivy leans her head back against the bookcases, closes her eyes her eyes and sighs. Then, she looks back at her goddaughter and smiles.

'His name was Cosmo Brown,' she begins to say. 'All throughout the 70s and 80s, we were a close group of friends. Cosmo, Emily and me. We would parade around the bookshop, screaming our opinions and singing our favourite songs, with flowers in our hair. But I remember watching Emily and Cosmo share something special, between them. She loved him more than anything else; I'd never seen her like that. He would play his ukulele and sing songs that he'd written for her; he made her laugh like no one else. Your dad was like a gentle giant, who would carry Emily to the ends of the earth if she needed it. When she was pregnant with you, the two of them were so excited to become parents. Even your grandma took him into the family. We all thought they were going to live happily ever after. But when he died of a heart-attack, your mum was beyond heartbroken and couldn't love anyone else. She couldn't laugh or find any reason to smile. But what always pulled her through, was the love from her family and the thought of you coming into her life. But there was never a day that went by, where she didn't think of Cosmo.'

'Grandma once told me that our ancestors are always watching over us.'

'I think she's right. Never think that you're ever alone, Penny. Sometimes, family goes beyond what you're born into.'

'I'm fine,' Penny quickly tells her. Although they both know it's not true.

'I'm sure you are. But are you happy?'

She opens her mouth to speak but doesn't know what to say. Instead, she stares straight ahead at the books in front of her. Eventually, Ivy slowly stands up and walks out of the bookshop.

Penny stays sat on the floor, hugging her knees to her chest. It's coming to the end of the day but she can't even be bothered to lock up. She rests her head on top of her knees, closes her eyes and lets her hair fall over her face. She thinks back to the morning after Emily's funeral, where The Author's Library wasn't as comforting as it usually would be. When all that surrounded Penny was darkness and a sense of loneliness that slashed into her life, like a blade piercing flesh.

Shaking herself away from what she remembers, Penny reaches behind her and grabs the first book she touches. It's Orwell's *1984,* which was one of

Emily's favourites. She read it at least once a year and used to be able to quote it from memory. Penny begins to absent-mindedly flick through the pages but doesn't bother to read the story. Right now, it just feels like a repetitive pattern of black and white. She quickly discards *1984* because books don't seem to be helping her today.

Meanwhile, Christopher hurries through the shop looking for Penny. A young man and woman try to keep up with him.

'Christopher, where are we going?' the young man groans.

'Just follow me.' Christopher takes long strides and jumps over stacks of books, looking in-between and behind every bookcase. 'There's someone I want you to meet.'

'I don't like meeting new people. We all know this.'

'You're never happy, are you?'

'That's not true. I was perfectly content with how my day was going until you came along and ruined it.'

Christopher abruptly stops and turns around to face him. 'Dexter, you've stepped into a world where hundreds of stories lie at your fingertips and you want to hide away from the world?'

'I want to hide away from you.'

'Miserable bugger…'

'Oi!'

'Hurry up,' Christopher cries, ignoring Dexter. He quickly turns around and continues to sprint through the bookshop,

'Why did we decide to follow him?' Dexter asks the young woman, who skips by his side.

'Why not? It's all so exciting,' she replies, giddy with excitement. 'You would never believe that this bookshop is bigger on the inside…'

'So many stories, all in one place,' Christopher says, slowing down so he can walk with his friends and admire all the books that surround him. 'Although, I have read this one…' He points out one book, as he walks past it. 'I've also read that one…' He points out another and continues to do so with every book that stands out on the shelf. 'Also, that one. I've read that one. I loved that one. Was disappointed with that one…'

'You've read a lot of books, Christopher, we get it,' Dexter cries.

Penny doesn't move when she hears unfamiliar voices, but sharply looks up when she overhears Christopher's name. As he emerges from behind the bookcase, she forgets everything else. She jumps up onto her feet and runs towards him.

'Christopher!'

'Hey, Penny!' He lifts her off her feet and spins her around, until they feel dizzy. She clings onto his biceps for dear life but their laughter echoes throughout the bookshop.

'I wanted to come back and see you,' he says, when he eventually puts her down.

'I hoped you'd come back.' she admits, blushing slightly.

They slowly begin to edge closer, with Penny standing on her tiptoes. However, she's soon swept off her feet, again, when a young woman throws her arms around her. It feels oddly comforting, even though it's left Penny feeling dazed and confused.

'It's so nice to meet you,' the young woman cries, holding Penny tight. 'I absolutely love your bookshop. I'm Millie, Christopher's sister.'

'Oh, I swear to Thor...' Dexter grumbles, although he can't help but smile.

However, Penny enjoys Millie's hug, even if it's cutting off all her blood circulation.

'Err... I'm Penny Figment,' she replies, nervously.

When the two of them break apart, Penny takes a moment to gaze upon Millie. Her hair is a mixture of pastel pinks, lilacs and turquoise and she has a heart-shaped face and deep blue eyes that twinkle at every angle. She's strikingly tall and as soft as a cushion Just standing in front of her, makes Penny feel all warm and fuzzy inside.

'I'm Dexter, by the way. Millie's husband and Christopher's only friend,' he says, shaking Penny's hand. Dexter's a short and scrawny man with a mop of copper-coloured hair and bushy eyebrows. A pair of thick-rimmed glasses makes his eyes look too big for his face.

'You're not my only friend,' Christopher cries.

'Fine. I'm his best friend.'

Millie turns back to Penny. 'Shall we have a cup of tea?'

'Err... I'd love to,' Penny replies, as confidently as

she can. She's still bamboozled as to what's happening.

Millie links arms with Penny and the two begin to walk further into the bookshop.

'You don't have to. You really don't have to,' Dexter calls out, in the distance.

'Ignore him.' Millie says. 'He's just grumpy because his favourite character died in *Game of Thrones…*'

*

With every step she takes, Millie becomes more and more fascinated by The Author's Library. She can't help but look all around her; her eyes widen in wonderment and the smile shines on her face. With her free hand, Millie gently runs her fingers across the spines of all the books on the shelf. She imagines opening a book and watching the pages fly out and form into paper birds and butterflies, gliding throughout the bookshop.

*

'So, what's your favourite book?' Penny asks, when the two of them are sitting in large armchairs and drinking tea from brightly coloured mugs.

'Oh, gosh. I'll be honest, I don't really read much.' Millie admits, trying to avoid Penny's gaze as she takes a long sip of tea. 'Christopher's the clever one in the family. Sometimes, I struggle to read for long periods of time and words confuse me. You probably think I'm so stupid…'

'No, I don't,' Penny quickly replies, while spilling tea down her t-shirt. 'There are loads of books that I've only pretended to have read, just so customers don't judge me.'

'You have no idea how good it feels to hear that.' Millie giggles. 'When Dexter tried to get me to read *Lord of the Rings,* I really didn't get it. So, Dexter insisted I read *Game of Thrones,* instead. He's always argued that he liked the series before everyone else did.'

'I read *Lord of the Rings* as a teenager, but it was hard,' Penny reassures her.

'Can I tell you a secret?' Millie asks. She takes out a packet of biscuits and offers them to Penny. The two of them nibble contently.

'Of course.'

'I only pretended to read *Game of Thrones*, whenever Dexter was around. I didn't want to seem dumb, but it's so baffling. Far too gruesome and not enough dragons, for me.'

'But Dexter thinks you've read the whole thing?'

'I know we shouldn't keep secrets from each other, but I didn't want him to judge me. So when the boys have their nerdy debates, I just nod along…'

'Don't worry, your secret's safe with me.'

Millie wraps her arms around Penny, but this time it's a lot softer. Penny hugs her back and doesn't want this moment to end; a new friendship is beginning to blossom.

Meanwhile, Christopher and Dexter stay amongst the fantasy books; a genre they loved, when they were growing up together. The two of them stay silent but they've known each other for long enough for it to never be awkward.

Dexter stares at Christopher. They're as close as brothers, but Dexter always knew that something wasn't right with his best mate. For the last few years, he used to think that Christopher was as boring as a history textbook; even though Dexter knew the reason why. Now, he wonders what Penny had said to Christopher that had made him change.

'I speak on behalf of myself and Millie when I say that we both approve of Penny,' Dexter loudly announces, breaking the silence and making Christopher jump a foot into the air.

'Why do I need your approval?'

'I'm a married man, Chris. I don't care about anyone else's love life. I frequently worry about yours.'

'It's not that bad?'

'Apart from my existence, Penny is one of the best things to ever happen to you.' Dexter places his hands on Christopher's shoulder and looks him straight in the eye. 'Don't lose her. I would hate to look after you for the rest of my life.'

'I don't need looking after,' Christopher says, breaking away from his oldest friend. 'Also, why is my romantic life any of your business?'

'I question the girls you date. Until recently, you're the human embodiment of a shit storyline between a hormonal teenage girl and her moody-excuse of a vampire-boyfriend…'

'Don't compare me to *Twilight!*'

'The last girl you dated loved *Twilight.*'

'Millie liked her.'

'Nah, Millie tolerated her.'

'She wasn't that bad.'

'She told me that my lightsabres were too childish. So I told her to piss off.'

'Don't remind me. She made me choose between my relationship with her, or my friendship with you guys.'

'You made the right choice. She was fit but she ain't no Princess Leia.'

'I knew you didn't like her. You two high-fived as she stormed out…'

'Don't you remember how horrible she was?'

'I remember…' Christopher grumbles.

'Plus, you said last week that you would…'

'…I would rather date Gollum dressed as Minnie Mouse than ever go out with her again.' The two of them laugh, thinking back.

'But on the night you went to break up with her, you met Penny,' Dexter cries, flailing his hands in the air. 'Coincidence? I think not.'

'You believe in this, as destiny?'

'I believe she's the kick up the arse your life needs, pal…'

Penny and Millie come back to the boys, with another cup of tea in their hands. Soon enough, the four of them sit cross-legged in a circle, as the evening falls on the bookshop.

'So, it's just you in your bookshop?' Dexter asks Penny.

'Err… Yeah, it is.'

'Doesn't that get lonely?'

'No,' Penny replies, almost too quickly. But during the few weeks after Emily's death, Penny felt lost and could do nothing else but float aimlessly throughout her bookshop, like a lonely astronaut, lost in space. She told customers that she was fine and told herself that it was better to be on her own where no one beyond her family can ever hurt her.

'I'll never be lonely, so long as I'm surrounded by stories,' Penny says, before realising just how odd that sounded.

'Your imaginary friends keep you company?' Dexter asks, sarcastically.

'No,' Penny says, although Dexter doesn't look convinced. 'There are ghosts in The Author's Library.'

'Ooh, tell us,' Millie says, looking at Penny and resting her chin in her hands.

'Well, my grandma once told me this story about my great-great-grandma, Ruth Figment. In 1917, her husband went off to war but was soon declared missing in action. No one knows what happened to him. We've always called it the mystery of Robert Figment.'

'Wow,' Christopher whispers.

'But Ruth promised that she would wait for her husband to return, one day. According to my grandma, she never lost faith. So every night, from the day he left, she waited by that window for her husband to come back. Apparently, her spirit still appears each night as she sits at the same window, waiting for him. Then, she disappears as the sun begins to rise.'

Penny points to the window opposite her; it's the largest one and overlooks for miles.

'Have you seen anything?' Christopher asks.

'My mum was convinced that she saw her, once. I love the tale but I don't know if it's anything more than a ghost-story. But once my mum made us stay up all night, hoping for a glimpse of Ruth Figment. She swears she saw something when I accidentally drifted off to sleep.'

A sudden gust of wind blows past outside, slamming the window shut. All four of them shriek and immediately huddle together.

'Do you think that was Ruth?' Millie whispers.

'Who knows?' Penny replies.

'Have you been back down to the basement?' Christopher asks.

'I have, actually. It seems my family have more mysteries than Robert Figment.'

'Could we maybe go down and see?' Millie asks.

'Absolutely not.' Dexter cries, shivering with fear.

The flickering light bulb loses its last remaining glow and suddenly the four of them are plunged into darkness. They all gasp and huddle closer together.

'I agree with Dexter,' Penny admits. 'I don't want to upset the ancestors.'

The Missing Puzzle-Piece

When Penny spends the second evening in the basement, she stands in the middle of the dimly-lit room and circles on her tiptoes, breathing it all in. The smell of old books that cuts through the stench of stale cigar smoke is familiar to her.

'I wonder if my great-great-grandmother had a secret life, down here? Maybe she never told anyone about it,' Penny mutters to herself, as she continuously walks around the circular table, in the middle of the room. She peers at the books that have been open and abandoned on the table and they're all a form of ancient Greek literature: tragedies, Homeric poems and philosophies.

'That's odd. I was told Ruth only ever read adventure books and Robert read mystery novels. So, this doesn't make any sense…'

Penny carefully treads over to the old bookcase at the back of the room. She straightens her glasses, and her eyes adjust to the dimmed light, as she leans over and studies every old book on the shelf. Just as Penny suspected, they're mainly old atlases and adventure stories, with a few mystery novels, too.

'That sounds about right,' Penny thinks, as she stands up straight. She begins to gently trace her fingers across the bookcase, collecting all the dust. 'These are the books that Ruth and Robert used to read. There's no mention of anyone in my family reading any ancient literature. So, who else could've been down here? This has never been mentioned in my family…'

Penny's thoughts trail off when she reaches the end of the bookcase. Underneath the flickering light, there's a door behind it.

'What are you doing there?' Penny mutters, shuffling from one foot to the other in excitement. She cautiously moves the bookcase to the left, until the door is exposed and her nose is almost pressed against it. An ecstatic grin starts to appear on her face.

'Eureka!' Penny cries, flinging her arms into the air. 'I can't believe I found this.'

The door appears to be made from the same dark wood as the bookcase and it's as tall as Penny. There's a small keyhole that lies hidden in the shadows of the large, bronze door handle.

'Why were you hidden away?' Penny mutters. 'You wouldn't have believed this…' When she looks behind her, Penny immediately realises that she's talking to an empty room.

She grabs the door handle, twisting it vigorously.

'Shit… Come on.' Penny huffs and puffs as she shakes the door from left to right and up and down. Even when she tries to heave the door with her shoulder, it still won't budge.

'Then, there must be a key that unlocks this,' she concludes. 'I know this door leads to something exciting.'

She frantically begins to search for a key. Penny spends an hour looking in-between every book on the shelf and underneath every artefact. She continuously circles the table, studying every inch of it. But no key is found.

'Someone once locked that door and hid it away. There must be a key, somewhere,' Penny says, as she ascends back to her bookshop. She doesn't realise how late it is, until she looks out of the largest window and sees the moon in the sky.

'Maybe it's hidden away in my bookshop,' Penny wonders, as she sits down in an armchair and rests her head in her hands. 'I lose myself in The Author's Library, all the time. I've got to find this key... but I don't think I can do it on my own...'

Penny takes her phone out of her pocket, her thumb hovering over Christopher's name in her contacts. She hadn't purposely called anyone for a long time and the thought of doing it now, fills her with dread.

'This is something me and Mum did together.' Penny thinks. Her heart's pounding beneath her t-shirt and her hands are slowly becoming clammy. 'But I can't do it on my own... But what if they think I'm stupid for doing this? But I want to see them again... Do they want to see me? I won't do it... Sod it, yes I will.'

With as much confidence as she can muster, Penny

stabs the call button and presses the phone close to her ear. She doesn't even know what she wants to say, her mouth has gone dry. A part of her wants to hang up straight away and hide in the depths of her bookshop.

When Penny hangs up the phone, Christopher, Millie and Dexter are on their way. She slides off her armchair and onto the floor, taking deep breaths as if she had just come up to the surface after swimming from the bottom of the ocean. Then, she scrambles onto her feet and paces throughout her bookshop, anxiously waiting for her friends to arrive. She ties her hair up with a purple scrunchie, to keep it out of her face.

Walking amongst the dystopian books, she stops and gasps at her reflection in the mirror. Some customers used to say that Penny and Emily Figment were incredibly similar. They both had the same piercing green eyes, an identical laughter and the same 90s fashion style. Emily would always wear dungarees and her lucky-purple-scrunchie in her hair. It was only lucky because Emily was wearing it on the day she won £2.50 on an abandoned scratch-card.

With her fingertips, Penny begins to gently rub the jigsaw puzzle tattoo on her collarbone. Emily had the same one on her wrist. The two of them had gotten it together a few years ago because they were like two pieces of a jigsaw that perfectly fit together.

Penny stares at herself in the mirror and sighs, the smile beginning to fade from her face. Without her mum, she feels as lonely as an abandoned jigsaw piece, with nothing to connect to.

'Hey, Penny,' Christopher says appearing from behind the bookcase soon followed by Millie and Dexter. They all tentatively walk up to her.

'Are you ok?' Millie asks.
Penny looks at her friends and the sight of them brings a smile back on her face.

'Yes,' she cries, her voice echoing throughout the bookshop.

Christopher and Dexter are fully dressed, although Christopher's hair is scruffy and Dexter's holding a flask of black coffee. Millie is proudly wearing her unicorn pyjamas and a pair of fluffy slippers.

'So, what do you need us to do?' Dexter yawns, stretching out his arms.

As soon as Penny tells her friends everything about the basement and the hidden, locked door, they immediately begin to look for the key.

'Have you found anything yet?' Penny calls out, an hour after consistent searching. The four of them decided to stick together, so no one gets lost.

'Nope,' Christopher admits.

'Nothing yet,' Millie replies.

'Couldn't this have waited until later?' Dexter asks, almost falling asleep on top of the bookshelf.

'No,' Penny says, as she climbs up every bookcase,

trying to reach the higher shelves. 'Where is your sense of curiosity?'

'Unavailable, at this time of night,' Dexter replies. 'Do you know what this key looks like?'

'Err... It's probably key-shaped,' Penny says.

'Do you even know what's behind the door?'

'If I knew that, then I wouldn't be searching for the damn key.'

'Have you asked anyone in your family about this?'

'Nope.'

'Why not?'

'There isn't anyone in my family who could've told me about this.' Penny admits. 'I could ask my grandma, but not just yet.'

'Why don't you want to ask her?' Christopher asks.

'She's a forceful woman. When I was younger, I used to believe she could scare monsters out of hiding, if she wanted to.'

'So, we're looking for a key and you have no other information about it,' Dexter says.

'I did say that it's probably key-shaped.'

'Why do you care so much about this door?' Christopher asks.

'It must be connected to the rest of the basement. I just have to know,' Penny replies, climbing down from another bookcase.

'What if it's not as exciting as you think it is?'

'I can't afford to think like that. I just know there's something sensational behind that door, I can feel it.'

'Do you always try and live your life, like you've just escaped from a storybook?' Dexter asks.

'Life is more exciting, that way,' Penny immediately replies. She begins to frantically look in-between every fairy-tale book. 'Why can't I find this bloody key?'

'What if you can't find it?' Dexter asks.

'Then, I'll go crazy.'

'You're already halfway there, love…'

'I won't stop until I've found it,' Penny says, triumphantly.

'Ok, here's what we're going to do,' Christopher says, as he emerges from around the bookcase. 'I'm going to thoroughly search amongst the adventure books, romance and family history. Dex, you can look around the children's books and mystery genre. Penny, dystopia and politics. Millie, stay awake.'

'Huh?' Millie cries, suddenly awake when Christopher nudges her with his foot. During the last hour, she had curled up and drifted off to sleep, snoring gently with dribble on her chin. She looks up at her brother and gives him a sleepy smile. Then, she falls back asleep in the same position.

'Excuse me?' Penny demands. She strides up to Christopher and leans against the bookcase, crossing her arms. 'Who put you in charge?'

'Do you have any better ideas?'

Penny marches right under Christopher's nose, with her hands on her hips.

'I have a plan,' she replies, as confidently as she can. 'You can… Why don't you… Just keep looking!' Penny quickly turns on her heel and walks away from Christopher and into the depths of The Author's Library.

'You just searched there,' Christopher calls out, teasing her.

Penny turns on her heel once more, and marches back past Christopher. She holds her head up high, pretending not to hear him. Although her cheeks are blushing scarlet.

'I knew that…' she says, unconvincingly.

Another hour passes. Millie is still fast asleep and the key hasn't been found.

'I've lived in this bookshop, all my life,' Penny says to, Christopher. 'If there was a key hidden in here, then I would've found it by now.'

Penny and Christopher simultaneously look up at the bookcases which tower over them. These bookcases are so high that they make them feel as small as specks in the universe.

'What about the books on the top shelves?' Christopher asks.

'It's possible,' Penny says. 'Some of the oldest and most fragile books live up there. I like to keep them out of harm's way because they're precious and worth a lot of money. I don't even climb up them because these ones are too frail.'

Christopher looks back at Penny and a wicked smile begins to grow on his face.

'What are you thinking?' Penny asks him.

Instantly, he grabs a set of heavy books from the bottom shelf and begins to evenly stack them into two separate piles.

'Hey, I had all those books organised,' Penny cries, although she's too intrigued to stop him. 'What are you doing?'

When the two piles are high enough, Christopher stands on top with one foot on either stack. 'If you climb up onto my shoulders, we could reach the higher shelves,' he suggests, leaning down and offering Penny his arm.

'That sounds ridiculous.'

'It's worth a try, though.'

Penny takes a deep breath and when she exhales, she takes his hand and swings onto his shoulders. He clings onto her legs as Penny tries to stable herself and peer onto the top shelf.

'I can't see a key,' Penny calls down. 'I think we need to be higher... Whoa!'

Christopher leaps down from the stack of books and runs to another spot.

'What are you doing?' Penny clings onto him for dear life. 'This is ridiculous. Aagh!'

When Christopher stops running he begins to jump up and down, on the spot. 'I'm trying to help you reach the top shelves,' he explains. 'Do you want to find this key, or not?'

'Yeah, but I don't want to plummet to my death.'

'I've got you, don't worry. Can you see anything?' he asks, still jumping on the spot.

With every jump, Penny quickly scans the top shelf.

'Nope,' she calls out.

'Then, let's look somewhere else.' Christopher stops jumping and leads Penny deeper into her bookshop.

They repeat this a few more times, until Penny finally loses her balance. They try to cling onto one another but she slips from his grasp; as she crashes to the floor, Christopher tries to catch her but ends up tripping over his feet. There's a moment of awkward silence, as Penny is strewn across Christopher's midriff. Then, the two of them burst out laughing.

'As fun as that was, we still haven't found the key,' Penny moans, out of breath. She sits cross-legged with a frown on her face.

'At least we had fun though?' Christopher says, sitting up.

Penny looks at him and giggles like a schoolgirl. For a second, the two of them forget about everything else and keep their gaze on each other, slowly edging closer.

'So, it's just me looking for this bloody key, now?' Dexter asks, as he walks around the corner and finds the two of them.

When Penny and Christopher quickly jump to their feet, Dexter leans against the bookcase, crosses his arms and raises his eyebrows.

'We'll keep looking!' Penny announces. She marches past Christopher and Dexter and doesn't look back. But the cheeky grin is still on her face.

They keep searching until the sunrise breaks through. Completely exhausted, they decide to give up. Penny makes them all a cup of tea and they gather beside Millie.

'Did we find the key?' Millie asks, slowly opening her eyes and resting her head in Penny's lap.

'No, we haven't,' Penny replies, gently stroking her hair. 'Thanks for helping me, guys.'

'The pleasure is all mine,' Dexter mumbles. He takes a swig of his coffee, which has now gone cold.

'I was really hoping we would find the key tonight,' Penny admits, with a tinge of disappointment in her voice.

'Are you going to ask your grandma, now?' Christopher asks.

'I don't want to. But now, I might have to,' she grumbles.

She is as Ill-Fated as a Greek Tragedy

The next day, Penny can't stop thinking about the basement and what could lie behind the locked door. While she organises all the new books and serves the old customers, she's mentally still searching for the key. She couldn't even get to sleep after her friends had eventually left; her mind was too preoccupied with the endless possibilities, thinking what the door could lead to. She dreamt of discovering hidden family treasure or releasing the ghosts of long-lost ancestors who float aimlessly around the bookshop.

Meanwhile, Nora Figment visits her granddaughter and her beloved family bookshop every Sunday at 3:30pm, although she always arrives exactly two minutes early. She has silver curls which are bound close to her head and dark green eyes which could pierce into your soul, if you said the wrong thing. Her facial features are pointed but soften significantly when she smiles, and square-shaped glasses hang on a pearlescent chain around her neck. She always wears the same suit that she wore back in 1950s, when she once took on the responsibility of The Author's Library.

Before she sees Penny, Nora takes a wander through the bookshop. It's been so long since she had the responsibility of being a bookseller, but she's always loved her family's bookshop. When she closes her eyes and breathes in the scent of old books, nostalgia flows throughout her body, sending goosebumps up and down her arms.

When Nora first came to the shop, aged ten, she used to practise the way she walked; back straight, confident strides and never losing her footing, like a strong and independent woman. Nora Figment had always wanted to prove to everyone that she was good enough to be a part of the bookshop that she was adopted into. She would carry a stack of children's books under one arm but the other was outstretched so she could gently brush the dust off the spines, revealing the story to everyone. She used to look up at the soaring bookcases that loomed over her and believed that they were magical and could protect her from any harm. She much preferred her home in The Author's Library than her dismal life on the streets of London, where she spent most of her childhood.

When she grew from a girl to a young woman, Nora loved to climb the ladder as high as she could and watch from above. She smiled whenever she saw the elderly man who found a book he hadn't read for years; or when a romance would flourish between two young people and the happy ending was in sight. Whenever she screwed her eyes tight, Nora would wish for her own romantic tale, but she never told anyone that.

In the beginning of 1940, Nora Figment was evacuated from London to The Author's Library. Before then, Nora had spent her childhood abandoned at an abusive orphanage before running away at the age of five and spending the next few years, homeless. From the moment she stepped inside the bookshop, she fell in love with it all, wishing every night that it could be her home. She soon became a part of the family and grew fond of Patrick Figment and his mother, Ruth.

In 1945, she was adopted into the family, as Patrick's daughter. She was gradually taught the responsibilities of becoming a bookseller and in 1953, Patrick gave Nora the responsibility of the shop while he travelled the world in search of rare and exotic books to sell. Nora was honoured, cherishing every moment spent working hard and demonstrating to everyone what she was capable of.

Then, over the next two years, her life as a bookseller became as exciting and dramatic as a Greek tragedy. She remembers the days of soaring high and achieving her dreams, before falling into a pit of despair and slowly having to crawl her way back up again. Nora thinks back to times when she relied too much on what her heart was telling her, rather than her head; it usually left her heartbroken and all she could do was look towards the future for herself, her daughter and The Author's Library.

As the remaining customers begin to leave the

bookshop, Nora peers through the cracks in-between the books and gasps when she sees Mr. Marblelight. Even though there's a row of books that separates them from touching, she still takes a tentative step back. After all these years apart, Nora's still taken aback by his beauty and she slowly leans forward to get a better look; his eyes still twinkle behind his glasses whenever he picks up a book and his nose almost touches the paper. She's always loved the way he treated every book with delicacy and respect, as if they were an old friend. As Nora's heart begins to flutter and her whole body trembles with anticipation, it reminds her of the way she used to feel back in the early 50s.

'Good afternoon, Nora,' Mr. Marblelight says, as he puts the book back on the shelf and takes another off so he can get a better look at her.

'Good afternoon, Michael,' Nora replies, in her clearest voice. She stands up as tall as she can and keeps her hands clasped around her walking stick.

'It's… It's wonderful to see you here,' he says awkwardly, while still keeping his gaze on her.

'I come back to my family's bookshop, every Sunday,' Nora says. 'to see my granddaughter, of course.'

'Of course. Penny is truly a wonderful girl.'

Neither of them know what to say because neither of them have spoken to each other since 1955.

'I guess I should…' Nora begins to say, taking a

tentative step backwards.

'…Remember the books we used to love?' Mr. Marblelight gently reminds her.

'Pardon?' Nora asks, her mouth ajar.

'Whenever I stand amongst these books, it always comes flooding back to me.'

Nora looks up, before taking a gasp and another step backwards. In front of her, is a bookcase filled with Greek tragedies and other forms of Greek literature. Tentatively, Nora takes a copy of Euripides' *Medea* off the shelf and begins to flick through the pages. Then, she looks up at Mr. Marblelight and gives him a small smile.

'I remember,' she whispers, just loud enough for him to hear. 'But it's been so long since I've read anything like this. It must have been 1955.'

To stop herself from getting too excited, she lets out a deep sigh and slowly puts *Medea* back on the shelf.

'I remember our passion for these tales,' Mr. Marblelight recalls. 'It was some of the happiest moments of my life.'

'It was such a wonderful time.'

There's another silence between them. Without realising, both of them place a gentle hand on the bookcase, over their favourite Greek mythologies.

'It was lovely speaking to you, again,' Mr. Marblelight finally says. 'Even if I…'

'I have to go,' Nora says, abruptly. 'I'm spending

time with my granddaughter.' Slowly, she begins to walk away.

'Nora…'

'Goodbye, Michael.'

She can hear his footsteps, as he begins to walk alongside the bookcase, hoping to emerge from the other side and properly see her. In an instant, Nora strides forward and when Mr. Marblelight turns left, so does she, wandering into the depths of her beloved bookshop. He doesn't chase after her but instead, he watches her disappear in-between the bookcases. Then, sighing with a heavy heart he slowly leaves.

When Nora walks around a bookcase of family histories and sees her granddaughter; they simultaneously give each other an endearing smile.

'Hi, Grandma,' Penny says, bounding over to Nora and gently taking a hold of the crook of her arm.

'Hello, Penny,' Nora replies, holding onto her tightly.

'Shall we?'

'We shall.'

Much like they do every Sunday afternoon, arm-in-arm Penny and Nora take a slow wander throughout The Author's Library. They follow wherever the bookcases direct them, twisting and turning in any way. Today, Nora looks over at her granddaughter with tears in her eyes that she fiercely blinks away.

'When I see you, all grown up, I can't help but remember when I used to take a wander with Emily.'

'Mum always walked much faster than I did,' Penny says.

'Don't remind me. That foolish girl lived her life at a hundred miles an hour.'

'It was from all the coffee she drank, every day.'

Nora sighs, but the smile's still on her face. 'But I remember when she calmed down and we always took a stroll, arm-in-arm. We could wander around in circles for hours but we would never notice. We always had the time for each other when we needed it. When you used to come with us as a child, you would sing your alphabet at the top of your voice. We were always so proud of you.'

'I remember when you taught me how to make a proper cup of tea,' Penny says. 'Then, Mum told me what to do if we were ever faced with the zombie apocalypse…'

'Well, someone had to teach you sensible life skills,' Nora says. 'Emily could speak such nonsense sometimes.'

'Yeah, she was the best.'

'I'm just glad that instead of inheriting her madness and foolish personality, you took on all of my sensible characteristics.'

'Err… Sure.'

When Penny and Nora tire out from their stroll, they eventually settle down in two armchairs, always amongst the adventure books. Penny brings them a pot of tea with matching cups and saucers. In silence, they sip their tea with their pinkies out.

'Shall I tell you the story of my father, Patrick Figment?' Nora asks.

'You always tell me this story, Grandma,' Penny reminds her.

'Well, it's a story I love to tell,' Nora says, confidently. She leans back in her chair, takes a deep breath and smiles. 'When I first came here, he was so nervous to take me in, as an evacuee. He never married and lived with his mother, who would later be known as my Grandma-Ruth. It was Ruth who convinced him to take me in. At first, we didn't know what to do with each other and in fact, we were both too nervous to say anything at all. But over time, as we got to know one another, we developed a special bond. Almost as if we could call ourselves father and daughter. He gained the confidence as a guardian to look after me and he taught me how to read and write. By the end of the war, he decided to adopt me into the family and ever since I've always been so proud to be a Figment.' Nora sits up straight with a confident smile on her face.

While Nora tells her favourite story, Penny slowly loses concentration and her thoughts begin to take control.

'Does my Grandma know anything about the basement?' she thinks, slowly slumping in her chair.

'Of course she doesn't, which is why she's never told me. But maybe she does know and she never wanted to tell me. There's no one else in my family that I can ask…'

'Sit up straight, Penelope,' Nora snaps at her, as she raises her teacup to her pursed lips.

Even though she's completely startled, Penny quickly sits up, while accidentally spilling scalding tea down her t-shirt; she doesn't want her grandma to clip her around the ankles with her walking stick.

'What's that matter?' Nora asks her. 'You look like you've seen a ghost?'

Penny doesn't reply and instead she looks ahead at the basement door, which is hidden by the velvet curtain.

'Why would Grandma tell my mum to never look behind the curtain, unless she knew what lies behind it?' She thinks.

'Penny? What are you thinking about?'

She looks back to Nora, drains her cup of tea and rests it down on the tray. 'This was Ruth's favourite spot in the bookshop, wasn't it?'

Nora chuckles. 'It certainly was. This was a part of the bookshop that she created herself. Then, she warned everyone that if it were to ever change, she would curse the family, forever. When I was a child, during the war, I used to sit at Grandma-Ruth's feet and she would tell me stories of her adventures, all from memory. I listened to every word she said.'

'Did she ever write her stories down?'

'Funnily enough, I asked her that, once,' Nora recalls. 'She always had so many amazing stories; I often wondered how she remembered them all. So when I asked her, she told me that she once kept a travel journal. She'd hidden it away when her husband left in 1917 and knew exactly where it was. I tried to look for it but I could never find it.'

'I could show you Ruth's travel journal, if you want to see it, Grandma,' Penny says, her heart beating with excitement.

'What do you mean?' Nora chuckles. 'Have you been looking for it, too? I doubt you'll ever find it…'

'No, I found it,' Penny cries. 'I also found all her old atlases and the maps she used…'

'How did you find all of that?'

Nora's voice slowly trails off. Her hands start to tremble and her empty teacup falls to the floor. She suddenly grips onto the armrests, keeping a stern gaze on her granddaughter.

'Where did you find all of this?' Nora asks.

Slowly, Penny leans back in her armchair and her eyes widen in fear. 'Maybe this wasn't such a good idea.' She thinks.

'Penny, you must tell me. Where did you find all of this?' Nora demands.

'Err… I found it in the basement,' Penny mutters.

'The basement…' Nora whispers. She quickly grabs hold of her walking stick with both hands, for stability. 'No…'

'What's the matter, Grandma?' Penny asks, leaning over to place a hand over hers.

Nora snatches her hand away. 'How did you find out about the basement?'

'Err… A while ago. I found it with Mum. But recently, I went back to it…'

'Of course, you found it with Emily.' Nora mutters. 'That foolish girl, could never curb her curiosity… I told her not to look behind the curtain…'

'Do you know anything about it, Grandma?' Penny asks, tentatively.

'No!' Nora snaps, slamming her walking stick on the ground. 'Don't ask me such personal questions.'

'It's just that… there's a locked door down there… I was wondering if you knew anything about a key.'

'I don't want you going back there,' Nora commands.

'Why not?'

'It's not important.'

'I'm hoping I might find something exciting…'

'Well, you won't.'

'I thought that maybe I would discover a long-lost family member.'

'Don't be absurd. You know of everyone in our family.'

'It seemed exciting to me and you're the only one who could've answered any of my questions?'

'I've already told you, that basement has nothing to do with me,' Nora snaps. 'There's nothing down there that's worth discovering.'

'So, why won't you tell me…'

'I know what you're like, Penelope. You're hoping there will be a mystery in our family, but you're wrong. Get your head out of the clouds and don't try and seek such foolish adventures. Everything you could ever want, is in our bookshop.'

'You can't expect me to have discovered something beneath our bookshop and not feel curious,' Penny whines. 'Mum wouldn't stand for this…'

'Well, Emily isn't here anymore.'

Penny sinks further into her armchair. Her eyes are filled with tears but she refuses to cry.

'I know that,' she mutters, running her fingers through her hair.

Nora slowly sits up straight and wipes the sweat from her brow. 'Now, let's forget all about this and have another cup of tea.'

Penny opens her mouth to argue but it's no use. She knows that Nora Figment will argue her case from dusk until dawn.

'Sure.'

A Little Bit of Mayhem

On Monday morning, from the moment Penny opened her bookshop, mistakes were made and everything seemed to go wrong. Soon enough, customers had crammed themselves in-between the bookcases, snatching books off the shelves. Penny spends two hours scurrying around customers and running up and down her bookshop. She accidentally bumps into a tall stack of hardback classics which topples over her and breaks up a couple who were about to engage in a very spicy cuddle.

At lunchtime, when customers slowly begin to disappear, Penny only has ten minutes to make herself a cup of tea and sink into Emily's old armchair. She gobbles down four digestive biscuits in a row, before jumping up and catching a group of teenagers ripping out the pages of various editions of *An Inspector Calls.* When they sneer at her, it reminds Penny horribly of secondary school bullies. Cruel teenagers who used to hide her books around the school and taunt her at lunchtime, while she usually ate alone.

'Little shits,' Penny grumbles, as she picks up the scattered pages and the torn book cover.

When her Mum was still alive, busy days in The Author's Library were never quite as stressful…

Despite the rush of customers and the piles of abandoned books that needed to be organised, Penny and Emily still found the time to high-five as they walked past.

They always encouraged each other, made rounds of tea or coffee, when it was needed. Neither of them was afraid to call on the other for help. Novels were stacked in organised chaos but their positive and enthusiastic energy radiated throughout the bookshop, drawing in more customers. They gave a warm welcome and their time to anyone who walked through the door. Everyone that day found a reason to buy a book.

'We can do this, Mum!' Penny cried, as she raced past her.

'Hell, yeah!'

However, the moment they closed the bookshop, Emily fell onto her knees and face-planted the floor, groaning and swearing. Penny sat cross-legged next to her and gently ran her fingers through her hair.

'Are you ok?' Penny asked.

'Can't move. Won't move,' Emily grumbled. 'Today was exhausting.'

'I don't think I've ever seen you so tired.' Penny giggled. 'Sometimes, I don't even think you go to sleep.'

Slowly, Emily began to sit-up, stretching out her legs. 'I can sleep when I'm dead. I'll be fine after one more coffee.'

'How can one person drink so much coffee, like you can? No wonder you have so much energy...'

'Tea?'

'Yes please.'

'I'll meet you by the armchairs.'

With a final cup of tea and coffee in her hands, Emily found Penny sat in one of their favourite armchairs either side of the largest window in the bookshop and they watch the sunset.

'What's wrong?' Emily asked, when the mugs were

empty.

'Nothing,' Penny replied, as she kept her gaze on the evening sky.

'You've not said anything for ages.'

'Usually, you don't let me get a word in edgeways...'

'Well, tonight you're not even trying. What's on your mind?'

'No, it's nothing...' Penny began to say.

'Tell me.'

'I'll be fine.'

'Ha! So, there is something wrong.'

'You're a clever bugger, aren't you?'

'If you don't tell me, I'll keep asking...'

'I don't doubt that for a second...'

Instantly, Emily lunged forward and began to annoyingly jab Penny in the arm.

'Tell me, tell me, tell me, tell me,' she cried.

'Fine. Get off me.' Penny laughed and pushed her mum back in her armchair. Then, she sighed and put her empty mug of tea to the side. 'I saw Echo today.'

Emily put her empty coffee cup down and clasped her hands in her lap. Just the mention of his name, makes her blood boil.

'I see,' Emily muttered, through gritted teeth.

'I didn't say anything to him,' Penny quickly added. 'He didn't say anything to me, either. He just watched me and then when I looked back up, he was gone. I tried to find him...'

'Why would you do that?'

'I wanted answers.'

'What did you want to ask him?'

'I would ask... I want... Ok, maybe I don't know what I

would say,' Penny admitted, as she hung her head in shame. 'I thought... maybe we could be friends again.'

Emily sighed and reached out for her daughter's hand. 'Penny, you said it yourself when he left you for the last time. You don't need him in your life. You have to move on.'

'It's difficult.'

'I know, darling.'

'He was like a brother, to me...'

'Oh, please. No one in our family would ever treat you, like that.'

'It doesn't mean that it hurts any less. It was as if he'd forgotten all about me. Or he wanted to forget all about me.' Tears started to fall down Penny's face and Emily immediately wiped them away, with her sleeve.

'It's his loss, Penny...'

'He left me, though, and it hurts. Sometimes, I wonder if I did anything wrong. Was I a bad friend to him? Or maybe I just wasn't good enough...'

'You were good enough. He's just not good enough for you,' Emily cried, throwing her arms around Penny. When she cried onto her mum's shoulder, Emily held her tighter. 'You always looked out for him. You hung out with his friends, even though they made you uncomfortable. You did everything you could, to make him happy. He was never a good friend, to you. Echo was an ugly, little shit and you're better off without him.'

'Thanks Mum,' Penny whispered, as she breathed in Emily's scent of books and strong, black coffee. 'You're my best friend.'

'I'm your mother. Of course I am.'

Penny remembers how isolated she felt, working

in The Author's Library straight after her mum had died. She thought she would be fine and it could keep her distracted from bereavement; instead, it felt as if Penny had fallen into a black hole and all she could do was drift, with nothing happy to cling onto. She didn't want to get out of bed in the morning and face the day. The bookshop became a sad place to be and there were hardly any customers. Not that Penny cared. She lost her ability as a bookseller and instead, she opened a book and cried within its pages. Nothing could make Penny laugh and everything made her irritable or heartbroken. All while telling everyone she was fine.

Penny glugs down her tea and slowly sinks her head into her hands. At least a busy day can distract her from the basement and all the questions that she cannot find the answers for. Her grandma's outburst last night had left Penny even more confused and too scared to look any further for the key.

'Maybe some mysteries are meant to stay undiscovered,' Penny thinks, staring at the floor.

'Where has your smile gone, Miss. Figment?' Mr. Marblelight asks, as he walks over to her. Penny doesn't notice him until he sits down in the armchair next to her.

'There's a lot happening, inside my head,' she admits, hiding her head in her hands. 'More so than usual.'

'You could talk to me about, if you'd like,' he asks, gently. 'Will that help?'

'Hold me and tell me that everything's going to be

ok,' Penny thinks, rubbing her jigsaw puzzle tattoo. 'No, I couldn't ask him that. That would be too weird…'

'Or I could just sit with you, if that would also help?' he asks, calmly.

'I discovered something exciting. But I promised my grandma that I wouldn't go back there,' Penny admits.

'What did you discover? Mr. Marblelight asks, his eyes twinkling in the daylight.

'Behind the velvet curtain is a door that leads to a basement,' Penny says. 'No one's ever told me about it before. I know nothing about it, but it's beautiful.'

'Nora doesn't want you going back there?' he mutters.

'Nope. She got quite angry about it.' Penny pauses and then stares at him, for a several moments. 'You know my grandma?'

'I did, once.'

'She's never mentioned you before?'

'We haven't spoken in years.' he sighs. 'I think if your grandma doesn't want you going down there, I'd say you should respect that. If that's what she definitely wants.'

'I thought you'd say that.' Penny grumbles.

He chuckles. 'I'm sure Emily would tell you something different. Looking for trouble was always her speciality.'

'Yeah and she always dragged me along with her,' Penny says. 'You don't happen to know anything about the basement, do you, Mr. Marblelight?'

He looks up at the copy of Plato's *Symposium,* just above him. He takes it off the shelf, smiles at Penny and hands her the correct amount of change.

'I used to adore the work of Plato,' He says, ignoring Penny's confused expression. 'But I lost my copy years ago and I never thought to buy another. Maybe it's time to read this again.'

He gets to his feet and slowly walks out of the shop, leaving Penny utterly bamboozled.

'That was odd,' She thinks, shoving the money in her shirt-pocket and chases after Mr. Marblelight. However, he's lost amongst another wave of customers and nowhere to be found.

Another hour of busy work commences. Amidst the chaos, Penny carries large stacks of books from one side of her shop to the other. Organising them gives her a sense of peace; Penny loves dealing with fictional characters much more than real people. She carefully slots each book onto the shelf, giving every book a home in and admiring every title.

Penny's phone rings, from her dungaree pouch. It's an unfamiliar feeling because no one's called her for a long time. When she hesitantly answers the call, she treats her phone as if it's a firework that's about to explode.

'Hey, Penny!' Millie explodes.

Penny almost drops her phone from shock. Her heart begins to flutter but she doesn't know what to say.

'Penny?' Millie asks again. Penny doesn't say anything. 'Have I got the right number? Christopher gave it to me. I thought I'd surprise you with a little catch-up, if you're free. Oh, shit. Have I scared you away?'

'I'm here, Millie,' Penny replies, taking a deep sigh of relief. 'You couldn't scare me away.'

'Oh, great. You ok?'

'Err… I'm fine,' Penny quickly replies, unconvincingly. She presses her phone against her ear and shoulder and jumps onto her book trolley; racing over to move an antique atlas out of grasp from a screaming toddler.

'How are you?' Penny asks.

'I've finished work early. It's been such a shit day. I could do with hearing a friendly voice,' Millie says.

'Well, it's actually complete chaos here.' Penny says as she steers her trolley away from a group of schoolgirls.

'Chaos sounds fun.'

'I'd much rather be hanging out with you.'

'Why don't I come over?' Millie asks. 'It sounds like you need help.'

'I can't ask you to help me,' Penny says, as she organises and re-organises the feminist literature.

'You're not asking. I'm insisting.'

'Come over when all the customers have gone.'

'You need help.'

'I'll be fine.'

'I'm bringing cake.'

'You don't have to… what?'

'I'll be there in ten minutes. I'm bringing cake.'

'Wait, Millie!' Penny cries, but Millie has hung up.

When Millie arrives, carrying a flask of hot chocolate and a tin full of cupcakes it's as if a Greek goddess has ascended upon Penny, showing her glorious mercy. She's dressed in a pastel pink trouser suit, a faded *Star Wars* t-shirt underneath and purple trainers. Penny sprints over and throws her arms around Millie. She has crayons sticking out of her hair and is incredibly sweaty.

'Thank you so much,' Penny says, gasping for breath.

'I tried to get Christopher and Dexter to come, but Dexter hates people and Christopher has to catch-up on work.'

'You're amazing.'

Millie puts down her flask and cake tin and rolls up her sleeves. 'What do you need me to do?'

Just before Penny can give Millie a stack of books to shelve, there's a thundering crash and if Millie wasn't ready to help, Penny would've hidden away in the basement and cried. Without saying anything else, they nod at each other and sprint over to find a fallen bookcase and small mountains of books, scattered across the floor. With every ounce of strength they have, they manage to push the bookcase upright and organise the books back onto the shelves. Then, they take it in turns to either serve customers or run errands around the shop. When the two of them pass each other, they reassure the other of their hard work. As they stack books together they try to make each other laugh and, soon enough, life doesn't seem as stressful for Penny.

At the end of the day, when there are no more customers, Penny shuts the door and takes a deep sigh of relief. She staggers into the depths of her bookshop and finds Millie sitting cross-legged and looking up at all the political and feminist books. She's discarded her pink blazer and now she's licking the frosting off a strawberry cupcake, clutching a hot chocolate with marshmallows.

'Thank you so much, for today,' Penny says, sitting down next to her. Millie pours her a cup of hot-chocolate and gives her a white chocolate and raspberry cupcake.

'Hey, that's what friends are for.' Millie gives her a grin.

'It's been a long time since I've had any friends to hang out with,' Penny mumbles, hiding her blushing face behind her hot chocolate.

'Me too,' Millie says. She takes a deep sigh when she sees the surprised look on Penny's face. 'Sometimes, when I get too excitable, I can scare people away.' She drains her mug and then lies on the floor, looking up at all the towering books. 'I don't mean to, I'm not a monster. I've just always struggled to make friends.'

Penny drinks her own hot chocolate and then lies down, next to Millie. 'Me too. Maybe we could stay friends?' Penny says, without thinking. 'Oh, God. You sound so bloody desperate.' she thinks.

'I'd love that.' Millie giggles. Her feet fidget with joy. 'Pinky-promise?' she asks, holding out her little finger.

Penny wraps her little finger around Millie's. 'I pinky-promise that we will stay friends.'

'How about best friends?' Millie asks.

Penny's heart begins to flutter. She'd never thought that she could ever share a moment like this again.

'I promise that we will be best friends,' Penny says. The two of them kiss their pinky fingers and then start giggling.

'Dexter always thinks I'm an idiot for swearing on a pinky-promise,' Millie admits, when they break apart.

'Me and Emily always used to swear on a pinky-promise,' Penny says. 'I don't think Dexter likes me.'

'What? Dexter does like you; he can just come across a bit cold at first. He's a miserable bastard, but I do love him. You'd know if he didn't like you. He swears at lot more.'

'That's good to know.' Penny giggles.

'Who's Emily, by the way?'

Penny's body completely freezes. She slowly sits up, cross-legged and fidgets with her hands in her lap.

'Err… Emily was my mum.' Penny looks down at her hands, avoiding eye-contact with Millie, trying not to burst into tears. 'She worked with me in The Author's Library, once. Err… She's not here, anymore.'

Millie sits up and slides over to Penny, wrapping her arms around her waist. 'I'm so sorry. You don't have to talk about it, if you don't want to.'

As Millie nuzzles her face into her friend's hair, Penny lifts her arms and clings onto Millie. Almost as if she might lose her best friend, at any moment.

'Thanks, Mills,' Penny mutters.

'I lost my dad, a few years ago,' Millie says, her voice beginning to wobble. 'He was strict and brutal, but I always loved him, regardless. It completely broke Christopher, though. He suddenly lost himself and became almost empty. He's always had me and Dex at his side but we both knew that he needed something else in his life. Then, he met you.'

I'm nothing special,' Penny mutters, as Millie pours her another drink and gives her extra marshmallows.

'Oh, you can shut up, right now,' Millie says, almost spilling her hot-chocolate over her t-shirt. 'You're everything special and more. You changed Christopher, for the better. Without even knowing it, you gave him that fulfilment that he never knew he needed. Actually, I think he's quite fond of you...'

'You're talking nonsense. He doesn't like me, like that... Does he?'

'Do you like him?'

'Err... No?'

'How convincing.'

'We're just friends.'

'That's what they all say,' Millie cries, spilling hot chocolate over herself. 'So were me and Dexter, once.'

'That's a completely different story.'

'It still had a happy ending, though?' Millie rocks

back and forth, giddy with glee and blushing cheeks. 'Destiny brought you two together…'

'Or it was just a stormy night?'

'The perfect setup for a romantic tale,' Millie shrieks, throwing her hands up into the air. 'Don't tell me you haven't thought about it.'

'Of course I have. But I'm not going to tell his sister that.' Penny thinks. 'Err… I'm too awkward for romance.' she says.

'So what? Do you think Dexter is Shakespeare? On our first date, he sorted me into my chosen Hogwarts house. On our second date, we played Dungeons & Dragons.'

'Oh, wow!' Penny says and the two of them giggle again.

'Can I ask? Why do you want to find this key, so badly? Why is it so important, to you?'

Penny sighs. 'My mum and I discovered that basement together. I know she would've loved to have gone back there. But I'm not allowed anymore.'

'What's stopping you?' Millie sits up with her legs outstretched.

'I had to promise my grandma that I wouldn't go looking for the key. Let alone go back to the basement, ever again. She's the only family I've got left. If I went back down there, I'd only go looking for trouble.'

'Sometimes, it's fun to go looking for trouble,' Millie suggests, cheekily. 'You can rely on your friends to help you with that.'

'Even if I were allowed, I wouldn't be able to. I

never found the key.' Penny hangs her head, ashamed of her own failure.

'Well, why don't we keep looking?'

'I've looked everywhere. Christopher and Dexter couldn't find it, either.'

'True. But you haven't looked with me yet,' Millie says, flashing Penny a charmingly wicked smile.

'You were there, when we were looking all night,' Penny reminds her. 'Well, you were asleep.'

'You'd be sleeping too, if you were having a lovely dream about riding a marshmallow into space.'

'I don't think we'll find the key, Mills. The basement underneath my bookshop seems like it'll always be a mystery.'

Penny lies back down and keeps her gaze up. The thought of disappointing Emily is too painful to bear. But when Millie peers over and sees Penny's blank expression, she grabs her hand and drags them both to their feet.

'What are you doing?'

'I haven't given up looking for that key. Neither should you.'

'We won't find it, Millie. It's hopeless.'

'No. It's hopeless when you look for something with Christopher and Dexter. I don't know which one's worse. You haven't looked with me yet. I don't believe in giving up. Come on.'

While still holding onto Penny's hand, Millie drags her into the depths of The Author's Library.

'Where are we going?'

'Here.' Millie cries. She suddenly comes to a halt,

with Penny crashing into her. The two girls are surrounded by romantic novels.

'I've already looked here,' Penny sadly admits.

'Maybe you have,' Millie acknowledges. 'But sometimes you need to look for something from a different perspective.' She places her hands on the floor and kicks her legs up into a handstand.

'Have you ever tried looking for something, while standing on your head?' Millie asks.

'No.'

'Well, why not? For God's sake, join me.'

Penny quickly copies Millie; both seeing the bookshop, upside-down.

'Have you found it, yet?' Millie asks, after a minute.

'Nope.'

Millie kicks her legs down, flipping herself upright and her cheeks are as pink as her hair. Penny does the same.

'Then, let's keep looking,' Millie declares.

The two girls spend an hour looking for the key; continuously flipping themselves upside-down and staring at anything the eye could see. They lead each other amongst several genres of books; laughing harder and becoming dizzier, every time they decide to move on.

'The boys would've never thought to search for something, like this.' Penny says. Both of them staring at a row of Greek tragedies, still upside-down.

'Have you found anything?'

'No, still nothing… wait!' Penny suddenly cries, almost toppling over from excitement.

All the Greek tragedies on the lowest shelf are perfectly in line with each other and tightly packed together. All except for a well-loved copy of Sophocles' *Antigone,* which has been placed at the end of the shelf, hidden in the shadows. The book doesn't seem firmly closed and it's as if something has been wedged inside, separating its pages.

Penny flips herself upright and takes *Antigone* off the shelf. She gently opens the book and a small key falls out of the pages and into the palm of her hand. She gasps in delight and clutches onto it, as if it could suddenly disappear. Penny drops the book and looks back at Millie, who's standing behind her.

'You found it,' Millie whispers.

'I found the key.'

The two girls suddenly explode in a fit of giggles and cries of triumph.

'Millie, call Christopher and Dexter,' Penny says. 'We have to go down to the basement, tonight. I can't wait any longer.'

While Millie calls the others Penny drifts to the other side of the bookcase and sinks onto the floor.

'If only you could see me now,' Penny mutters. Her cheeks begin to ache from smiling so much.

When Millie gets off the phone, she finds Penny and joins her. Penny throws her arms around her and they hug for several moments, revelling in the moment. Penny has a funny feeling that what lies beneath the bookshop is about to become a lot more intriguing.

However, she hasn't noticed the message in *Antigone,* handwritten on the same page the key was found.

My heart has been broken. Yet, I never thought it would be from you.

Hidden Stories

'Who thought this was a good idea?' Dexter asks, clinging onto Christopher.

'Will you let go of me? I'm losing all the feeling in my arm.'

'Well, it's a good job that you're left-handed, then.'

'I can't wait to see what's behind that door,' Penny says, clutching onto the key. 'Maybe it'll explain everything.'

'This is so exciting,' Millie squeals.

'I'll ask again. Who thought this was a good idea?' Dexter asks.

'I did,' Penny cries. 'You didn't have to come with me.'

'Well, someone has to look after Christopher,' Dexter replies.

'I can look after myself,' Christopher says, trying to release himself from Dexter's grasp.

'You tell yourself that, mate. I care for you, so no one else has to.'

The four of them continue their descent to the basement. When they stand beneath The Author's Library, Penny re-lights all the candles and everything in the room is revealed.

'Wow!' Millie breathes. 'You'd never expect to find this beneath your bookshop.'

'I can understand why you're obsessed with finding the answers to this place,' Christopher admits to Penny. He slowly begins to circle the table, looking at the books abandoned on random pages. Penny and Millie follow him.

Meanwhile, Dexter hangs back at the entrance. 'It's just another room,' he grumbles, with his arms crossed.

'I'm not obsessed. I'm just curious,' Penny tells Christopher. Then, she shoots Dexter a scathing look. 'It's a secret that no one's ever told me about. Where's your sense of adventure, Dexter?'

'I left it upstairs, in your bloody bookshop.'

'Three chairs… Three different books… Three rum glasses,' Christopher mutters, gently stroking his beard. 'So, there must have been three people who once met down here.'

'Good point.' Penny mutters. 'Why didn't I think of that?' she thinks.

'Could this have anything to do with your great-great-grandma? Or the mystery of Robert Figment?' Christopher asks.

'You know, what? I did think of that,' Penny triumphantly says, with her hands on her hips. 'Everything that belonged to Ruth is on that bookshelf. But I don't know if it connects to everything else.'

'Penny? Do you know anything about this?' Millie asks, pointing to the wall that's right next to her.

Penny walks over to her. When she looks up close at the wall, she gasps. 'No, I don't.'

The entire wall is covered in handwritten messages, in different scripts; all disguised by the midnight-blue wallpaper:

I wish we could spend forever together...
Why must the time fly so quickly, when I spend such precious moments with you?

'Who wrote this?' Millie asks.

'I don't know,' Penny says. She rushes over to the bookcase and carefully takes out Ruth's journal and the copy of *Sherlock Holmes,* with Robert's message on the back page. Then, she walks back holding up each book, in turn.

'The handwriting doesn't match,' Penny confirms. 'So, Ruth must've hidden most of her stuff down here, but that's all she used it for. It still doesn't explain who else was down here.'

Penny turns away from the wall and looks back at the table, secretly hoping that the answers will suddenly appear in front of them.

'My grandma has to know something about this. There's no one else in my family, that I can think of, who could answer this for me.'

'Didn't you mention that your grandma told you not to go back to the basement?' Christopher asks.

Penny cheeks flush pink. 'Err... Maybe. I just chose not to listen...'

Avoiding more awkward questions, Penny quickly

runs over to the locked door with the key still clutched in her hand.

'I'm not going to give up, not just yet,' she mutters.

'We're definitely not going to tell you to give up,' Christopher reassures her, as he stands to her left.

'We're gonna help you, Penny,' Millie tells her, standing to her right. 'Whatever you need, we're here.'

'Thanks, guys,' Penny says, with a warm, fuzzy feeling in her tummy.

'I hate to break up a tender moment between you three, but I am not enjoying this,' Dexter announces, with his arms crossed and a scowl on his face.

'What's your problem?' Christopher says, as the three of them turn to face him, with their eyebrows raised.

'Don't look at me, like that,' Dexter says, stomping over to them. 'I'm standing in a basement, where no one can hear you scream...'

'I forget that you're scared of the dark.' Christopher chuckles.

'Don't worry, Dexter. The ghosts in my bookshop are perfectly friendly,' Penny teases.

'Boo!' Millie cries, as she creeps up behind Dexter and slams her hands on his shoulders. He shrieks and stumbles backwards, making the books rattle on their shelves.

'S... S... Screw you.' he snarls at Millie. 'I'm not afraid of the dark.'

'Are we going to unlock this door, or not?' Millie asks.

Penny stares back at the locked door and then looks down at the key in her hand. 'Sure,' she mumbles.

'What's wrong?' Christopher asks.

'Well, what if it's not what I expected?'

'You won't know until you try,' Millie replies, softly.

'It's just that… I've had so many ideas about what could be behind there. But what if it's boring?'

'I don't believe that for a second,' Christopher tells her. 'So instead of imagining, why don't we find out?'

Penny screws her eyes shut, clutching the key tightly until it makes a groove in her palm. 'This is for you, mum.' She thinks. When she opens her eyes, a brave sense of confidence washes over her.

'Let's do this,' Penny triumphantly says to her friends.

As predicted, the key fits perfectly in the lock. Penny wiggles it for a few seconds and with a shove against the door, it finally gives way and gently opens.

They're faced with a dark corridor, where the walls are bare and no lights to guide them. The tunnel seems never-ending. Even Dexter is curious enough to peer over Penny's shoulder to have a look. There's only enough space for one person at a time because on either side are stacks of paintings, bursting notebooks and abandoned books, all covered in dust and cobwebs.

'Eureka,' Penny mutters. She quickly pinches herself to make sure it's all real.

'It's all real,' Christopher whispers.

'Let's go,' Penny says, striding confidently into its depths with Christopher following behind her. They're several feet in when they suddenly look back at Millie and Dexter, who are still standing by the entrance.

'Aren't you coming with us?' Penny asks.

'Are you crazy?' Dexter exclaims.

'Yeah,' Penny replies.

'I think I'm gonna stay back,' Millie admits. 'This is all very exciting, but you guys can go on. It's starting to give me the heebie-jeebies.'

Tutting and turning back, Penny and Christopher take slow, cautious steps, deeper into the tunnel. When they finally reach a dead-end, Penny illuminates everything with her torch. All the books are Greek tragedies, philosophies or epic poetry; some are translated into modern English and others are still in the ancient language. Most of them appear to be in good condition, with just a few cracks in the spine and no loose pages.

'They're the same types of books that were found on the table,' Penny observes.

'Even the handwriting seems the same as the

messages on that wall,' Christopher tells her. 'So all this has to connect with everything else.'

He gently takes out a copy of Euripides' *Medea* and shows it to Penny, carefully turning the pages. She shines her torch on the notes written around the text:

Medea, you beautiful priestess. Your spirit of determination has always inspired me.

'Why does this handwriting seem familiar?' Penny asks. 'Where have I seen this before?'

She picks up a leather-bound notebook and opens it to a random page. Once again, it's the same as the handwriting on the wall:

You can define a person by their actions. Yet, you can see who they are, by how and why they made that decision.

'It's like fragments of a story, hidden in other books. I just need to piece it all together, like a jigsaw-puzzle.'

'It seems like someone wanted all these books and paintings hidden away,' Christopher suggests. 'Perhaps they wanted everyone to forget all about the basement.'

'But why? That's what I want to know.'

'Wait. Look at this.'

Christopher shows Penny a pencil-sketch, drawn on a rough piece of paper; it's no bigger than a paperback but it's incredibly detailed, even though some of the lines seemed to have faded over time. It's of a young man and woman, sitting with their knees tucked under their chin, smiling at each other.

Penny looks up close at the female in the drawing. The wicked grin sketched on her face and her curly hair flying free seems all-too familiar. She then looks back at the notes written in *Medea*; it's almost as if she knew that these notes came from her.

'Do you recognise any of these people?' Christopher asks.

'No, but I feel like I should.'

Penny reaches for another drawing. It's significantly larger and has the same two figures, as well as a third; a slightly older man, who strokes his beard with his fingers. The three of them are gathered around the table, with open books in front of each of them. A half-full bottle of rum and a lit candle sits in the centre. The woman is hovering above her seat with a glass in one hand and a cigar in the other. Her mouth gaping open as if she'd just had an epiphany.

There's another painting which depicts the woman and the bearded man looking lovingly at each other. Christopher finds another of an ancient Greek warrior, who's ready for battle. At the bottom of every piece, it's signed: B. Figment.

'B. Figment,' Penny mutters.

'I thought you'd know who that is,' Christopher says.

'Nope. It seems like I've got more questions than answers, now.'

The two of them turn around and head out of the tunnel and back to the basement, carrying as many books, notebooks and drawings as they can.

'How did it go?' Millie asks, as she and Dexter follow behind the other two.

When Penny and Christopher scatter their finding across the floor, the four of them gather around it.

'You found all of this?' Dexter asks, with a slight intrigue in his voice.

'This and much more,' Christopher tells him.

'There were definitely three people who met down here, once,' Penny confirms, pointing to all the figures in the paintings.

'One of them was called B. Figment...' Christopher says.

'But I don't know who B. Figment is,' Penny admits. 'We also don't know why they met down here.'

'They all seem really fancy, what with all the rum and cigars?' Millie suggests.

'Or maybe there were pretending to be fancy,' Christopher adds.

'Penny, do you know who owned The Author's Library, back in 1955?' Dexter asks.

'My grandma took over the responsibility in 1953. Why?'

Dexter points to the back of several paintings. 'All

of these are dated back to 1955.'

Penny gasps. But when she checks each painting, Dexter's right. They're all dated from the same year.

'Surely not…' Penny mutters.

'Maybe your grandma is keeping secrets from you,' Dexter says, gently.

'Could she be one of the three?' Millie asks.

'Would she know who B. Figment is?' Christopher asks.

'Why would she hide a family member from me, or from my Mum, for so long?' Penny's heart begins to ache from the mention of Emily.

'Are you going to ask her again?' Christopher asks.

'I think I might have to. But she told me that she knew nothing about it…'

'She also told you not to go back,' Millie reminds her. 'Maybe she wanted to hide everything away.'

'But why?' Penny asks, for the umpteenth time. None of it made any sense.

She stands up and moves over to the wall covered in messages. She reads each one in turn, trying to piece together the story.

'It has to match up, somehow?' Penny thinks. She gently shuts her eyes and places a hand against the wall. 'If my ancestors can hear me, then send me a sign as to what this all means. I'll be a good Figment-girl, I promise…'

'Penny? Are you ok?' Christopher asks, as he walks up behind her and places a gentle hand on her shoulder.

Despite the kind gesture, Penny is abruptly shaken back to reality and her shriek echoes throughout the basement. Instantly and without thinking, she spins around and punches Christopher on the nose. He groans in agony and staggers backwards, covering his nose with his hands and gently bumping into Dexter, who screams even louder and sprints back upstairs.

'Dexter, wait.' Millie cries, as she chases after her husband and tries to stifle her laughter.

Ten minutes later and the group are sat amongst the fantasy books, each with a cup of tea to calm themselves down. Although Millie's still got the giggles.
'Why did you feel the need to punch me in the face?!' Christopher asks Penny.

'It was an immediate reaction. Your nose isn't broken, is it?'

'Nah, I should be fine. Dexter's already broken my nose once.'

'You deserved it,' Dexter says, loudly. He puts an arm around Millie, who snuggles into him.

'You're the one who thought it'd be funny to start a fight with Christmas decorations,' Christopher cries.

'It was funny. Besides, you're the one who started it in the first place...'

'No way. I called you a twat and you decided to

throw a bauble at my face.'

'That was a very messy Christmas,' Millie tells Penny. 'Mum still can't get the blood out of her favourite tea-towels.'

'Besides, Christopher,' Penny says. 'It's your fault, anyway.'

'Oh, yeah? Why's that?'

'You're the one who crept up on me. I thought you were a ghost.'

'You'd punch a ghost in the face? Surely, you'd just go right through it?'

'Don't question my logic.'

'You use logic?'

'Ha. Ha. You're not funny.'

'Order! Order!' Dexter cries, all of a sudden.

'What?' Penny doesn't realise that she's been edging close to Christopher the entire time and couldn't stop gazing into his eyes. Also, she completely forgot that Millie and Dexter were even there.

Millie and Dexter look at each other and nod, in unison. Then, they look back at the other two and smirk.

'We need to interject, before you two start making out, right in front of us,' Dexter declares.

'Huh?' Penny asks.

'We need to discuss the elephant in the room,' Millie adds.

'Here we go…' Christopher mumbles, shuffling

from one foot to the other. 'Why must you two always interfere with my life?'

'Who knows what would happen to you if we didn't?' Millie replies.

Christopher turns to face Penny. 'Look, there's something I want to tell you…'

'Take a look at yourself, Christopher.' Dexter swiftly interrupts. 'You're good-looking and single, but your romantic life is as lame as a donkey wearing a bowtie. You've dated so many questionable women…'

'I second that,' Millie adds.

'Anything else you'd like to add?' Christopher asks, loudly and sarcastically.

'The list is endless…' Dexter mutters.

'What is it, Christopher?' Penny asks. When he puts his hands into hers, she just wants to melt into a puddle.

'You two are so meant to be together!' Millie explodes, giddy with glee.

'What?' Penny shrieks, internally. She's frozen to the spot, with her hands stuck by her side and her eyes wide in shock. She can feel her heart flutter at a million miles an hour. 'This shit doesn't happen to me! I've dreamt about it enough times, but that's not enough… I should've read more books to prepare me, for this moment…'

'Penny?' Christopher asks. 'Are you ok?'

'…Romeo and Juliet were far too depressing… I

never read the end of *Pride and Prejudice* to know what happened… So, what do I do?' she thinks, frantically.

'Err… I really like you,' Christopher says, awkwardly. He blushes beneath his beard. 'I've felt this way for a while and I was just wondering if you felt the same way about me?'

'Umm… That's groovy?' she says, before instantly regretting it. 'Shit, what's wrong with me!?' she thinks.

While Christopher stares at her, totally baffled, Penny quickly tries to come up with every possible way to rectify the situation.

'Look, Christopher,' She says, with an odd amount of confidence. 'Being with you, is like I'm falling into a void. I have no idea what's happening…'

'What?'

'Should we help them?' Dexter mutters to Millie.

'You're not helping them,' Millie hisses back.

In this moment, Penny just wishes she could disappear in a puff of smoke. But instead, she keeps her eyes on Christopher and takes a deep breath.

'No,' Penny cries, clinging onto Christopher's hands. 'What I mean is… I really like you, too. Ever since you came to my bookshop, it's been wonderful and you've made me so happy. Maybe we could go from there.'

'I'm so glad it's not just me,' Christopher admits, with a chuckle. 'I thought I was going mad.'

'Welcome to my world.'

Just as they're about to kiss, Penny and Christopher slowly look back at Millie and Dexter.

'I think I'm going to cry,' Millie squeals, with her arms around her husband.

'I think I'm going to be sick,' Dexter grumbles, although there's a smile on his face.

'Are you two still here?' Christopher asks them.

'Apparently,' Dexter replies, sarcastically.

'We should leave you two alone.' Millie says. She rushes forward to give Penny and hug. 'Love you.'

'Love you too.'

'Come on, Dexter!' Millie grabs his hand and marches him out of the bookshop.

'Have fun, kids.' Dexter calls out.

Night slowly begins to fall over the bookshop. Suddenly, Penny and Christopher don't know what to say to each other.

'So… Where were we?' Penny asks, awkwardly.

'Was I going to kiss you?'

'I think so.'

Christopher takes a step forward. So does Penny. Neither of them say anything again, for several moments.

'Does this feel weird, to you?' Penny asks.

'It does and it doesn't.'

'Thank God. I thought it was just me.'

The two of them sink to the floor, with their backs against the bookcases. When they look at each other, they begin to giggle.

'Millie and Dexter have not helped, at all,' Christopher admits.

'But if we like each other, then we should do something about it,' Penny says.

'True.'

'We were fine, earlier.'

'Things were great.'

'Why should it be weird now?'

'It shouldn't be.'

'Then, I really want to kiss you.'

'We'd have beautiful children.'

'What?'

'Nothing!'

Christopher holds Penny in his arms but does this too quickly. As he tries to bring her closer, they accidentally knock their heads together.

'Ooff!' The two of them groan, simultaneously. They look back at one another and start laughing.

'What's wrong with us?' Christopher asks, still holding her in his arms.

This time, Penny places a hand on his cheek and draws herself in closer, until their lips are locked together, and they kiss for several, glorious minutes. Penny clings onto Christopher's biceps while he gently runs his fingers through her hair. Even when they break apart, they keep their gaze on each other and the smiles never fade from their faces.

'Stay with me, tonight,' Penny says, as she rests

her head on Christopher's shoulder. He puts an arm around her and she snuggles in, close.

'Of course.'

Uncovering the Past

Night continues to fall on The Author's Library. Penny grabs the duvet from her bedroom and brings it to her bookshop and she and Christopher huddle underneath it, amongst the fantasy books. When he puts his arm around her, she snuggles into his chest.

'So, what's your story?' Penny asks.

'I would've thought Millie told you everything.'

'Some things, but not everything. I want to hear it from you.'

'I haven't really told anyone before. Apart from Millie and Dexter, who were there when it happened.'

'You can trust me.'

*

Christopher slowly lays down and rests his head on Penny's duvet-covered lap. She gently runs her fingers through his hair, which makes him feel at peace and he fully relaxes into her. She's the first person he can trust after everything that had happened; almost as much as Millie and Dexter. Whatever he said to her, Penny would never laugh or mock him. Instead, she would listen and that in itself gave Christopher a warm, fuzzy feeling in his tummy.

'I haven't been able trust anyone in a long time,' he begins to say. 'A few weeks after Dad died, I slowly began to drift away from Millie and Dexter. Which sounds mad, considering how close we are now and I couldn't live my life without them…'

'They're so wonderful.'

'Even when I didn't know it, Millie and Dexter always kept an eye out for me. They warned me about the people I was hanging out with, but even when I didn't listen to them, they never held it against me. They never made me feel bad for the mistakes I've made. Their support throughout it all, made me stronger.'

Christopher slowly sits up and leans his head back against the bookcases. He likes it when Penny rests her head on his shoulder.

'A few years ago, I used to hang out with a group of lads who weren't there when I needed them most,' he says, quietly. It's almost as if he's ashamed to admit it. 'We used to go out and party every weekend. I drank so heavily, that I could never remember what I'd done. I'd snort and smoke whatever they had, which scared me but never stopped me. I'd pick up girls and then break their hearts, the next day.'

'That doesn't sound like you?' Penny says.

'I remember when Millie and Dexter said that to me. But I just wanted to fit in with the crowd and I wanted to find a way to forget all the pain. Maybe it wasn't the best idea, but I followed them wherever they went, like a sheep.'

'We've all been there,' she reassures him.

'You probably think I'm such an idiot.'

Penny links her fingers with Christopher's and gives them a comforting squeeze. 'Listen. Everyone screws up, it's what makes us human. Otherwise, we may as well be robots. Plus, you're better now because you don't do that anymore.'

Christopher smiles and kisses the top of Penny's head. 'That's true. I was trapped in a world I didn't want to live in and was just too scared to walk away. I thought that if I did, I'd be on my own and that was too painful to bear, even though I always had Millie and Dexter. Two years ago, they found me lying unconscious in the middle of the road. If it wasn't for them, I could've died that night.'

'What happened?'

'I was on a night out with the lads, but I'd finally had enough and decided to walk away from them. I couldn't do it anymore and wanted to go back to Millie and Dexter. But the leader of the group didn't like that, and he hit me in the back of the head with a piece of pipe. I collapsed onto the road face first, barely conscious. Two of my back teeth were knocked out and they continued to beat me up. When I stopped moving, they thought I was dead and they scarpered.'

Tears begins to fill Christopher's eyes and he begins to sob. When he tries to hide his face in his hands, Penny wipes away his tears and holds him close. For a few moments, she becomes his shoulder to cry on and he doesn't feel ashamed or weak. Instead, it's a cry for help that can finally be released.

When Christopher eventually sits up, he lifts his t-shirt and shows Penny the scars across his back; there are even deep slashes across his shoulder-blades, where his skin had to be stitched back together. When he turns back to Penny, she holds him in her arms, again.

'I'll always have these scars,' he tells her. 'Even though I don't always see them, I know they'll always be there. I guess it's my mark for trying to do the right thing.'

'You did do the right thing,' she says. 'Those guys were bastards.'

'I remember hearing Millie's screams and Dexter checking to see if I was still alive. They found me, just as the lads were running away. If it wasn't for them, I would've been left for dead. They took me to the hospital and stayed by my side. When I was discharged, they wanted me to live with them and that's where I've been living ever since.'

'They're such good people.'

'They really are. I never saw those lads, again, not that I ever wanted to. Millie and Dexter stood by me through every doctor's procedure and helped me get back on my feet. That's when I decided to go back to my studies, work hard and became an academic in English literature. I decided that the party-animal life wasn't for me.

'But even though I tried to get to get my life back on track, I knew I wasn't happy. I was too scared to let go because the last time I did that, it got me into trouble. There were times when I wouldn't leave the house after dark, for fear of getting attacked again. Despite Millie and Dexter's reassurance, I lacked a lot of confidence. It took me a long time to hang out with anyone else, because I was too scared to trust anyone, and I couldn't put myself through that. That was, until I met you.'

'Me?'

'Yeah. You sussed me out and I couldn't deny it, for much longer. From the first night we met, I knew I could trust you and I could trust my instincts again.'

'There was a part of me that thought I had scared you away,' Penny admits, shyly.

'Never.'

Christopher kisses Penny gently, placing both hands on either side of her face. When she wraps her arms around his waist, he can feel the butterflies in his stomach.

When the two of them break apart, they look out of the window and notice the sun rising. Christopher holds her close and kisses the top of her head, nuzzling his nose into her hair.

'So, that's my story,' he concludes. 'What about you…'

But when Christopher looks at Penny, she's fallen asleep and gently snoring. He smiles and gently falls asleep, too. Both of them feeling safe in each other's arms.

*

Penny and Christopher sleep all throughout Sunday morning and straight through lunch. They probably would've slept all day, if Penny's grandma hadn't woken them up.

As always, Nora arrives at two minutes before 3:30pm, like she does every Sunday. At first, she thought it was strange that the bookshop wasn't bumbling with customers. But it all made sense, when Nora found her granddaughter asleep in another man's arms. She begins to jab Penny in the ribs with her walking stick, with a scowl on her face. When Penny doesn't wake up, Nora prods her harder.

'Huh?' Penny grumbles. She slowly opens her eyes and is greeted by her grandma, looming over her.

'Good afternoon, Penelope,' Nora announces, loudly.

'Hi Grandma!' Penny cries, throwing the duvet off herself and Christopher and scrambling onto her feet.

'What was that for? I was enjoying...' Christopher mutters, running his hands through his hair, with sleep still in his eyes. Instead of seeing Penny, he catches Nora glaring back at him.

'You won't be enjoying anything for much longer,' Nora snarls at him.

'Err… Good morning,' Christopher mumbles, jumping to his feet and awkwardly standing at Penny's side.

'Good afternoon, to the both of you,' Nora says.

'Grandma, I can explain everything…'

'Penelope! You've left the bookshop in a right state,' Nora cries. She looks behind her at the abandoned books on the floor and then drags her glare back to her granddaughter. 'Ruth Figment would be very disappointed in you…'

'Oh, that makes me feel great,' Penny thinks. 'I'm sorry?' she mutters.

'Now, who are you?' Nora sharply asks Christopher.

'Er… It's nice to meet you.' Christopher's cheeks flush pink.

'Who are you?' Nora demands, again.

'Err… I'm not sure…'

'You don't know your own name?'

'No…' Christopher mutters.

'Are you an idiot?'

'I don't know…'

'Grandma, please don't scare him away,' Penny moans.

'Listen, Penelope,' Nora says, still glaring at Christopher. 'If you're going to take someone as a lover, at least makes sure he's not an imbecile.'

'My name is Christopher.'

'Don't try and change my mind, Christopher,' Nora says, with her nose in the air. 'You're a fool and I've made up my mind about you.'

'He was just leaving,' Penny quickly says. She pushes Christopher away from her grandma before it can get any worse.

'Go,' She hisses to him.

'It was lovely to meet you,' Christopher calls out to Nora, as Penny hauls him out of the bookshop. He quickly kisses Penny on the top of her head and darts outside.

When Penny walks back to her grandma, she's standing in the same position with both hands clutched around her walking stick.

'Listen, Grandma,' Penny says. 'Before you judge me...'

'You don't know what I'm going to say,' Nora says, her face expressionless.

'Christopher really is just a friend of mine...'

'Did he stay the night or not?'

'He stayed the night!'

As if it couldn't get any more humiliating, Penny freezes in fear when she hears Millie's voice thundering throughout the bookshop.

'Shit.' Penny thinks.

Penny slowly turns around, in dread. She usually would've been fine with Millie and Dexter marching towards her and dragging Christopher by the hand; it just doesn't help that her grandma's gaze is burning into the back of her head.

'What is all of this nonsense…?' Nora begins to say.

'He stayed the bloody night,' Dexter cries.

Millie and Dexter throw Christopher forward and he stumbles into Penny's arms. Almost collapsing from the force of his weight, the two of them quickly stand up straight and neither of them look at each other. Penny keeps her eyes on her grandma's and Christopher looks down at his shoes.

'Couldn't this have waited, until later?' Christopher mumbles. Then, he looks up at Nora and awkwardly waves at her. 'Err… Hi, again.'

'Hello again, Christopher,' Nora says, bluntly.

'Hiya. You must be Penny's grandma? I'm Millie and this is Dexter.' Millie bounces up to Nora and offers her hand. To Penny's relief, her grandma accepts.

'Nora Figment,' She says, before quickly retracting her hand.

'Grandma?' Penny mutters. 'These are my friends…'

'Christopher's more than a friend to Penny,' Dexter mutters, loud enough for everyone to hear. Penny glares at him, but Dexter gives her wicked smirk.

'I knew you two would make the perfect couple,'

Millie says to Penny and Christopher.

'Guys, this is not a good time,' Penny hisses, wishing she could evaporate on the spot.

'Nora? Don't you think that Penny and Christopher are meant to be together?' Millie asks.

'Oh Gods, Mills. Please don't ask my grandma that,' Penny thinks, hiding her face in her hands.

'He seems like a blithering idiot, to me,' Nora declares.

'That makes two of us,' Dexter mutters.

'Well, it was lovely to see you guys,' Penny says. 'but it's time for you all to go.'

Before anything else can happen, she hauls her friends out of The Author's Library.

'Thanks for that,' she murmurs, sarcastically.

'You're welcome,' Dexter replies, with a grin on his face.

'Sorry, Penny,' Millie says. 'Did we get you into trouble?'

'I might have to answer some awkward questions, from my grandma.'

'Did you and Christopher cuddle?' Dexter asks loudly.

'Oh, for God's sake!' Penny cries, although she's trying to stifle her laugh. 'Yes, we did.'

Millie and Dexter swiftly leave. Before Christopher heads out, he looks back at Penny, one last time.

'Will I see you soon?' Penny asks, standing on her tiptoes so she can look deep into his eyes.

'Do you even need to ask that question?' He smiles and places a gentle hand on her waist.

'I guess not.'

Just before the two of them can kiss goodbye, Christopher gets quickly dragged away by Dexter.

'Come on,' he yells. 'If Penny wants us out of her bookshop, that includes you!'

'Don't ruin their magical moment, Dexter!' Penny can hear Millie cry, just before the front door slams shut.

Dazed and filled with happiness, Penny begins to sway from side to side and revels in the moment. She jumps out of her skin, when she turns around and sees Grandma standing behind her. Suddenly, what's just happened has all come screaming back to her.

'Err… Hi Grandma? Shall we…'

'Don't think you can get away with this, Penny! You've known Christopher for some time, haven't you?'

'Shall we have a cup of tea?' Penny asks, her cheeks flushing scarlet.

'Answer the question.'

'He's a nice guy?'

'All those friends of yours were foolish…' Nora mutters, as Penny quickly links arms with her and swiftly leads them into the depths of The Author's Library. 'Have you always acted this inanely?'

'I learnt it all from Mum.'

'Of course, you did.' Nora tuts, but a smile begins

to grow on her face. 'My daughter was as mad as a box of frogs, getting you into all kinds of mischief. I was the one who taught you how to read and write properly.'

Penny squeezes her Grandma's arm, lovingly. 'I'll always be grateful of that, Grandma. You know that. But surely, you had fun at some point in your life.'

Nora looks away from her granddaughter. When she was a young woman in the early 50s, Nora loved being passionate and carefree; running in-between the bookcases, with no heels on and letting her hair fly free. But when customers wouldn't take her seriously, still seeing her as a little girl, she had no choice but to change her ways.

'I had to prove something back then,' Nora replies. 'Every morning, I set myself expectations and I did everything I could to achieve them. I would never let what other people think of me, dictate the way I worked. I would wear my highest heels, my smartest suit and my glossiest pearls. I sold more books every day, so nobody could argue with the figures.'

Penny and Nora walk past the ancient Greek literature. *Antigone* is still discarded on the floor.

'Oh really, Penny.' Nora huffs, breaking away from her and shuffling forward to pick it up. 'You must take better care of the books you sell. Have some respect for someone else's story…'

But when Nora picks up *Antigone,* she sees the page with the handwritten message inside:

My heart has been broken. Yet, I never thought it would be from you.

Nora stares at the message, with tears filling her eyes. She can feel the ground sway beneath her feet and clings onto her walking stick.

'What's the matter, Grandma?' Penny asks, walking over towards her.

Nora doesn't respond, but instead remembers when she wrote that message back in 1955. She wanted to forget everything and so she hid it all away, along with the key. She doesn't even notice her granddaughter looking over her shoulder and gasping.

'This book should not be sold. It's been tarnished,' Nora mutters. But before she can put the tragedy in her handbag, Penny snatches it out of her hands.

'Penelope!' Nora cries. 'What on earth…'

But Penny doesn't listen. She looks at the message in *Antigone* and suddenly, all the pieces of the puzzle begin to fit together. It's a similar piece of literature that's also found in the basement. Penny thought that the handwritten messages seemed familiar as well as the woman in all the sketches; she was wearing square-shaped glasses and a formal suit.

'Why are you gawking at me, like that?' Nora asks, although her voice begins to tremble when she sees her granddaughter staring back at her. 'Give that book to me.'

'You taught me how to write, when I was younger,' Penny whispers.

'Yes, Penny. We've already established that.'

'You sat with me and wrote out the alphabet, for me to copy.'

'Are we going to have this cup of tea, tonight? Or are we going to stand around, repeating the same conversation?'

'Did you write this?' Penny blurts out, pointing to the message in the book.

Nora snatches *Antigone* and stuffs it into her bag. 'You would never find me writing such foolish thoughts in such precious works of literature,' she cries, almost too defensively.

'You were one of them, weren't you?' Penny asks, just loud enough for her grandma to hear. 'You were one of the three who went down to the basement. Back in 1955.'

'Are we really going to have to discuss this, again?' Nora asks, crossing her arms and scowling. 'I've already told you, Penny. The basement is of no importance…'

'Who's B. Figment?' Penny blurts out.

Nora's face suddenly turns a deep shade of red. She clutches onto her walking stick, as if she's strangling someone.

'I have no idea who that is,' Nora tries to say, as confidently as she can.

'Yes, you do.'

'He's no one important.'

'So, you do know who he is. I've never heard of him before.'

'That's how it should always be.'

'But is he a part of our family?'

'No, he isn't!' Nora shrieks, slamming her walking stick on the ground. 'He hasn't been a part of this family in years.'

'Who is B. Figment?' Penny asks again, loudly.

'A useless man, Penelope! There's an answer for you!' Nora shrieks. 'He's a coward who betrayed our family.'

'There were three of you, who went down to the basement. What happened?'

'I told you to never go back there,' Nora snaps.

'What happened down there?'

'Why must you persistently ask questions, Penelope?'

'I have to know.'

'Why do you want to know?' Nora cries, tears now falling down her cheeks. 'So you can fall into another story, but forget your own? That seems to be what you've always done; you never want to face your own reality. You've been this way ever since Emily died…'

'Shut up! Just shut up!'

Penny drops to the floor, with her head in her hands. Her entire body is trembling.

'No, no, no…' She thinks, trying to forget.

Tentatively, Nora edges towards her and places a hand on her shoulder.

'Come on, Penny. Talking about all of this isn't bringing out the best in us. Why don't we forget all about it and have a cup of tea?'

Penny opens her eyes and slowly looks up at her grandma smiling at her but for once, Penny doesn't smile back.

'It's ironic that you accuse me of trying to forget the past, when you have appeared to do the exact same thing, Grandma.'

'Excuse me?'

'I know you're keeping secrets from this family.' Penny's voice hardens as she slowly stands up. 'You kept them for such a long time, too. You might not want to tell me about the basement, but I've discovered so much already. I'm not going to stop until I have all the answers to my questions.'

'Penny…'

But Nora doesn't have a chance to say anything else; Penny begins to sprint into the depths of the bookshop. She knows exactly where she's going and doesn't look back.

'Penny, please don't go back down there,' Nora begs, but she can't keep up with her.

Penny doesn't listen. She pushes the curtain aside, flings the door open and begins the descent. She's already reached the basement, by the time her Grandma has reached the door.

Madness Abundant

Penny staggers into the middle of the basement and collapses onto her knees. She stares at every book and drawing that's been laid out in front of her; hoping that if she stares at it for long enough, the answers to her questions will suddenly be revealed.

'Why did you all meet down here?' Penny asks, as she looks at a drawing with a trio gathered around the table; they're all smiling and lifting their glasses, presumably cheering each other. Penny points at the female in the picture.

'I know that's you, Grandma. Even if you won't admit it. But why did you hide this away from us, for so long? What's the story behind all this?'

Penny holds the sketch up close, until her nose is almost touching the paper. She keeps her focus on the two male figures, squinting and taking in every detail until her eyes begin to water.

'Which one of you was B. Figment? Who's the third person?'

Next, Penny flicks through every book, reading every note and message that's written around the text. Now, she recognises her grandma's handwriting, in Greek tragedies and written on the wall:

You have enlightened me with pure happiness. Let us stay together, for the rest of our lives.

Why should we allow fate to dictate our lives? Let's take a hold of our own future, together.

'Who was my grandma talking to?' Penny asks, as she wanders over to the wall and reads every message. 'She never mentioned falling in love with someone. Clearly, that's something else she forgot to mention…'

Penny circles the table, countless times until she becomes dizzy. Then, she stands over every armchair in turn, trying to work out the person who once sat there. She looks across the table, from every perspective.

'Three people must have met down here, often,' Penny mutters, as she kneels down at the first armchair. 'They discussed ancient literature… a lot.'

At the foot of the first armchair is a gold and emerald scarf that's fallen on top of a pair of brown moccasins. There's still a faint lipstick stain on the rim of the rum glass. A copy of Euripides' *Hecabe* and *The Trojan Women* lie open at random pages in front.

'I'm sure that my grandma sat here,' Penny says, as she cautiously turns to each Greek tragedy:

These women feel trapped under the pressure of mankind, as their world is collapsing around them. But we are women: stronger, as always.

At the second armchair, there's a ruby-red blazer that hangs over the back. Even though it feels like she's intruding on someone else's privacy, Penny delves into the pocket. In one, there's a half-empty tin of cigars and a box of matches; in the other is an old pocket-watch, engraved with *M.M.*

'M.M must be the third person,' Penny says, dancing on her tiptoes. 'Grandma, B. Figment and M.M. So, who is M.M?'

Neatly laid out in front, is a small pile of ancient Greek philosophies in pristine condition. But the suede notebook beside it is packed with intellectual notes and musings:

We make decisions, every day of our lives. Some are life-changing and others are mundane. Nevertheless, they define who we are as a person. But what direction would our lives take, if we made different choices, on that day?

'So, who are you, B. Figment?' Penny asks, as she kneels beside the final armchair. Disappointingly, there isn't anything that suggests who this person is. There's a few pencil sketches of Greek warriors, all of them signed: B. Figment. At the bottom of one of them, it's written:

I am not a coward. I am as strong and as brave as a Greek warrior.

Homer's *Iliad* and *Odyssey* have been abandoned to the side. However, as Penny flicks through, she notices faint pencil sketches of all the characters across the text, on various pages. Each sketch is incredibly detailed: there are sharp lines to depict the perfect male body and perfect shading around every contour; almost as if the characters could fly off the page and jump into life.

Penny looks at every sketch in both epic poems, then she looks up at the mural on the ceiling. She gasps. She's been so focused with what was below, that she never thought to look up. The ceiling is completely sketched-out but only half-painted. There's a bright blue sky and clouds that part way for three figures riding on a golden dragon-led chariot. It's the same three figures as the ones in the sketches; only this time, they're painted like ancient Greek Gods and Goddesses. The sun glistens in the background and lights them up spectacularly. The dragons have determined looks on their faces but are controlled by those in the chariot. All three figures look off into the distance, at a hopeful future; there's a man with a long beard who has his arm around the woman, stood in the centre. She has a wicked grin on her face and her hair's flowing free.

'Wow,' Penny whispers. She sinks to the floor and hugs her knees to her chest. For several minutes, she doesn't take her eyes off the ceiling.

Eventually, Penny stumbles back upstairs. She doesn't bother heading up to her bedroom. Instead she finds her duvet and crawls under it, falling fast asleep.

The next day is a quiet one. Towards the end of the day, Penny finds Ivy Thistlethwaite in and amongst the dystopian books, flicking through the pages of *Fahrenheit 451* with tears in her eyes.

'Hey, Ivy?' Penny says, offering her a tissue. 'What's the matter?'

Ivy looks back at her goddaughter and wipes her tears away. Then, she collapses into Penny's arms and continues to sob.

'Oh, Penny. Normally, I would hate it if you found me like this. But today, I felt like I had to be here and feel sad. I don't know how you're staying so strong. Just like Emily.'

'I don't understand.'

'Do you know what day it is today?'

'Yeah? It's…' When she realises the date, Penny voice trails off. Her limbs become heavy which forces her to drop to the floor. 'Thirtieth June… Two years ago…'

As she hugs her knees to her chest and stares into the distance, Ivy sits down next to her and weaves small, blue hydrangea's throughout her hair.

'How could I forget?' Penny whispers.

'It was an incredibly sad day, for all of us.' Ivy reassures her…

Emily stood in front of her mum, her daughter and her best friend. Up until now, Emily was too scared to admit the truth because it was too painful to even share it with herself. She knew it was stupid to hide this sort of thing from her family. Her palms became sweaty and before the tears could roll down her face, she screwed her eyes tight. When she lowered her head, her hair fell in front of her eyes; she lost her lucky-purple-scrunchie yesterday.

The truth was, Emily was afraid of dying but she knew that it was going to happen, even if it became sooner than expected. When she first found out that she was terminally ill from the doctors, she convinced herself that if she forgot all about it, it would magically disappear. So Emily tried to get her life back to what it was, with Penny in The Author's Library. All she ever wanted was to have a good time but it soon became clear that something was wrong with her. Penny and Emily would always chit-chat in the evenings but there were awkward moments, where the truth should be; Penny and Emily never kept secrets from each other. When Emily spent time with her mum, she dodged every question thrown at her, with a joke or a sarcastic comment. With Ivy, Emily reminisced the good times, back in their youth.

For weeks leading up to the announcement, Emily knew that she wasn't acting herself, no matter how hard she tried. Even though she sought to hide her secret with laughter and a smile on her face, Emily Figment was in agony. She quickly became exhausted just from stacking books on the shelves and felt bad for being irritable with customers. Emily began to look deathly pale and had bright red sores over her arms and legs which wouldn't heal, although she tried to hide them as much as possible. Sometimes, Penny couldn't find her mum for several hours because she'd disappeared to throw up in the bathroom. The twinkle in her eyes had begun to fade. But whenever she was asked, Emily told everyone she was fine and laughed through the pain. It had been weeks since she had a cup of coffee in her hand. There wasn't anything in The Author's Library that sparked any joy or curiosity, within her.

Emily's illness became worse. When she tripped over her own feet, she didn't have to strength to pick herself back up. As Penny carried her to bed, that's when Emily knew she couldn't hide it for much longer; that's when Emily decided to tell them.

Soon enough, when the silence was too painful to endure, Emily told them. It was barely more than a whisper, but it was loud enough to hear and it was worse than what anyone could ever imagine. The truth that Emily's life was abruptly coming to an end. The stories of hospital appointments and endless medication that hadn't worked. The reasons for her change in behaviour and wellbeing, all while pretending to be fine and hiding the truth for as long as possible. Yet, that was nothing compared to the ache in her heart, when she had to tell her family.

Instantly, Nora broke down into tears and sank further into her armchair; her head buried in her hands and wishing it weren't true. Emily walked over to her, fell at her mum's knees and held her close. Ivy knelt by Emily's side and wrapped her arms around her waist.

'You'll stay strong, Emily,' Ivy whispered. 'I know you will.'

'I'm not going down without a fight.'

Emily looked up at Penny but neither of them said anything to each other. Instead, Penny's gaze became blank and expressionless. She tried to imagine living her life without Emily in it but couldn't see it. When Emily showed her daughter the jigsaw-puzzle tattoo on her wrist, Penny placed her hand on her collarbone. They were two pieces of a jigsaw puzzle; soon to only be one...

'I just don't understand why she had to hide it for so long,' Penny says, her heart beginning to ache. 'We never kept secrets from each other.'

'Emily kept it a secret from everyone, even herself. It was scary for her to come to terms with.'

'She stood by my side, after everything I'd been through. I was so wrapped up in my own anxieties that I couldn't even see...'

Penny buries her head in her hands, before she can start sobbing. Ivy wraps her arms around her goddaughter and gently kisses the top of her head.

'She wanted to make sure you were ok,' Ivy reassures her. 'You meant the world to Emily.'

'My mum meant the world to me.'

'Don't be afraid to feel this way, Penny. It's perfectly understandable…'

'I'm fine.'

'Are you sure?'

'I think so.'

'You haven't been driving yourself mad, have you?'

'I've always been mad. It runs in the family.'

'I don't deny that for a second.' Ivy chuckles, through her tears. 'Sometimes, I could never understand what you Figment girls were talking about.'

'Neither could we, sometimes.'

'Emily would be so proud of you, Penny. Just try not to drive yourself into insanity.'

'I'll try not to.'

When the day comes to an end, Ivy eventually leaves. Penny watches her go, before immediately disappearing into the basement, once again.

For the rest of the week, Penny closes The Author's Library and spends most of her time down in the basement. If anything, it gave her a sense of fulfilment and made her forget about all her anxieties. Every day, Penny felt that she was so close to uncovering something amazing that she never stopped until she was exhausted. There were even nights where she fell asleep in the basement and when she woke up, she carried on with her work.

It soon becomes an obsession. She only ever

appears in the bookshop to make herself a cup of tea; when that isn't strong enough, she switches to coffee. Penny hates the bitter taste but at least it keeps her awake. She wears the same clothes for days on end and only showers when she's increasingly sweaty and unbearable. Her muscles ache from staying in the same position for too long, trying to figure out what happened in the basement. Penny studies every book, every note and every drawing; she comes up with the most ludicrous conspiracies, each one more bizarre than the next.

'I have to keep going… No time to sleep,' she mutters to herself, her teeth chattering on her mug of tea. 'I have to solve the mystery… If I don't, I'm a bad Figment and I shouldn't be a part of the family…'

Only Christopher, Millie and Dexter know what Penny is up to. On some nights, they would receive calls and voicemails from her; she'd gibber some nonsense, laugh hysterically and hang up. When they decide to visit the bookshop and confront Penny on her insane determination, they know exactly where to find her.

At first, they gawk at Penny, who's pacing around the basement and muttering to herself in different voices. It's been too long since she's spoken to another human being.

'Penny, we need to talk,' Christopher says.

'I'm all ears,' Penny replies, as she collapses onto

the floor in front of all the scattered books and sketches. She doesn't look up at her friends but continues to twitch from the lack of sleep.

'We think you've gone mad,' Dexter tells her.

'I'm always mad.'

'You're not *this* mad.'

While reading *The Oresteia* upside-down, Penny repeatedly rolls onto her back, kicking her legs up into the air and then rolling herself back upright. Millie sits next to her and gently places her friend upright.

'Penny,' Millie says, tentatively. 'The three of us are just worried that you're not looking after yourself. You've been working so hard that we think you need to take a break.'

'I'm fine, Mills. Honestly, I am,' Penny says, leaning forward to study every sketch for the umpteenth time. She also wipes the dribble off her chin with her sleeve.

'Penny, when was the last time you slept?' Christopher asks.

'Sometimes,' Penny replies, now bopping along to an imaginary song.

'You need to stop, just for a bit,' Dexter tells her.

'No, I need to work harder!' Penny cries. Her eyes wide like a lunatic, she slams her hands onto the floor and crawls over to the wallpaper messages.

'No, Penny…' Millie begins to say, crawling after her.

'No, Millie.' Penny turns to her best friend and ecstatically smiles at her. 'Look what I've found.'

'What is it?'

With one hand pushing her glasses up her sweaty nose, Penny reaches over and picks up a thin, golden thread. She holds it in front of Millie's face and clasps their hands around it.

'Look at this,' Penny says, with trembling hands. 'This could be something…'

Unconvincingly, Millie smiles back at Penny. Then, she looks back and gives Christopher and Dexter a look of extreme concern. The three of them dart their eyes at one another, in agreement.

'What if a princess lived down here and once wore beautiful, golden clothes?' Penny mutters to herself, as she stares intently at the golden thread and completely ignores her friends.

'Penny…' Dexter says.

'Evil witches, named Deborah…'

'Penny…' Millie says.

'The king was one of them…'

'Penny Figment!' Christopher booms.

'Whuh?' she says, dumb-founded. 'When did you guys get here?'

'For the love of Odin, you need some help,' Dexter says.

Penny rubs her hands all over her face, covering herself in dust and dirt. 'How long have they been standing there?' she whispers to Millie and points to

Christopher and Dexter.

'Long enough,' Millie replies, through clenched teeth.

'Look, Penny. If you're not going to give yourself a rest, then you've left us with no choice.' Christopher looks at Dexter and they nod in agreement.

'I'm fine,' Penny says. 'Whoa!'

But before she knows it, Christopher and Dexter have grabbed her by the arms and begin to haul her upstairs. Millie follows behind them, with a triumphant smile on her face.

'Put me down!' Penny cries. She tries to wriggle herself free but the boys are holding on tight.

'This is for your own good.' Dexter says.

'I need to go back to the basement,' Penny groans, still trying to escape. 'I need to…'

'You need to sleep. That's what you need to do,' Millie tells her. 'No offence, Penny, but you look awful.'

'Offence taken.'

'Millie's right,' Christopher adds. 'We're only doing this because we care about you.'

'Do you guys really care about me?' Penny asks, dreamily.

'Penny, I've given up my Friday night, to keep you away from insanity,' Dexter grumbles. 'Don't make me regret that decision.'

Christopher and Dexter carry Penny as far away from the basement, as possible. They only put her down, when they reach the door that leads upstairs to her flat.

'Now, promise us you'll get some rest?' Christopher asks, as they gently put her down.

'Fine.'

'Pinky-promise?' Millie asks, holding out her pinky finger.

'I won't stop searching until I've found my answers,' Penny tells them.

'We know and we'll always be here to support you,' Christopher reassures her. 'We think you just need to stop, for tonight at least.'

Penny stares at her kind-hearted friends. She could never break a pinky-promise, just like Emily never would've. Instead, she shakes her head.

'I can't stop,' she whispers. Then, she swiftly dives past her friends and sprints back towards the basement door.

'Bloody hell,' Dexter grumbles.

'Penny!' Christopher cries, as the three of them begin to chase after her.

'I have to know.' Penny twists and turns in-between every bookcase. For a second, she looks back at her friends instead of looking forward.

'Watch out!' Millie cries.

Penny doesn't see the bookcase in front of her and she runs into it head first; she immediately knocks herself out and falls peacefully into a deep sleep.

'Penny!' Christopher's the first one to reach her

and crouches beside her. Millie and Dexter do the same.

'Oh, shit,' Millie says. 'Is she breathing…?'

'I can fight the Minotaur… King Theseus,' Penny mutters in her sleep before gently snoring.

Christopher, Millie, and Dexter laugh.

'I think she'll be ok,' Dexter says.

'Help me carry her to bed,' Christopher says.

Gently, he and Dexter lift Penny up with her arms draped over their shoulders. When they reach her bedroom, Millie takes off Penny's glasses and tucks her best friend into bed. Then, she switches off the light and the three of them head back downstairs.

Penny sleeps for sixteen hours. It then takes her two hours to regain consciousness and then another half an hour to put her glasses on and drink a cup of lukewarm tea that's been left on the side for her.

'I don't remember making a cup of tea.' she thinks. 'Or even getting to bed. Why am I… Oh, shit!' She drops her empty mug, falls out of bed and sprints downstairs.

While Penny was asleep, Christopher, Millie, and Dexter spent the entire day working in the bookshop. Every few hours, one of them would check on her and make sure she was ok; it was Millie who quickly made her a cup of tea when she noticed Penny stirring in her sleep.

Throughout the day, Christopher handles orders and deliveries, Millie deals with customers and

Dexter organises all the books on the shelves. It's been a fairly quiet but successful day.

Meanwhile, Ivy wanders gracefully in-between the bookcases, observing Christopher, Millie and Dexter while they work. The way they happily deal with customers and carefully handle books brings a smile to Ivy's face; it's almost as if The Author's Library was their home and they were a part of the family.

'Are you friends of Penny's?' Ivy asks Millie, when she spots her amongst the feminist books.

Startled, Millie quickly shoves *The Female Eunuch* back on the shelf and turns to face her. 'Err, hi?'

'Hello.' When Ivy smiles at her, Millie gives her a small smile back.

'Penny's my best friend,' Millie mutters. Her cheeks turn pink and she looks down at her trainers. 'We're looking after her bookshop, while she rests. She's been sleeping all day.'

'Oh, gosh. Is she ok?'

'She went a bit mad, so we decided to help her out.'

'Who else is here?'

'It's just me, my husband and my brother.'

'You seem like very kind people, to take care of Penny. It's what she needs.'

'We all care about her. But she's been on her own, for a long time. We're worried about her.'

'You're not the only one,' Ivy mutters and leans back against the bookcases, breathing in the familiar scent of old books.

'Do you know why? She briefly mentions her mum but doesn't want to talk about it.'

'It's Penny's story to tell and she will, in time. For now, she just wants to lose herself in every fantasy she can find, to distract herself from the pain. But Penny will fall back to earth, eventually. All we can do is stand at her side.'

'Of course. She's so wonderful and I hope she knows that.'

'She will, one day.'

Millie looks at all the feminist books and brushes the dust off the spines, making them stand out and shine. But when she looks to her left, the unknown woman has disappeared.

'I've just closed up the shop and Dexter's cashed everything up,' Christopher says to Millie, when he and Dexter emerge from around the corner.

'Who were you talking to, Mills?'

'It was… I don't know,' she admits.

'Hi, guys,' Penny mumbles, when she eventually finds her friends. She's still wearing the same clothes from last night and her hair resembles a bird's nest.

'Penny!' Millie cries, running over to her and throwing her arms around her neck. 'I'm so glad you're ok. Do you need another cup of tea? How are you feeling?'

'Geez, Millie,' Dexter says, calmly. 'You don't want to knock Penny out, again.'

'I'm feeling better,' Penny admits, nuzzling into Millie's embrace. 'A little dazed, though.'

When Penny and Millie let go of each other, Christopher wraps his arms around Penny and kisses the top of her head.

'We're glad you're alright,' Dexter says to her.

'Thanks guys. What did I miss?'

'Not much,' Christopher says. 'It's been a quiet day, today.'

Penny suddenly notices the neatly stacked books on the shelves; they're all in alphabetical order and she would never normally be this organised.

'Did you…' Penny whispers, looking all around her as if she's seeing The Author's Library for the first time.

'We did,' Christopher tells her.

'You needed to rest, so we thought we would help you out,' Millie says.

'That's what friends are for,' Dexter adds.

Penny doesn't know what to say; she can't remember the last time someone did something like this, for her. Instead, she wraps her arms around Christopher and draws Millie and Dexter into the embrace.

Nothing else matters. All Penny can think about is how grateful she is to have such wonderful friends. It's something she's wanted for so long, even though she always convinced herself otherwise. She closes her eyes and wishes that this moment will never end;

maybe she can trust people, after all.

But then, a familiar sense of loneliness begins to creep across her body. When Penny snaps her eyes open, she remembers why she always chose to be alone. Memories flash before her eyes, of friends who once abandoned her; as well as losing her mum, Penny's best friend. She couldn't do that to herself, again. Emily wasn't here this time.

Without warning, Penny breaks away from the group and stumbles forward.

'Don't do this to yourself.' she thinks. 'It may seem so wonderful now, but what about when it all comes crashing down and you're on your own again? In no time, they're going to run away from you, just like everyone else did.'

'Penny? Are you ok?' Dexter asks, moving tentatively towards her.

'Eventually, you're going to scare them away because you're just not good enough…' she thinks. 'You'll never be good enough to have any friends…'

'Penny. Please talk to us?' Millie asks, gently.

Penny turns to face the rest of the group. They all have such kind faces and for a moment, she thinks that maybe they won't do her wrong. But she's believed all this before.

'I can't go through it all, again,' she mutters, just loud enough to hear.

'What do you mean?' Christopher asks. When he takes one step towards her, she takes one step back.

Penny looks into the depths of her bookshop and thinks of the basement. It feels safe there, as a distraction from everything else. So, she runs away. She knows exactly where she's going and tries to forget about everything else. It's not long before she can hear Christopher, Millie and Dexter chasing after her.

'Penny, wait!' Christopher cries.

'Leave me alone!' Penny sprints even faster, with tears streaming down her face.

Eventually, they lose sight of her but Christopher keeps searching until he's out of breath. But Penny is already staggering downstairs, to the basement.

She stumbles to the furthest and darkest corner. There, Penny sinks to the floor and sobs and wails, loudly. The darkness is somewhat comforting and she's glad that no one will find her crying.

'It's for the best,' she thinks. 'It's better to be on your own…'

Just a few feet away from her and hidden in the shade, is a crumpled sheet of paper that's been torn in two. Once she's dried her eyes, Penny crawls over to it and holds both ends together. It's a letter in a familiar handwriting:

January 29th, 1956

Nora,

I have to leave *The Author's Library*. Unfortunately, I can't tell you why and it kills me, because we've never kept secrets from each other. But this is something that I must do. Trust in me, as a fellow Figment, that I will come back to our bookshop, one day. Then, I promise I will explain everything.

I know that Father has always been proud of you. You're determined and passionate and I'm proud to call you my sister. Keep selling books and being brilliant. Now, it's my turn to show everyone what I can do.

Best wishes,

Bradley.

Penny reads the letter over and over again, trying to take it all in.

'Bradley… B. Figment!'

She takes deep breaths and sits with her back against the bookcase. She looks at the entire basement and tries to gather her thoughts.

'My grandma has a brother?'

Much like a jigsaw puzzle, everything was beginning to fall into place.

The Author's Library
1955
I

9th February 1955

Around The Author's Library, Nora stretches out her arms and totters in her highest heels, which are a size too big for her. She closes her eyes and directly places one foot in front of the other, with her fingertips brushing against all the books she's shelved. For a moment, she stops worrying about her creased suit and judgemental looks from customers. She smiles at them regardless and never gives anyone an excuse to think that Nora Figment's not good enough to work in her family's bookshop.

But when Nora opens her eyes and drops her arms to her side, she can already count three customers giving her raised eyebrows with hands on their hips. They're all wanting her attention, at once.

'They would never treat my brother, like this,' Nora thinks, as she deals with them all. Customers like this have never given her the respect she craves. Then again, she's used to it by now.

When he left on his travels to find rare and exotic books to sell, everyone thought it was mad that Patrick Figment would give responsibility to both of his children. While Nora worked in the bookshop with pride on her shoulders, it was tough at times. No matter how hard she worked, she still encountered petty complaints from customers; they always praised Bradley, but never Nora. She was critiqued on the way she looked and frequently told to only read books on being a good housewife and nothing more.

Yet, Nora always persisted with her work as a bookseller. All she ever wanted to do, was make her family proud.

When there's another quiet moment she kicks off her heels, shrugs off her blazer and releases her auburn curls from her topknot. Then, she clambers up her ladder and looks over the whole bookshop, watching her customers go by.

At first, Nora observes all the girls in dresses that float effortlessly around her knees, all while clinging onto the arms of their male companions. She sees young lovers, newly-weds and old married couples; all sharing the same passion for books and too busy falling in love to think about anything else.

'I wish I could be like them.' she thinks. 'To wear pretty dresses and fall in love with the man whose arm I'm clinging onto. He'd be intelligent, handsome, kind and love me for who I am. But that's not a priority, right now – I'm a bookseller and I must be taken seriously…'

But when Nora spots Michael Marblelight in-between the bookcases, her thoughts begin to trail off and her heart begins to flutter. Her entire body feels as light as air, as she watches him browse the ancient Greek philosophies. Michael Marblelight stands tall and proud, while twiddling his perfectly trimmed beard with gentle fingers. When he's in deep concentration, he adjusts his hexagon-shaped glasses. Today, he wears an amethyst-coloured suit.

'He's so beautiful and wonderful,' she thinks. 'But I could never tell him that. I know Michael doesn't feel the same way about me…'

'Good afternoon, Nora,' Michael calls, when he's standing by her ladder. He looks up at her and smiles.

Thankfully, Michael doesn't see Nora blushing as she scampers down the ladder. She awkwardly slips her feet back into her heels and quickly puts on her blazer.

'Hello, Michael.' She quickly ties her hair up out of her face.

He gently takes Nora's hands in his own, allowing her curls to fall gracefully around her face.

'Leave your hair down, for once. It's so pretty, that way.'

'Thank you. Will I see you tonight?' she asks, as she tucks a strand behind her ear.

'Of course. I wouldn't want to be anywhere else.'

Michael slowly edges towards her and rests a gentle hand on her upper arm. Nora looks at his hand which is delicate but firm. Then, she traces her gaze across his body, looking at every defined muscle beneath his skin, before looking deep into his twinkling-blue eyes. Michael Marblelight is as beautiful as a Classical Greek statue. For a preposterous second, she thinks that he's going to kiss her. She stands on her tiptoes, to meet his gaze and she breathes in his scent of rum and cigars.

'I'll be back, later,' Michael tells her. He slowly turns away and disappears into the depths of the bookshop.

When the sun begins to set, Nora sees her twin-brother emerge from behind the bookcases.

'Are you ready?' Bradley asks, quietly. He gives his sister a small smile, but he's nervously shuffling from one foot to the other.

'Of course,' she replies, placing the rest of the books haphazardly on the shelf. 'I don't why you're so nervous, Bradley. We've been doing this since the beginning of the year.'

'It's still something I need to get used to,' he admits, his cheeks blushing a deep red.

Neither of them says anything else, but they link arms and delve in-between the bookcases. When Michael joins them and links arms with Nora, the three of them look forward and know exactly where they're going.

Silently, the trio go through the door and descend one hundred and twelve steps until they reach the basement. They sit in their designated armchairs, gathered around the table. Nora illuminates all the candles and Michael lights himself a cigar and pours them all a thimble of rum. Meanwhile, Bradley shuffles in his seat, clutching a copy of Homer's *Iliad*.

'Cheers,' Michael says. The trio clink their glasses and down the rum in one. Then, Michael pours them another, which they sip throughout the evening.

'I thought I would do a reading, tonight,' Bradley squeaks, as he fumbles with *The Iliad*. It's a well-loved copy and the spine is heavily cracked, with a few loose pages tucked away inside.

'That sounds like a marvellous idea,' Michael tells him.

'Then tell us the tale,' Nora says.

With blushing cheeks, Bradley opens the book and stands to face his companions. Even though his audience only ever consists of two people, Bradley's hands become clammy and his mind goes blank; he's been practising his Epic Poem recital all day. But when he looks to his sister, who gives him a reassuring nod and his heartbeat falls to a reasonable rate, he clears his throat and begins to read the tale.

This all began in the beginning of 1955. Nora, Bradley and Michael would meet in the basement every night as a trio of companions, and it soon became part of their nightly routine, an escape from daily struggles. They were brought closely together by their fondness of ancient Greek literature and discussed it every night. They tried to sound as eloquent as possible and pretended to be more extravagant than they were; almost as if they were trying to be completely different people. Michael would even sneak in a bottle of dark rum and a cigar that he stole from his family's business. Sometimes, they would write a message on the wall in black ink and it'd be camouflaged by the navy wallpaper.

Nora, Bradley and Michael would discuss different mythologies and philosophies until the early hours of the morning. Then, the trio would head back up to The Author's Library, say goodnight and nothing else. It became a well-loved secret between three people.

The basement was first discovered by Nora and Bradley, out of sheer curiosity. At first, it only had two bookcases that lurked at the back of the room; but the twins were determined to make it their own and they soon filled it with their favourite things. When Michael Marblelight knew about it, he was intrigued and soon invited to join them.

While Bradley recites his favourite passages from *The Iliad,* Nora looks at her brother but can't stop thinking about Michael. She can almost imagine the sparks flying between them. But what Nora doesn't know, is that Michael Marblelight feels exactly the same way.

If only we could spend the rest of our lives down here, together!

Another wonderful night, spent with beautiful people...

We shall meet again...

II

17th March 1955

It's a busy afternoon in The Author's Library. As she weaves her way through the crowds, Nora carries stacks of books that are taller than her and serves as many customers as possible. Her glasses slowly slip down her nose and her hair flies around in a mad panic. There's barely even a moment to breathe.

'Look here, woman.' A burly man storms up to Nora. His presence alone causes her to drop a stack of books she was carrying onto her foot, but despite the unfathomable pain, she doesn't flinch.

'Can I help you?' Nora asks in her clearest voice, although she's frozen on the spot, in fear. She clasps her hands together to stop them from shaking.

'Why can't you do your job properly? Are you stupid, or something?'

Customers begin to stare at Nora and raise their eyebrows at her. Even though she wants to shrink to the floor, she stands up straight and it makes her back ache.

'What's the matter, sir?' she asks, meekly.

'The romance novels are mixed up with mystery.' He barks, rolling his eyes in frustration. 'Foolish woman… I bet you can't even read.'

'I… I can read…'

'You can't even talk, either! You're pathetic. A woman should never be left with the responsibility of a bookshop.'

'Actually, my grandma was the first female owner of this bookshop…'

But he doesn't listen to her. He spits on the floor in front of Nora and throws a copy of *Rebecca* at her. It's hits her hard in the chest as he storms out of the bookshop. There's a sharp pain in her ribs but it's nothing compared to the embarrassment. Customers are still staring her and probably thinking that she's incompetent. But instead of breaking down and crying, Nora slowly disappears into the basement and cries.

Bradley and Michael find her there, sobbing.

'It can all be too much, sometimes,' she utters. Her eyes begin to fill with tears, again. 'But I just want to make my family proud.'

When Michael puts his arm around Nora, she snuggles into him.

'You have made her proud, Nora,' Bradley reminds her. 'Grandma-Ruth and Father. They've always adored you. That's why they trust us with the bookshop…'

Nora wipes the tears from her eyes and slowly

takes her place at the table. Even though they give each other confused looks, Bradley and Michael join her.

'I don't want to talk about it, anymore. Shall we begin?' Nora sits up straight and looks down at the Greek tragedies, in front of her.

Michael pours them all a drink but Nora knocks it back before they have a chance to clink glasses. Tonight, they spend the evening in silence. Michael studies his favourite philosophies and writes it all down in his notebooks. Bradley begins to sketch out an Amazonian Queen.

Meanwhile, Nora re-reads all her favourite Greek tragedies and knocks back two more thimbles of rum, which she pours herself. All she focuses on is Medea and Clytemnestra: independent women in Greek tragedy who were feared when they couldn't gain respect from mankind. They took control of their own story, even if their hubris led to their inevitable downfall.

In the early hours of the morning, Bradley begins his ascent back to the bookshop, with Michael following behind him.

'Are you coming with us, Nora?' Michael asks, when he notices that she's still in her armchair.

'I'll be there... I'll be there soon...' she slurs, swirling the remains of rum in her glass.

Michael gives Bradley a nod and walks back over

to her. Bradley watches the two of them for a second, before disappearing upstairs.

'I think you've had enough to drink,' Michael tells her. When he tries to move the glass away from her, she snatches it back.

'Another man who thinks… who thinks they have the right… to control a woman!' she shrieks, gulping the last of her rum. When she tries to reach for the bottle, Michael's quick enough to move it away from her.

'Leave me alone,' Nora whines.

'You're very drunk.'

'It eases the pain…' She begins to sway from side to side. 'You'd do the same if you were in my predicament…'

'Don't put yourself down, Nora. You're an incredibly intelligent woman…'

'I know I am.' She slams her hands down on the table. 'So why can't other people see that?'

'What happened today, was just one man…'

'Oh, it's easy for you to say that.' Nora suddenly stands up and looks down at Michael, her face turning red. 'I get this treatment, every day. People cannot stand the fact that I'm an independent woman, but it's fine for you. You'll always be respected and so will Bradley. Even though I work ten times harder than him. So what's the point, anymore? Maybe I should just give up.'

Nora sinks back into her armchair and tears start

to fall down her face, which she furiously wipes away. Gently, Michael interlinks his fingers with hers.

'Not everyone thinks that, of you,' he reassures her. 'The two people that don't, join you in the basement every evening. Those that judge you just know that they will never be as wonderful as you are.'

'You think I'm wonderful?' When more tears fall down Nora's face, Michael gently wipes them away.

'You're wonderful and beautiful.'

'Do you ever think we were destined to be joined together?' she asks.

He slowly sits back in his chair and strokes his beard. 'Maybe our stories were meant to connect together, like three woven tapestries, sewn into one.'

'I'm extremely glad, that I can spend this time with you...'

Soon enough, Nora becomes doe-eyed and flutters her eyelashes at Michael. She leans forward, hoping to finally kiss him or touch more of his skin. But instead, she closes her eyes and sleepily rests her head on his shoulder, wrapping her arms around his neck. He holds her for a moment, nuzzling his face into her hair.

'I think you need to sleep,' Michael tells her and she doesn't object.

He gently lifts Nora out of her seat and allows her to lean on his shoulder. But before they leave the basement, Nora grabs a pen and writes a message on the wall as a drunken, free-spirit. Michael does the same, inking his own response.

I thank you for wiping away my tears and being my shoulder to cry on

You're an intellectual force of nature. Anyone who cannot see that are merely fools.

The next day, Nora nurses a bad headache and gives herself a stern talking to, after what happened last night. She doesn't know if she can ever face Michael Marblelight again, because she's so embarrassed.

There's no one else in the bookshop when Michael finds Nora amongst the Greek tragedies and strides towards her. He swiftly gathers her in his arms and kisses her passionately. She slowly melts into his arms, her lips fitting perfectly against his. Whilst Michael holds her close, never wanting to let her go.

Meanwhile, on the other side of the bookcase, Bradley watches his sister fall in love with Michael Marblelight.

III

<u>16th May 1955</u>

Quick and nimble, Bradley Figment scampers up the bookcases. When he reaches the top, he doesn't look down, but instead he holds his head up high and imagines he's the captain of his own ship at sea; just like in the stories that Grandma-Ruth used to tell them. When Bradley imagines himself as the hero in another story, he's filled with an unfamiliar sensation of confidence that warms his entire body. He's usually so used to hiding behind the bookcases, allowing Nora to deal with customers. He hates busy bookshop days; when a customer approaches him, he doesn't know what to say.

Fortunately today is a quiet day. Bradley looks down and sees his sister, walking arm-in-arm with Michael; he takes long strides, while Nora has to walk twice as quick to catchup with him. Even standing up straight, Nora only manages to reach Michael's shoulders and she can't keep her eyes off him.

Recently Bradley's been watching his sister fall in love with Michael Marblelight. Every night in the basement and all throughout The Author's Library. Nora hangs onto every word he says and obsesses over his elegant handwriting and intellectual mind. She finds any reason to touch him. Michael responds in a similar way, when he kisses her hands and listens to everything she says. Meanwhile, Bradley keeps his nose close to the sketchpad and illustrates what he sees.

When he clambers down the bookcase, he walks in front in front of the mirror and stares at his own reflection.

'You will never be as grand as him.' Bradley thinks.

He closes his eyes and stands up straight; Bradley's a lot taller than people think. He pushes his hair out of his face and straightens up his glasses. He forces a grin on his face, with his head held high and slowly opens his eyes. But to his disappointment, Bradley sighs and quickly hunches back down and his ginger curls fall over his eyes, just like they always do. He's a lot skinnier than Michael and wearing an oversized linen shirt and trousers makes him look even smaller.

Gradually, his face retracts back to its usual expression of anxiety.

'I'll never be good enough.' he thinks.

Bradley sees a few customers emerge from behind the bookcase; his heart beats as hard as a drum and he cowers, before running in fear to the other side of the bookshop. He eventually sinks to the floor with tears in his eyes, resting his back against the bookcases and hugging his knees to his chest.

'Why can I be brave?' he thinks. 'Oh, God. I'm just a coward. I could never outsmart the Cyclopes or kill the Minotaur… I can barely talk to another human being…'

Reaching behind him, he grabs the first book he touches; it's a copy of Homer's *Iliad,* which Bradley quickly delves into. He imagines strong, Greek warriors with beautiful weapons fighting in the

Trojan War; admiring their courage and bravery but also longing for that same connection that Achilles and Patroclus once had.

At the end of the day, Michael finds Bradley in the basement, pacing up and down and running his fingers through his curls.

'Hello, Bradley.'

When he looks up at Michael, Bradley's whole body becomes numb. His face begins to sweat and he suddenly doesn't know what to do with his hands.

'Good evening, Michael,' he mumbles, slowly walking over to the table.

'How are you?'

When Michael sits beside him, Bradley's heart begins to flutter. He looks up at the blank ceiling and briefly thinks about the magnificent masterpiece he could create.

'I'm feeling curious, tonight,' Bradley eventually says, looking back at him.

'How so?'

'I've always admired you, Michael…'

'That's very kind of you.'

'…You're handsome, intelligent, loyal and charismatic. I've longed to be everything that you've become.'

'What's with all this flattery?' When Michael smiles at him, it sends butterflies in Bradley's stomach. 'I'm sure there's a woman out there who'll love you for who you are.'

'When I hear you recite Greek philosophy, I find it sensational. I've read every romantic note on the wall that you've written to my sister. Sometimes, I wish it were me you were writing them to. I watch you walk arm-in-arm with her…'

'Bradley, if you're worried about what's happening between me and your sister, then you have nothing to worry about.'

'You care a great deal for Nora, I can see that. You have my blessing because you make her so happy. She just adores you. But if I never tell you this, then I'll regret it for the rest of my life.'

'Then, what are you trying to tell me?'

Bradley leans in closer, towards Michael. They're almost nose-to-nose from an embrace but Bradley holds back.

'I wish I could walk arm-in-arm with you,' Bradley says, quickly. He cheeks flush a deep red.

'You have feelings for me?' Michael whispers.

'Yes, ever since I first saw you. At first, I thought you inspired me. But soon, those feelings only grew stronger and soon enough, I wanted to be the one you hold in your arms. To be the one you kiss behind the bookcases…'

Michael leans back into his armchair and rests his head on his fingertips. The awkward silence between them is unbearable but Bradley can't keep his eyes off him.

'Have you told anyone else?' Michael asks.

'I've been too scared to do so. But I had to tell you.'

Michael rests a hand on Bradley's shoulder and gives him a comforting smile. It immediately makes him feel a lot better.

'I'm flattered, Bradley. If you want to keep this a secret between the two of us, then I will do so.'

'Yes please.'

'But I'm falling in love with Nora...'

'You should tell her that. She'd want to hear it.' Bradley advises him. 'But I know you make my sister happy and that means a lot to me.'

'I have a lot of respect for you, Bradley. I hope you know that.'

'I do, now.'

Michael pours the two of them a drink. They clink their glasses and drink it in one gulp, just as Nora enters the basement.

'Wait for me!'

Nora slumps into her armchair, with a wide grin on her face. She grabs the bottle and takes a large swig. Then, Bradley watches Nora and Michael kiss, before starting the evening.

The evening plays out as it usually does. Michael recites some of his favourite lines from Plato and Nora hangs onto his every word. All while Bradley listens to his soothing words and sketches out a strong, Greek warrior.

At the end of the night, Nora and Michael go back upstairs and kiss each other goodnight. Then, Nora descends back to the basement and finds her brother still sketching.

'If you ever had a choice, you'd be drawing forever,' Nora says, as she walks towards him. She peers over Bradley's shoulder and looks at every detailed sketch on Gods and Goddesses.

'It's something I want to show Father, when he comes back,' Bradley tells her, as he puts his pencil and paper down while Nora joins him at the table.

'I miss him so much. I've kept every letter he's written but he hasn't written to us for ages. I hope he's alright.'

'I just want to make father proud.'

'So do I.'

'You definitely have. You're determined and loyal. I reckon I'm the disappointment, in the family.'

'No, you're not!' Nora snaps. 'Don't ever say that about yourself.'

'It's true, though…'

'No, it's absolutely not.'

'Grandma-Ruth used to tell us stories about her bravery and adventures and Father's gone exploring, which takes huge amounts of courage. I could never be like that when I can't even talk to anyone, apart from you. Father told me to have confidence, in myself. But I don't think I ever will.'

When Bradley hangs his head in shame, Nora nudges his ankle with her foot. He looks up at her and she has a smile on her face. Bradley gives her a small smile, in return.

'Acts of bravery come in many different ways,' Nora tells him. 'So, you may never defeat the hydra. But you show more and more courage with every book you sell. Your talents lie beyond what the customers see. I can see that and so can Michael and Father.'

'Thanks. I don't know what I'd do, if I didn't have a sister like you.'

'We'll always stick together.' Nora slowly stands up and heads for the stairs, but Bradley remains in his seat. 'Aren't you coming up?'

Bradley looks up at the ceiling and then back at his sister. 'No, not yet.'

Before Nora leaves the basement, she writes a message on the wall. Alone, Bradley closes his eyes and thinks about what to create, on a grand scale. Colours and shapes begin to form in his mind, with his imagination whirring alongside.

He opens his eyes and runs upstairs. He comes back, five minutes later, with a ladder in one hand and a box of paints in the other. With a sharp pencil between his fingers, Bradley shoots up the ladder and begins to sketch out a mural on the ceiling of three beautiful and heroic figures, riding through the sky on a dragon-led chariot.

For hours, Bradley darts about the basement and covers the ceiling with a magnificent pencil-outline. When his arm begins to ache and his eyes become droopy, he stops his work. He'll return to it, another time. Before he leaves the basement for tonight, he writes a message on the wall.

We will always overcome any storm...

Any adventures I take, I wish to conquer them with you.

I hold the highest respect, for you. You will never be a coward, but a true gentleman.

IV

29th July 1955

At the end of another evening together, Bradley is the first one to make the ascent back to the bookshop.

'I'd like to stay here a bit longer, if that's alright?' Michael asks, as he looks up from Plato's *Symposium*.

'Of course,' Bradley says, before disappearing upstairs.

'I'll stay with you,' Nora says. When she walks over to Michael, she wraps her arms around his shoulders and gently kisses his neck.

'I'd like that.'

There's a twinkle in Michael's eye tonight. He tries to keep his eyes on his notes, but Nora is too beautifully distracting. Soon enough, Michael's pulled her onto his lap and they're kissing; his arms are wrapped around her waist and her hands are on either side of his face. They keep each other as close as possible and their eyes are shut tightly, revelling in the moment.

Over the last few months, Nora's loved every moment she's secretly spent with Michael, beneath her bookshop. She wishes it could be that way for the rest of her life and they could live happily ever after. But it wasn't completely perfect. Their affair only lasted for a few hours every night and when they go upstairs they're nothing more than companions. A part of Nora wishes for more romantic outbursts, like the first time he kissed her. But it seems that Michael wants to keep their romance a secret and she goes along with it, always hoping it will develop into something more.

But Michael can't tell her the truth because he doesn't even want to admit it to himself. He knows he loves her and being with Nora every evening brings out a side to Michael that he's always hidden away. It's where he truly wants to be. The other side of him is spent with his parents; where he does what he's told and tends to keep quiet. His parents are too rich to consider anyone else's feelings and think books are a waste of time. They want Michael to become an accountant for the family business but never ask what he wants. Whenever they see Nora Figment in The Author's Library, they stick their noses up at her, through the shop window.

So Michael has to make a choice. To stay with his

parents or to leave them and be with Nora. The latter is a huge risk and he could lose everything, but a part of him feel it's right. He could never hurt her. But for now, Michael continues to kiss Nora and lives in the moment. He'll worry about it later.

When Michael and Nora eventually break apart, they still hold each other with their foreheads pressed against each other; feeling the other one's breath on their own skin.

'I love you,' Nora whispers.

For a few moments, Michael doesn't say anything. Nora can feel her heart drop slightly, almost as if she's preparing herself for what's to come.

'You mean a lot to me, Nora. There's no denying that…'

Nora leans back and stares at him. When Michael tries to draw her close, she refuses.

'I see,' she says, sharply.

'Allow me to explain…'

'You can't say it back to me…'

'Nora…'

'I'm not good enough for you. That's it, isn't it?'

'It's not that at all.'

'That's why you wanted to keep this a secret for so long…'

But her words trail off. Nora looks down at Michael's notebook. There's a loose sheet sticking out in unrecognisable handwriting and at the bottom, its signed by a woman.

'What's this?' she asks, taking the letter out of the notebook.

'Nora, don't read that…'

But she's already jumped off his lap and walked away from him. She reads through the letter several times.

'Please let me explain,' Michael begins, as he paces towards her. He snatches the letter away but it's too late. Nora stands a foot away from him, staring him in disgust.

'This letter was written to you, from your fiancée. She wants to know where you are every evening.' Nora's eyes begin to fill with tears but she refuses to cry in front of him. 'You're getting married?'

'It's not what it looks like…'

Nora doesn't even give him a chance. 'It seems perfectly clear to me! You kept this a secret from me, the whole time. After all the time we've spent, together? I have to get away from you…'

Nora shoves Michael and runs upstairs. She can hear him behind her and quickly wipes the tears that are streaming from her face.

'Wait!' Michael calls out, but Nora's already pacing throughout the bookshop. 'Please, listen to me.'

'Why should I?' she yells, turning to face him with her hands on her hips. Her eyes are bloodshot and her face is bright red with fury. 'I put my trust in you, Michael. Now, everything makes sense to me. I'm just your little secret. I was never good enough for you, so you found someone better. You're ashamed to be around me…'

'I would never think that about you!' When he takes a step towards her, Nora takes a step back.

'Leave me alone, Michael. I don't want to see you, ever again.'

Nora tries to walk past him, but he grabs her hand before she can disappear. She quickly turns back to face him.

'I don't love her,' Michael says, clinging onto her. 'She doesn't love me, either.'

'So, why are you marrying her?'

Michael lets go, thankful that Nora doesn't run away from him. 'My parents made the decision. They think they know what's best for me, but they haven't got a clue.'

'Why didn't you tell me about this?'

'Only because when I'm with you, I don't want to think about anything else.' There are now tears in his eyes. 'I've always savoured every moment with you. But now I must make a decision, to either follow my heart or the duty I have to my parents.'

'Have you decided?'

'I have, right now. I can't continue to live my life without you in it.'

'It would break my heart to lose you.'

'Me too.'

Without saying anything else, Michael draws Nora in to kiss her. This time, it's much more passionate.

They wrap their arms tightly around each other and Michael lifts Nora off her feet. They're locked in an embrace that they don't want to break.

'I love you, Nora,' he says, between kisses. 'I want you and nobody else.'

'I love you, too,' she replies, as the two of them kiss harder and fall to the floor in a dither.

Later that night, Nora and Michael write on the wall:

Maybe I am good enough, after all...

I have made my choice. If I spend the rest of my days with you, it will make me the happiest man alive.

V

12th December 1955

As it comes towards the end of the year, the basement is filled with joyful epiphanies. Bradley paints the mural on the ceiling, while Nora and Michael sit around the table. Cigars are smoked with the ash scattered everywhere; the rum is merrily drunk, swirling around in the crystal glasses. There are books stacked across the table and some left on an open page. Everyone in the basement continues to live in the moment, with not a single worry about what the future could hold.

Her male companions remain silent and wouldn't dare interrupt, as Nora discusses some of her favourite moments in Euripides' *Hecabe*, and when she gazes at Michael, it makes her heart sing with joy. When Nora gets excited, she gently hovers over her chair. When she recites certain passages, she climbs onto her chair and reads it as loud as possible. Eventually, when Nora's voice has gone hoarse and she sits back down, Bradley and Michael applaud her, proudly. Michael closes his notebook and gives Nora a kiss.

While she'd been speaking, Michael had been taking notes. He looks at Nora, his entire face lighting up in ecstasy; he could listen to her for hours. He cannot wait until it's just the two of them and he can sweep her off her feet.

Meanwhile, Bradley keeps his focus on the mural, with Nora's voice comforting him like a familiar tune. He mixes the paints together until he has the perfect colour. Bradley paints bold strokes, but with a gentle hand. He makes the Gods and Goddesses in the mural seem powerful, determined and unfazed by the future. The paintbrush becomes a part of Bradley's hand, as he plots out shading and gives extraordinary detail to everything.

The trio of companions know that they will always be by each other's side, no matter what. They wish to always meet in the basement and to share the passion for ancient Greek literature. They see this night in the basement, like any other and they expect to return to tomorrow.

Before they leave, the three of them write another message on the wall.

Let us spend the rest of our nights, down here! How wonderful would that be?

Another glorious night, spent together. I cannot wait to see you again, tomorrow.

When I sit with you, my confidence grows. I couldn't have done it without you.

The three of them walk back up to the bookshop, leaving their glasses and books on the table. The cigar butts are left to fester in the ash tray. Bradley takes his paints with him and hopes to finish the mural before the end of the year. Nora holds hands with Michael and is so fixated on him, that she forgets her scarf and shoes. Michael's leaves his blazer hanging over his chair, with his pocket-watch tucked away inside.

They slowly leave the basement and appear in The Author's Library, leaving behind the echoes of their laughter and joy.

But what they never knew, was that someone else now knew their secret, too.

Fear and Laughter

It's almost a week since Penny ran away from her friends and, although she desperately wants to, she doesn't look back. Instead, she's only been looking forward and keeping her focus on solving the mystery of Bradley Figment. When she opens up the bookshop, she tries to spend every waking moment looking for answers; but her days are so busy that she can barely think of anything else. As she rushes around The Author's Library, serving customers and organising all the new books, it's seems more overwhelming than usual. Penny wishes that she had six other clones to help out, or at least grow another set of arms, to multitask.

When she sells old sci-fi novels to her customers, it regrettably reminds her of Christopher; she remembers on hectic days, when Millie came over to help. It makes her heart ache to think about the friends she chose to leave behind. But then Penny remembers busy days in the bookshop with Emily and it makes her feel worse.

'You're better off on your own?' she thinks, as she always does. But this time, she doesn't seem to fully convince herself.

But today, it's been a quiet morning and Penny feels a lot better than usual. Almost as if she knows her luck's about to change. With a cup of tea to her left and pens sticking out of her plaits, she sits at her till with a stack of directories in front of her. A notepad and pen are on her right, ready to take contact details.

Now that she knows the name – Bradley Figment – she begins to look him up. At first, she tried to look him up online but there was nothing; so instead, Penny checked out every directory she could get her hands on.

'Bradley Figment doesn't seem to be a common name?' Penny taps her pen in frustration, as she moves onto another directory. Her notepad still remains blank.

'He's definitely someone in my family. A long-lost relative maybe? I found all his sketches, so Bradley Figment had to exist at one point… he can't have disappeared into thin air the moment he left the bookshop. Oh God, what if he's dead? I really hope not… Wait!'

BRADLEY FIGMENT
SET DESIGNER
(SPECIALISING IN SET PRODCUTION FOR GREEK
TRAGEDY ADAPTATIONS)
CONTACT DETAILS BELOW:

Penny jabs her finger over the name and swiftly writes down the phone number and address. 'That must be him!'

She looks up as if to tell someone, but she's faced with an empty bookshop. When she thinks of her friends who helped her with the mystery, her entire body is washed over with a wave of guilt. But she's one step closer to getting all her answers and can feel the tingling sensation of excitement.

But just before Penny can pick up the phone, she

hears an ear-deafening crash that sounds like a bookcase that's been deliberately toppled over. Then, she hears a gaggle of raucous laughter which feels horribly familiar. Penny drops the phone, in fear. Her whole body suddenly freezes and her heart drops to the pit of her stomach.

'Oh, bloody hell… Shit. Not them, again…' she thinks, as three men with cold-blooded expressions stagger towards her. Without thinking twice, Penny quickly hides behind her till and waits for them to go away.

Meanwhile, Dexter muddles his way through The Author's Library, looking for Penny.

'I wish she'd include a map for this place,' he mutters to himself, as he twists and turns around the bookcases.

Over the last week, Christopher, Millie and Dexter had become more worried about Penny. None of them could understand why she ran off and hadn't returned any of their calls, since then and it had left them utterly baffled. They all wondered if any of them had done something wrong and went over what had happened. But it was a perfectly wholesome moment and that just left them even more confused.

After hearing absolutely nothing from Penny, Christopher began to mope around and Millie became increasingly anxious and flustered. So Dexter decided to go and find her. Maybe she wouldn't tell him why, but Dexter could at least see if Penny's ok.

Eventually, Dexter finds Penny. He would've

missed her, if he hadn't caught her gaze from behind the till. The mad woman crouching behind it, her eyes peering over, wide with fear; she's clutching onto the countertop with her fingertips, as if her life depends on it.

'Penny?' Dexter asks, slowly walking towards her. 'What are you doing?'

'Sshh!' Penny beckons him over, before dragging him down next to her.

'Who are we hiding from?'

'I'm hiding from them.'

Penny continues to scan what's in front of her and stares hard into the depths of her bookshop; as if a monster could come crashing through, causing mass destruction.

'Who?' Dexter asks, sarcastically. 'An invisible dinosaur, on the rampage? An evil, camouflaged unicorn? Anything similar to that?'

'Shut up.' She sharply points at the three young men and cowers in fear. Dexter looks at them and then back at Penny in bewilderment.

However, the three young men all look terribly similar, each expressing the same lack of kindness. They're taking books off the shelves and sneering at the titles, before flinging it behind them. Their designer belts still have the price-tags on and they're carrying an array of solid gold golf-clubs.

'They just look like posh boys,' Dexter mutters.

'They are posh boys,' Penny replies.

'I do find that the poor are always funnier when they try to run away from us,' one of the posh-boys announces to the others.

Dexter looks back at Penny and guffaws. 'Seriously? You're afraid of a group of pretentious kids?'

'Yes, I am,' Penny admits, defensively. 'Every time someone like that comes into my bookshop, I just hide and let them do what they want.'

'Why would you let them get away with that?' Dexter asks, before watching the posh-boys rip out the pages from *The Lord of the Rings* and throwing it up in the air. He clenches the desk, his breathing intensifies. 'Those bastards...' he growls, through gritted teeth.

'I'm afraid of them. It's simply better to hide, until they go away.'

'Can't you get rid of them?'

'You don't think I've tried? Once, when I asked them to leave, they pushed a bookcase over me. If they'd have killed me, they told me their lawyer-daddy could make it look like an accident.'

'Geez... Couldn't you call the police?'

'They're rich boys, Dexter. They have credit cards that are brighter than my future. Daddy pays for everything, so they can afford to be bailed out of jail.'

'So, what are you going to do?'

'I'm going to hide, until they go away.'

'What the...'

'Weren't you ever bullied in school?'

'Of course, I was.' Dexter mumbles, his face turning red. 'But I usually managed outwit them.'

'Oh yeah? Well, I hide until everything's fine

again.'

'Is this how you face all your problems?'

Whenever Penny was faced with her secondary-school bullies, Emily used to find creative ways to get rid of them. Usually, Penny would jump onto Emily's shoulders, clamber into her home-made monster costume and scare the bullies away. At least then Penny could always face her fear with laughter.

'I'm not answering that,' Penny eventually replies.

When the two of them look up, the three posh-boys are standing in front of the counter. Immediately, Penny and Dexter bounce onto their feet, brushing the dust off the till and pretending that everything is normal.

'Oi. Peasants.' One of the wealthy teens snarls at Penny, before spitting on the desk. 'Watch me do a magic trick.'

'What are you going to do?' Penny whispers. Her entire body quaking with dread. Both she and Dexter are frozen to the spot.

'We can make this book disappear,' the second one mutters. He dangles a copy of Lord of the Flies, in front of them. Then, he whips out a silver lighter from his blazer pocket and hovers it just below the book.

The white-hot flame begins to flicker and grow, slowly setting the pages alight. Penny and Dexter watch in horror, as the book begins to crack and crumble under the pressure, before falling into ash and dust. The specks of burnt paper slowly begin to drift downwards in front of Penny; she has tears in her eyes but she refuses to cry in front of anyone. Then, her cheeks flush red with rage. She's dreadfully reminded of cruel moments when she was a teenager and schoolkids would hide her books up in trees or use them to conduct science experiments. Penny refused to cry in front of them, too.

Swiftly falling back to reality, Penny clenches her fists and leaps over the till; lunging at the first posh-boy she can get her hands on. She manages to grab one of them by the scruff of their neck and with a forceful tug, she drags him down to her eye-level. While furious tears are streaming down her face, Penny doesn't take her eyes off the boy. He still has a smug smile on his face, but Penny can see the fear in his eyes.

'You bastard!' she shrieks, like a banshee. 'How dare you? You little shit!'

Just as Penny is about to take a swing at him, she's dragged back by Dexter.

'Whoa, Penny!' Dexter cries. He too, has also leapt over the till and throws his arms around Penny's waist, flinging her to the side. 'I'm not going to let them hurt you…'

'Dexter! Didn't you see what they just did?'

'I did,' Dexter says, trying to calm her down. 'Let me deal with it.' He slowly turns around and walks up to the posh-boys; who are still sniggering.

'Look, lads,' Dexter says to them. 'You can't just…' He takes a step back and looks back at Penny. Then, he looks back at the group of lads and stands up straight. 'Just piss off and leave my friend alone.'

One of them patronisingly bends down to Dexter's eyesight. Dexter's cheeks flush crimson with fury.

'Ooh, look gentlemen,' one of them cries to his cronies. 'Isn't he just so damn small? I could stick my hand up his arse and use him as a puppet.'

'I'd rather you didn't.' His voice trembles but he clenches his fists. 'Leave Penny alone. Get out of her bookshop.'

'What are you going to do about it?' another rich - teen asks him.

'Umm…' Dexter stutters, thinking too much about the perfect comeback. He stands on his tiptoes and puffs his chest out. 'Leave her alone, or… I will bite off your ears and scoop out your eyeballs with a blunt spoon. You rich Daddy Scum…'

'Oh, Dexter… No,' Penny grumbles, hiding her head in her hands.

As expected, the three boys erupt into a fit of mocking laughter. Dexter doesn't back down; his cheeks keep burning with embarrassment.

'Did I stutter?' Dexter asks, sarcastically.

'Piss off, midget,' one of the boys says, before violently head-butting him.

Dexter staggers backwards, his hands clasped over his forehead, swearing loudly. Penny runs up to Dexter and stands in front of him, scowling up at the posh-boys.

'Hey!' she cries, pointing her finger at them. 'Get out of my bookshop. Now.'

'What if we don't want to leave?' one of them asks,

with a sneer.

Penny's expression is blank, but her mind is whirring with ideas. Then, she relaxes her shoulders and begins to play with strands of her hair. 'Well, you've upset them, now.'

The three boys look at one another, confused. 'Tell us what you mean?' one of them demands.

'Yeah, what do you mean?' Dexter asks her. But Penny turns to face him and gives him a nod, telling him to go with it. He nods back.
'I can hear them,' she says. 'You've woken them up...'

'Who have we woken up?' the other one demands.

'The ghosts, of course,' she replies softly. She pretends to listen, intently. 'Can't you hear them?'

'I can hear them...' Dexter replies, following on with Penny's torment.

'You're talking utter shite,' a posh-boy says, although his voice is beginning to shake. The clan take a step back, nervously.

Penny raises her hands, calling for silence and pretends to listen out for something. 'Oh, shit. You've angered them now.' Penny chuckles. When she takes a step towards them, they take another step back.

'Why's... Why's that?'

Penny and Dexter look at each other. Then, they begin to edge forward, slowly walking the posh-boys out of The Author's Library.

'They'll come for you in the night...' Penny begins to say.

'With a thirst for blood…' Dexter continues.

'They'll slash through your soul with their fingernails…'

'…And they'll rip out your heart and eat it before your very eyes…'

'So, I'd leave now, if you want a good night's sleep, tonight,' Penny advises them, with a sickly-sweet smile on her face.

The posh-boys cower together. 'You're crazy,' one of them whispers.

'I don't believe you,' another one states.

But before Penny and Dexter can go any further, the lights begin to flicker and there's a sudden chill that runs through the bookshop.

'Aagh!' One of the boys shrieks. A selection of Mary Shelley books suddenly fall off the shelf, followed by a stray, black cat with white paws. While the falling books shower on the boys, the cat pounces on one of their shoulders, digging its claws into his flesh. The other two boys shriek, in unison.

'Tiny-Dancer,' Penny whispers. Then, she looks directly at the three boys, with a wicked smile of her face. 'Boo.'

It's enough for the three posh-boys to scream and sprint out of The Author's Library. Penny and Dexter chase after them, shrieking like banshees and flailing their limbs. Dexter continues to call them Daddy Scum.

When the posh-boys are gone, Penny and Dexter sink to the floor, with Tiny-Dancer at their feet.

'Thanks,' she mutters, to the cat. Tiny-Dancer gives

Penny a nod and then struts out of the shop. 'Seems like you were right, Dexter. All we had to do was outwit them…'

'Whoa, now! You didn't outwit them… You scared them off.'

'It worked, though…' Penny looks at the bump on Dexter's head. 'Are you ok?'

He gently rubs his forehead. 'I'll be fine. It's my battle wound. The mark of a true warrior…'

'You're an idiot.' Penny chuckles.

'Fine,' Dexter replies, grumpily. 'You can fight your battles alone, next time.'

Penny lowers her head and stays silent.

'Where have you been, Penny?' Dexter asks, his face softens but is accompanied by a concerned look.

The smile from Penny's face immediately drops. She starts to rub the tattoo on her collarbone and drags her gaze to the floor. 'I'm always here.'

'Don't mess about. You know what I mean.'

There's a hint of concern, in his voice, which still seems to surprise her. Up until this morning, she didn't think Dexter cared that much about her. Trying to dodge the conversation, Penny jumps onto her feet and wanders into the depths of the bookshop. Dexter quickly shuffles beside her.

'Don't try and dodge the question. We're worried about you. What happened? Why did you run away and disappear off the face of the earth?'

'You guys were worried about me?' she thinks.

Penny stops to face Dexter. She can feel herself becoming lighter with exhilaration, before the same anxieties quickly drag her back down.

'Don't worry about me, I'm fine,' she eventually says, although unconvincingly.

'I don't believe that,' Dexter immediately tells her. 'There's something you're not telling us.'

'I'll be fine.'

'So, there is something wrong…'

'I don't want to talk about it.' Penny runs further into her bookshop. She thinks she's hidden herself away, but Dexter comes and sits next to her.

'If you keep running away, I'll just keep on chasing you.' he tells her.

'I'd rather be on my own.'

'You don't mean that.'

'Yes, I do,' Penny says, bluntly. Although it's incredibly painful to say. 'At least if I'm alone, no one or nothing can hurt me…'

'Really? I used to think that, when I was sent to boarding school.' Dexter says. 'I was on my own and had to defend myself from bullies on a daily basis. It was shit. But what got me through it was writing home to Millie and Christopher. I always had my pals by my side and so did they.'

'Lucky you.'

'You can rely on us, Penny.' When Dexter rests a hand on her shoulder, it feels awkward but she appreciates the sentiment. 'We're your friends.'

Hearing that sounds so wonderful, but then she remembers when it all came crashing down before her eyes. Being lonely once a connection is broken, can sometimes be too painful to bear.

Penny looks away from Dexter and lowers her head. 'I can't do it to myself.' she mutters. 'I just want to forget it all.'

'Is that why you've become so obsessed with the basement? All your family mysteries?'

It's partly the reason. But Penny doesn't want to admit that. 'One day, the laughter stops…'

'Not if you've got good friends who'll always make you smile,' Dexter says. 'Why do you think we come to see you?'

'Why?'

'It's not exactly for the sci-fi books. It's always to see you. When we're all together, we forget about everything else and just have fun. We love you for who you are.'

'I wish I could believe that myself…' she thinks.

'You've helped us,' Dexter reminds her. 'Now, we want to help you.'

'I don't want any help,' Penny says, although they both know it's a lie.

'Sometimes, friends will help you whether you want it or not. None of us want to hurt you, Penny. But if you want to be left alone, then that's what I'll do.'

'I want to be on my own,' Penny mumbles but it's loud enough to hear.

Slowly, Dexter gets onto his feet and walks out. Penny watches him leave and it breaks her heart, knowing that she pushed her friends away. They seemed like good friends, too.

Penny spins around to face the books in front of

her. She looks up and tries to breathe it all in, but the books don't excite her like they usually do. Feeling slightly defeated, she closes the bookshop and then takes a lonesome wander.

'Now that I'm on my own, I can make my own fun. Nobody can hurt me.' she thinks.

But the silence in deafening and it all comes screaming back to her. As the bookcases loom over Penny, they don't seem to be as comforting as they usually are; it's as if they're growing taller and Penny's shrinking to the size of Thumbelina. She walks further into the depths of her bookshop, the passageways getting darker and eerily longer, as if there's no end in sight. When Penny begins to run, it's as if she can feel her demons following closely behind her.

Suddenly, painful memories come crashing into her mind. No matter how hard she tries to shake them away, she just makes herself dizzy. She remember when people tried to change her, tried to forget about her or act like she never existed. Those times made Penny doubt herself about everything: wondering what she did wrong and whether it she would ever be good enough to have friends.

Penny stumbles into the centre of The Author's Library, collapses onto the floor and cries.

'I don't deserve to have friends.' She thinks. 'I'm just a weirdo...'

Her thoughts trail off when she looks up and sees all the directories behind the till, as well as the notepad and pen she's discarded, with the contact details of one, Bradley Figment. She wipes her tears away with her sleeve and crawls behind the till. Sitting cross-legged, she holds the notepad in one hand reaches for the phone with the other.

She slowly dials the number and triple-checks it, to be sure. Penny holds the phone to her ear; she can hear her heart pounding in time to the phone ringing. It seems like it's going on forever. Her hands begin to sweat, so she holds the phone, even tighter.

'Please… let it be you,' she mutters.

Just as she's about to give up, a nervous voice answers the phone.

'Hello? Who is this?'

Penny opens her mouth, but she's speechless. She hadn't given any thought as to what she wants to say.

'Who's calling?' he asks, again. 'I don't recognise the number?'

'Are you Bradley Figment?' Penny asks and it's barely louder than a croak.

'I am.'

'Good start.' she thinks.

'May I ask who's calling?' he asks, again. He sounds more nervous. 'Please?'

'I… I'm Penny Figment… The Author's Library.'

There's a silence, between them. For a moment, Penny wonders if he's fainted from shock.

'Hello?' Penny mutters.

'The Author's Library. As in the bookshop?' he asks.

'Err… Yeah?'

'You say you're a Figment?'

'I am. I'm Nora's Figment's granddaughter…'

'Nora…' Bradley whispers, but it's loud enough for Penny to hear. 'I haven't heard from her in so long…'

'Is she your sister?'

'Yes. My twin sister.'

'Can you come to the bookshop?' Penny asks. She can't keep it in for much longer.

'You want me to come to your bookshop?' Bradley asks. Penny can hear some excitement rising in his voice. 'I can be there tomorrow.'

The Mystery of Bradley Figment

When Bradley Figment received that phone call from Penny, at first he couldn't believe it. He had wanted to come back to bookshop for so many years but had eventually given up. When Nora never replied to his letters, Bradley just had to accept the fact that his twin sister had axed him from the family. It was the worst feeling ever, as if he'd had his heart ripped out by a chimera. He had no choice but to move on with this life and, eventually, he did. But he'd always dreamt of one day, coming back to The Author's Library and now, he could finally explain everything.

Stepping back into the bookshop, it feels as if it's been perfectly frozen in time. Bradley takes a slow wander in-between the bookcases, peering around each one, just like he used to. When he finds himself amongst the ancient Greek literature, he takes in all the surrounding stories and a smile creeps across his face. He catches a glimpse of the Greek tragedy next to the Epic poetry and remembers all the times he loved the most; when happiness was as high as the walls of Troy, before they came crashing down.

'Can I help you?'

Bradley turns around and sees the young woman with green eyes and auburn hair; he clings onto his satchel with sweaty palms. For a moment, Bradley thinks he's looking at a young Nora Figment; but he knows that his twin sister would never wear so much colour. So this Nora's granddaughter.

'Have courage.' he thinks. 'Are you Penny Figment?'

'Yeah, I am.'

*

At first, Penny hasn't a clue who this man is. Although, he seems oddly familiar, as if she's known him before. But when she looks into his eyes, sees the pencils sticking out of his shirt pocket and the paint splotches on his shoes, she can guess who he is.

'You don't happen to be Bradley Figment, do you?'

'I am.'

Penny stares at him, for several moments. For starters, she didn't think he'd be the first customer to walk into The Author's Library and she hasn't prepared anything to say to him. All her hours of searching and curiosity had led to this: Bradley Figment standing right in front of her. Penny can only imagine what Emily would say. Finally, she'll get some answers.

'Is it just you who lives here?' Bradley asks, walking hesitantly towards her.

Penny blushes and looks down at her shoes. 'Err… Yeah, it is.'

'I tried to come back to the bookshop, in 1969,' Bradley mutters. The two of them now awkwardly standing next to each other. Neither of them know whether to look the other in the eye. 'I tried to catch Nora, but I knew that she didn't want to see me, even though I could explain everything to her. But I think I met her teenage daughter.'

'Emily Figment?' Penny's heart begins to pound heavily, in her chest. She looks away from Bradley and gently twiddles her hair.

'Was that her name? I never knew. But she was so friendly and didn't even know who I was.'

'That sounds like her. It's just me now, though.'

'I see.'

There's an awkward silence. Neither of them seems to know what to say next. Suddenly, all of Penny's questions have vanished from her mind.

'Would you like a cup of tea?' Penny asks. 'Then, you could tell me everything.'

Bradley smiles. 'I'd love that.'

'Then, make yourself comfortable.'

First, she closes the shop an hour after opening. Penny finally being a step closer to solving the mystery seems a lot more important than selling books, today. Then, as she makes them a pot of tea, excitement and exhilaration begins to bubble in her tummy. Penny can't believe that she's finally getting the answers to her questions. She dances on her tiptoes as the teabags brew in the teapot. For a moment, her friendship anxieties have been pushed to the back of her mind.

*

Meanwhile, as he finds his way to the armchairs amongst the adventure books, Bradley remembers when he was a boy, and he would build whatever he wanted out of stacks of books. Hundreds of heavy, hardback books were transformed into entirely new worlds: cities that were soon destroyed by imaginary monsters. Or planes and submarines, which Bradley would pilot and captain. He used to make stories from the books which already had their tales tucked inside their pages.

As Bradley sits in Grandma-Ruth's old armchair, he remembers when he used to sit cross-legged at her feet. Nora would sit next to him and they'd look up at Ruth with glee, as she told them stories of her adventures. During the childhood that Bradley spent in The Author's Library, he only once dreamt about when he and Nora were homeless children.

'Did Nora teach you how to lay out a perfect tea?' Bradley chuckles, when he sees Penny return with a tray holding a pot of tea at the perfect temperature, two teacups with matching saucers, fancy silver teaspoons and a plate of biscuits.

'Err… yeah. She taught me, when I was little,' Penny says, pouring the tea. 'We used to have proper tea-parties while my mum ran the bookshop.'

'I'm assuming you know Nora's story?'

'Of how she came to The Author's Library?'

'It's actually the story of how we came together,' Bradley says. He takes a long sip of tea, with his little finger sticking out. Just like his twin sister still does.

'We always stuck together, when we ran away from the abusive orphanage. We comforted each other, when we were homeless and we held onto each other, when we were evacuated to the country-side. Actually, it was Nora's idea. She fought our way, amongst all the other children, for us to be seen. That's how we were found by Patrick Figment and Ruth. I wouldn't have survived, if it weren't for my sister.'

'You were by her side, the whole time?'

'I was. She took me by the hand and I followed her to a better life. She never stopped fighting for our happiness and for our safety.'

'So, what happened, after that?' Penny asks, nibbling on a biscuit.

'Has Nora told you anything about what happened in 1955?'

'She never mentioned anything. Most of it I found out myself.' There's a hint of pride in her voice.

'You seem like a clever girl, Penny. So, I can only assume that no one's ever gone back to the basement?'

'Everything's been locked and hidden away.'

'I guess Nora wanted to forget all about it.' Bradley sighs, with disappointment. 'After everything we'd been through, it all came to a crashing, bitter end. But maybe, with your help I could explain myself and everything that happened.'

'I think so. I'll be honest, Grandma never wanted to me go back to the basement. In fact, she's never mentioned you.'

'I don't blame her.'

'You're a lot softer than your twin sister.'

Bradley chuckles. 'Why does that not surprise me? Nora's always been a born leader. Does she still wear her smartest suit and a string of her shiniest pearls?'

'Yeah, she does.'

'Aah, I remember it all so well. I've missed her so much.'

'Why have you left it so long to talk to her, if you left in 1955? I found the letter you wrote to her.'

'This isn't my first time, wanting to come back. Like I said before, I tried to come back but she didn't want to even hear of me. I wrote her countless letters, but never heard a response. Eventually, I gave up. Until I received the call from you.'

'What happened in 1955?' Penny asks.

'What have you discovered already?' Bradley asks.

'There were three people, who used to meet, down in the basement. Although I don't know why. Do you all love ancient Greek literature?'

'Yes, we did,' Bradley replies. 'It was our passion that really brought us together. We kept so many secrets and made so many memories, beneath our beloved bookshop.'

'Everything's still there,' Penny tells him, as she pours him another tea. 'The books, the paintings and the messages.'

'I'd love to go back there. None of us expected our time together to be cut so short. One day, we left the basement like we always did. Then, we never went back. It was like leaving an old friend behind.'

'Wait here.' Penny slips away for a few moments. She returns, less than three minutes later, with stacks of old books and sketches in her arms, all while tripping over her shoelaces.

'What about all of this?' Penny asks, when she presents it to him.

*

Bradley gasps and takes a while to look at every book and every sketch. He never thought he would ever see them again. There are tears of joy in his eyes and a wide smile grows across his face.

'I haven't seen all of this, in over fifty years,' he whispers. 'I feared that Nora had burnt it all.'

'Maybe Grandma didn't ever want to completely forget you.'

'We always told each other that we were family, no matter what. I still stand by that, even after I left.' He looks up at Penny and gently rests a hand on her shoulder. 'Thank you for showing me this.'

'You're welcome. So, tell me what happened, down in the basement? I'm dying to know!'

'You're certainly due an explanation, Penny. The truth is, we all suffered with our own struggles but that's what brought us together. When we headed down into the basement every evening, we left our problems at the door and found comfort in an ancient story. We created our own world beneath the bookshop, where no one could hurt us. The three of us shared moments of companionship, loyalty and romance.'

'Who was the third person?' Penny asks. 'You, Grandma and someone called M.M.'

'That would be Michael Marblelight. Do you know him?'

Penny's mouth hangs open, in shock. 'Mr. Marblelight? I know him! He's been coming to my bookshop for years...'

'I'm guessing Michael's been coming to The Author's Library, for longer than you thought?'

'Well, yeah. I've known him for as long as I can remember.'

'I always found him so intelligent and handsome.' Bradley blushes slightly. He opens one of Michael's notebooks and flicks through the pages. While Bradley never fully understood what Michael was always talking about, he loved listening to his voice; it was almost like velvet.

'Every night was similar, but we never tired of it,' Bradley continues, smiling at the memories. 'We'd have discussions about our favourite books, or sometimes we'd study them. On other nights, there'd be a raucous rabble of epiphanies. We took it in turns to do dramatic readings. It was a much loved time, shared between friends. We never wanted it to end.'

'So why did it end?'

Bradley sighs. 'Love may seem like something wonderful but Aphrodite is dangerously powerful. She cast her spell over Nora and Michael.'

'My grandma and Mr. Marblelight?' Penny gasps. 'Why didn't she tell me this, either?'

'There seems to be a lot that my sister has hidden from you.'

'Apparently so.'

'I can understand why. She'd been embarrassed, heartbroken and didn't want to handle the truth.'

'What happened between them?'

'No one else suspected anything. Michael was the one who wanted to keep their affair a secret and Nora went along with it, completely blinded by love. I knew they loved each other, but something didn't seem right.'

'Did you find out what that was?'

'Not until it was too late. In the beginning of 1956, Michael disappeared out of our lives. We didn't know why or whether he'd ever come back. It broke Nora's heart and we never went back to the basement, knowing it wouldn't be the same again. She'd wait all night and sit by the phone, trying to call or waiting for him to ring. She wrote him letters, but never received a response. As she slowly went mad, love was feasting on her entire body, from the inside-out. Soon enough, Nora was left with a broken heart. Customers didn't know why she was suddenly like this. But there were only ever three people who knew.'

'So that's why Grandma never mentioned him.' That's why Mr. Marblelight wouldn't tell me anything.'

'It gets worse.' Tears begin to fall down Bradley's cheeks, which he gently wipes away. 'Two weeks after Michael's disappearance, Nora and I received a note that our father had died. He'd contracted a fatal illness while on his travels.'

'Grandma used to say that Patrick Figment was a great man.'

'That's true. There's so much that I owe to my father. But on the day we found out about his death, I received a letter from him. This should explain everything.'

Bradley reaches into his satchel and takes out a crumpled letter, slightly torn at the edges.

Penny reads through the letter, once. Then, she reads it several more times:

20ᵗʰ January 1956

Bradley,

I want you to read this carefully, but do not show it to Nora. If she read this, she'd only worry. I know that you'll stay open-minded as I explain this all to you.

I don't know how long this letter will take to get to you. As you read this, I may already be dead. I have contracted pneumonia in Gothenburg and it's unlikely that I will survive.

When I left The Author's Library, it was initially to find great stories to share and eventually sell to the world. Yet, it soon became a mission to uncover the mystery of my father, Robert Figment. I'm doing this for my mother, so her soul can finally be put to rest.

Now, I need you to continue my journey. My father was reported missing in action but I have evidence that suggests he was caught by German troops and taken prisoner. However, his trail disappears at the shores of the Baltic Sea. I know that there is more to his story and I have trust in you, to find it.

Leave as soon as possible and take as much time as you need. Don't tell Nora what you intend to do but keep her updated, so she doesn't worry herself into a sickness. She'll want to come with you, but I need her to stay in The Author's Library. It's a world that she belongs in and I have faith that Nora can run the bookshop on her own. I choose you to do this because I feel like this is your time to shine. I have confidence that you will do our family proud, Bradley.

This will be the last time that you'll ever hear from me. But I want you to know that I am so proud of the both of you: From what you have achieved so far and I know my children will go on to do great things. You are an honour to the Figment name and I love you both so very much.

Yours

Patrick.

Bradley watches Penny reading the letter and it looks like she's absorbing every word. When she slowly hands back the letter, she appears to be speechless.

'The mystery of Robert Figment?' Penny whispers. 'That's why you left the bookshop. To solve the mystery of my great-great-grandfather.'

'It took me over two decades, to find out,' Bradley admits. 'I never knew him. But he seemed like a good man, from the stories Ruth used to tell us. My father grew up watching his mother wait for her husband by the window, every night. Me and Nora saw it too. So I wanted to make him proud.

'What did you find?' Penny asks, eagerly.

'I've waited so long to share the mystery of Robert Figment, but I'll save it for when I see my sister.' Bradley chuckles when he sees Penny slouch back down her chair, with a pout on her face. 'Don't worry. You'll hear it, soon enough. That mystery is long overdue to be told.'

'So, if you had your reason to leave, how did you tell her?'

'I want to let you know that this was one of the hardest decisions I ever had to make,' Bradley states. 'At first, I told myself I wasn't going to do it. I couldn't leave Nora, alone in The Author's Library. She'd already lost so much.'

'But you did leave her?'

'I have to admit, Nora's heartbreak soon became unbearable. Not just towards me, but to the customers as well. She became so distraught, that it turned her ugly and any love in her heart was soon replaced with animosity. She would scream and bark at people, all day until her voice was sore. No one wanted to approach her, not even me. Her descent into madness scared people away and then she would cry herself to sleep.'

'No wonder she never spoke about this.'

'I wanted to help her. I really did. We'd already been through so much together and I hated seeing my sister endure such internal agony. But when I offered her help, she refused it. When I wanted to comfort her, she'd run away. We were slowly drifting apart.'

'So, that's when you decided to leave?'

'Almost. I never told Nora about the letter but the mystery of Robert Figment called to me, like a Siren. I knew I couldn't leave my sister, or even have the courage to tell her. I needed one last sign, before I made my decision. Then, there was no going back.'

'What was it?'

'One day, a customer came to the bookshop. It was someone I'd never seen before. He asked me if this was the bookshop owned by the Figment family and I said yes. Then, he asked me if Robert Figment still worked here and I told him that no one knew what happened to him, since he left for the war.'

'Why did he want to know?'

'Well, the two of them fought together. His name was Tommy Broadbent and if it weren't for Robert Figment, he would've died long ago. He was a hero and none of us knew about it. So that's when I knew I had to leave and solve the mystery. Much like my father, I wanted Robert Figment to be remembered as a man who was more than missing in action.'

'I'm guessing Grandma doesn't know why you left the bookshop?' Penny asks, tentatively.

'This is why Nora's so angry with me. I remember it well. It was the following day and all was quiet. I approached her, with a suitcase in my hand and she didn't understand what was happening. I told her that I had to leave and I didn't know when I'd come back. But I promised I would. For a long time, she was silent. But I could see in her eyes that she was furious. I told her that one day, I would explain everything, but I needed her to trust me. Immediately, that had been shattered. Nora told me that if I left now, I could never come back. She thought I was leaving her because of her heartbreak.'

'That must be why she never told me about you.'

'It's upsetting that her anger towards me could last for so long. But I guess she never thought her own brother, would be the final one to break her heart. Nora's has always been standing strong, but she's equally as fragile...'

'I'm glad you came back.' Penny reassures

Bradley, as he hangs his head in shame. When she holds his hand, he's filled with a warm sense of comfort. 'You've always been a part of this family. You were just as big a mystery as Robert Figment was. No one else in this family has achieved what you did and it's amazing.'

'Thank you, Penny,' Bradley says, smiling at her. 'I've spent years trying to apologise to her. But I heard nothing back and I never knew what to do.'

'I could try and help you.'

'Will you?' Bradley gasps with tears of joy in his eyes. It's been so long since he's had any hope of seeing his sister again.

'Of course I will. After all, we're family.'

The Mystery of Robert Figment

Over the next few days, Bradley helps Penny in The Author's Library. She's glad to have some company and it feels familiar. Yet, it's odd because Penny now has to get used to the fact that she had more current family members than just her grandma.

While the last few days in the bookshop have been steady, Penny has thrown herself into her work. It was about time that she did, since she'd been giving all her attention to uncovering her family mysteries. She enthusiastically serves every customer that walks through the door, selling more books than ever. When she sees Ivy out of the corner of her eye, Penny smiles at her before delving back into the depths of her bookshop. Ivy's always there, watching over her goddaughter.

At least Penny's distracted from her thoughts that race at a million miles an hour. Penny's so desperate to hear the mystery of Robert Figment that if she stops for a minute, she'll become impatient and her head will explode from excitement. A part of Penny also feels guilty, for knowing so much: Her grandma told her not to, but she didn't want to listen. Also, Emily isn't here and Penny knows that her mum would've loved to know the story.

*

Bradley arrives at the bookshop the moment she opens up, he's eager and enthusiastic. It has been so long since he's stepped back inside, he can think of nothing better to do; besides, it distracts him from the impending reunion with his sister.

When he thinks about it, even for a moment, he's filled with excitement and nervousness. He can feel the butterflies in his tummy but his hands begin to tremble. While Nora doesn't know it yet, Bradley knows what's coming. He just hopes that his sister will at least listen to what he has to say.

Penny told him that she sees her grandma every Sunday afternoon, for a cup of tea and a wander around the bookshop. That's when he'll tell the mystery of Robert Figment. It's a few days away and he's been waiting long enough. Bradley can't believe that the time has finally come. He has all the information stored in his head and the evidence in his hands. He's wanted to tell his sister all of this for so long, before it's too late. He just wanted to make his ancestors proud, every step of the way. While Bradley organises all the books on the shelves, he goes over the story again and again in his head; making sure that no information is missing and every word is understood, like he's learning lines in a play.

He may be elderly, but Bradley's still strong enough to carry heavy stacks of books and tall enough to reach the top shelf. He thinks back to when he was a young bookseller. While his anxiety was much worse back then, he always found it comforting to be amongst the books and that never seems to have changed.

'How do I tell her?' Bradley asks on Sunday. It's almost 3:30pm and he's pacing back and forth, nervously. 'I haven't fully prepared myself, for this. It's been so long and I have so much to say to her…'

'I'm sure it'll all be fine,' Penny says, reassuringly. She's sitting in an armchair, drinking a cup of tea, with her little finger sticking out. 'When you sit her down and explain everything, she'll understand.'

'Are you sure of that?'

*

As always, Nora arrives just a few minutes before half-past three. But as she bustles her way into The Author's Library, she bumps into someone walking out.

'Ooff!' She huffs. 'Watch where you're…'

But before she can snap anything else, Nora looks up and into the eyes of Michael Marblelight. It's been so long since she's been this close to him. It sharply takes her breath away.

'Good afternoon, Nora,' he replies, with a kind smile. Much like a gentleman, he lets Nora through first. 'Are you seeing Penny again today?'

'Of course. It's always just the two of us.'

'How lovely.'

There's an awkward silence, between them. 'So, I guess I shall…' Nora stutters, as she slowly turns around.

'I just want you to know,' he says, quickly. He's relieved when Nora turns back to face him. 'That what we used to share, has always had a place in my heart.'

'Same here. More so than you could ever imagine,' Nora thinks, holding back her tears. 'Why are you telling me this?' she asks.

'Recently, I've been feeling sentimental and reading the books we used to love.'

'That's nice.'

'Do you ever think back to who we used to be? When we were younger and living in our own, precious world?'

Nora takes one last look at Michael. 'Yes, I do,' she says, before turning away and heading into The Author's Library.

Quickly, Nora shakes herself back to reality. Seeing him almost feels like she's coming face-to-face with her past, after she spent so long hiding it all away. It was once such a wonderful time in her life, but now Nora tries so hard to forget. All she can do, is tell herself that she grew stronger from it. But she will never erase the memories and, recently, they've been becoming stronger. Today, Nora's nervous to visit her granddaughter, after she went back to the basement. She's not sure if she can deny it all, for much longer.

*

But when Nora Figment emerges from behind the bookcase, Bradley instantly recognises his sister. The same square-shaped glasses on the pearlescent chain; the suit is identical to what she wore back in the early 50s. As well as her confident stance, even if she has to lean slightly on her walking stick. But Bradley knows that she doesn't recognise him.

'Hello, Penny. Shall we have a cup of tea?' Nora says, with a smile. As she walks towards them, she slowly looks up at Bradley and gives him a frown.

'Who are you?' she asks, bluntly.

Bradley takes a deep breath, before answering. He's almost speechless. 'Nora. It's been so long.'

'How do you know my name?' she demands. She takes a step forward and looks at him intently. 'Do I know you?'

'Err… Yes, you do.'

When Bradley looks at Nora, he'd forgotten how similar they still look. They even have the same, deep-set lines around their facial features and the twinkle in their eyes. It seems like Nora finally recognises him, too. The familiar figure of her identical twin-brother.

'Bradley?' Nora whispers.

'Hello, Nora.'

There's a moment of silence. Nora inhales deeply and she lifts her head up high. There's a moment where Bradley thinks that she'll be overjoyed to see her long-lost brother, again. She'll welcome him back into the family and all the Figment mysteries will finally be answered. But it's a moment of mad thinking.

'What. Are. You. Doing. Here?' She spits at him, prodding her walking-stick into his chest with every word she says. Her face slowly turns scarlet, with rage.

'Err… I've come back,' Bradley stutters. He looks at Penny and she has the same look of fear on her face.

'Don't you remember what I told you, when you left?' Nora shrieks. She swings her walking stick back onto the ground.
Bradley flinches, as if Nora were about to hit him on the head. 'I told you I would come back, one day.'

'Yet, I told you to never come back.' Nora stamps her foot on the ground and glares at him.

'But let me explain myself. Please, Nora? After all these years…'

'No! You broke my heart, Bradley. How could my own brother leave me, when I was feeling so low? But here you are, to remind me of it all. I tried so hard to forget all about you…

'I didn't want to leave…'

'But you did.'

'He has his reasons, Grandma…' Penny begins to say.

Penny's Grandma quickly snaps her head and glares at her. 'You did this,' Nora whispers, her voice trembling in anger.

'Grandma, I…'

'I told you to stop going down to the basement, Penelope. How dare you disobey me.'

'Listen, Grandma,' Penny replies, firmly. She keeps her voice steady but she clenches her fists to stop them from trembling. 'I only went looking because you refuse to say anything at all. How do you expect me to live my life, when there are so many mysteries in this family?'

'There are no mysteries in this family,' Nora shrieks, slamming her walking stick on the ground, again. 'There are simply moments that need to be hidden and my brother was one of them. If only you knew, Penelope.'

'I do know, actually. Bradley told me everything.'

'Then, why do you side with him?' Nora snarls.

They look back at Bradley, who cowers and then looks down at his shoes. A part of him wishes he could blend into the bookcases and never return to the real world.

'Robert Figment,' he whispers.

'What about him?' Nora demands. Bradley opens his mouth to speak but he doesn't know what to say.

Penny looks at Bradley Figment and then back at

her grandma. 'I found Bradley's name written all throughout the basement. I invited him to our bookshop, so he could explain everything.'

'So, why are you here?' Nora demands, to her brother. She crossed her arms raises her eyebrows.

'I've uncovered the mystery of Robert Figment.' Bradley announces.

'Don't be absurd.'

'Nora, I have.' Bradley's voice is getting louder.

It's takes a while for Nora to process this. She opens her mouth but for once, she's speechless.

'That's why I left,' he adds. 'It was our father's dying wish for you to succeed in The Author's Library and for me to leave and uncover the mystery. I was going to come back, one day, honestly.'

'So, you're telling me that for over fifty years, you've been investigating the greatest mystery in our family?' Nora scoffs.

'It took me over two decades to gather it all,' Bradley admits. 'I spent the rest of that time, trying to get back in contact with you.'

He rummages around in his satchel and takes out a folder with a few pages tucked inside. 'I have evidence of where he went, since he left in 1916. This could be my last chance to tell you everything.'

'Well, come on then,' Nora demands. She sits herself down in her armchair, back straight and knees crossed. 'I haven't got all day.'

Bradley sits in the armchair next to Nora and she

gives him a scathing look, as he does so. Penny sits cross-legged on the floor, between them.

'First of all, Nora,' Bradley begins to say. 'I want you to know that leaving you was one of the hardest decisions I have ever had to make.'

'Clearly,' Nora replies, with no empathy in her voice.

'I did this for Father and Grandma-Ruth. I wanted to honour our family.'

'Well, I made this family proud by working hard in The Author's Library, every day. No matter what.' Nora snaps back. 'Even when I was heartbroken and I didn't feel like I could go on. I've given so much to our family and I would do it all again. So, don't think that because of all this, I'll instantly forgive you. I swear to you...'

'Grandma. Let Bradley talk.'

Bradley doesn't dare look back at his glaring sister. Instead, he fumbles with the evidence at his fingertips and takes a moment to think about what to say.

'Where to begin?' Bradley mumbles.

'At the start, usually,' Nora grumbles.

'We all know that Robert Figment went to war as a stretcher-bearer,' Bradley begins to say. 'But we never knew what happened after that.'

'Yes.' Nora tuts.

'Well, at first I spoke to a man named Tommy Broadbent. He was another stretcher-bearer who trained with Robert, in the same regiment. He told me that throughout their training, Robert would tell his companions all about his family and his relationship with God. He was remembered carrying his *Bible* underneath his trench-coat and a photo of his family was tucked inside.'

Bradley delves into his folder and shows Penny and Nora two pictures. The first one is of the Figment family, dated back to 1913. Ruth and Robert are sitting in their armchairs, with baby Patrick sitting on his mother's lap. She's sitting up straight, her hair tucked messily underneath her hat. Robert wears a dark suit and he holds onto his *Holy Bible.*

 The second picture depicts four stretcher-bearers carrying a weighted stretcher, up a muddy hill. It was taken in 1916. Every soldier seems identical, wearing the exact same uniform; with steel helmets over their heads, hiding the fear that lurks behind their eyes. Robert Figment is noted, on the page of the photograph. He's the man with a faintest smile and the deep-set lines that carve out his perfectly defined face.

'Robert was the one who encouraged his companions, when morale was low,' Bradley continues to say. 'A chap who could lift anyone's spirits.'

'Grandma-Ruth always told us that Robert was an incredibly brave man, in many ways,' Nora replies. She uncrosses her arms and looks in Bradley's direction. 'If only Ruth was still alive to hear about all of this…'

'So why was he declared missing in action?' Penny asks.

'It was during the Battle of Arras, in 1917,' Bradley replies. 'I got speaking to another soldier, named Edmund Middlemost. Amidst the battle, Robert saved Edmund's life from a German bullet but was shot in the arm. The two of them laid in a shell-hole, holding onto one another for survival. Edmund told me that they were frozen in the same position, for hours. It wasn't until the guns fell silent, that Robert and Edmund had to find their own way back to their trench. Edmund could barely move due to trench-foot. So, Robert began crawling back to his trench, dragging Edmund to safety.'

'Did they make it?' Penny asks.

'It took them until the next morning. But they were so disorientated, they had accidentally entered a German trench. Both of them were captured and taken away for questioning.'

Nora gasps, with a tear running down her face. 'That's why Ruth never heard from him, again. What happened next?'

'Robert was taken to a Prisoner-of-War camp in Berlin,' Bradley replies. 'I found his name in the POW records. A POW called Sidney Gordon told me that Robert had lost the letters from Ruth but he still studied his *Bible,* every night. Towards the end of

1917, the two of them helped each other escape. They trekked the north of Germany and then went their separate ways.'

'Is this where Robert's trail ends?' Penny asks.

'I have missing information, to tell you the truth,' Bradley admits. 'But after many years of searching in so many places, I found out that Robert was washed up along the harbour of Nyhavn, Copenhagen, in May 1918…'

'How did he end up there?' Nora cries. 'That's absurd?'

'I have the evidence, to prove it,' Bradley replies, gently. 'Robert was found injured and unconscious, by a Catholic family. I spoke to the daughter about it, Klara Kristensen. She told me that her family took him in and nursed him back to health. Robert stayed with them, until the end of the war. He told the Kristensen's all about his wife and son, back in England. He even gave Klara the photos that had managed to survive. It was Klara who gave it all to me, after so many years. When she met him, Klara was engaged to a Danish gentleman. Yet, over time, she told me that she started to fall in love with Robert…'

'Oh no,' Nora utters. 'He didn't…?'

'No. Of course, he didn't.'

Simultaneously, Nora and Penny let out a sigh of relief.

'Klara told me that Robert always remained

faithful to Ruth. When she declared her love for him, he kindly rejected her but promised to never tell anyone else about it.'

'What a good man,' Nora says.

Bradley sighs and takes an old letter out of his pocket. 'When Robert found safety in Copenhagen, he did write to Ruth. He gave the letter to Klara to post.'

'I never found any letters about Robert arriving in Denmark,' Penny admits.

'That's because Ruth never received any letters. This is it.' Bradley passes the letter to Nora, who begins to read it. Then, she passes it to Penny. 'Klara told me that she never sent it and kept it for herself, even after he left.'

'Why would she do that?' Nora asks, spitting out every word, as if it were poison.

'She told me that she loved him and wanted to keep a part of Robert, always. Some people can go mad, when they're in love. Klara really hoped that he would fall in love with her and she'd convince him to stay in Nyhavn and marry her instead.'

21st June 1918

To my darling, Ruth,

I hope you find this letter in good health, for you and for Patrick. You haven't heard from me in some time, but I am far from the battlefield. I have been taken in by a kind Catholic family, in Copenhagen and I intend to stay with them until the end of the war. But I am alive and safe, which is all that matters, right now. While the family I am staying with are kind and generous, I

will return home: to you, Patrick, Max, and The Author's Library.
We shall all be together, soon. I pray for it, every night. Nothing
will ever stop me from doing so and I will make my way back to
England, when it is safe to do so. The storms do not scare me and
the perilous journey won't stop me. I would rather die, than be
without you for the rest of my life.
  Your loving husband,
  Robert.

'Klara gave me this letter, to settle the guilt that she was internally battling with,' Bradley says.

'She should feel extremely guilty, for what she did.' Nora snarls. 'Grandma-Ruth would've known, otherwise.'

'People don't always think logically, when they're in love,' Bradley replies. Nora shuffles awkwardly in her seat. 'Klara never told anyone about this. She didn't even try to stop Robert, when he began to plan his route home.'

'But Robert didn't make it back to England, did he?' Penny asks.

Bradley lowers his head, as if he's done something wrong. 'This is where his trail disappears. He left the Kristensen family in the beginning of 1919, when the war was finally over. No one else has heard anything since. He travelled alone, with no other witnesses to conclude his story. I've spent so long and extended my research, to finish this tale, but this is all I could find about him. I don't think we'll ever know how his story ends.'

Tears begin to fall down his face, as if he's failed in

what he was meant to do. He thinks back to the years he spent travelling around Europe, researching and investigating an age-old family mystery. Reading every piece of evidence that he could connect to Robert Figment. He was desperate to find anything about him and wanted to connect the story together, like a jigsaw puzzle.

Yet, it always felt right to uncover the truth about this man. Knowing that Robert Figment spent his life doing good for others made his story worth discovering. Bradley lets out a long sigh, in relief but also in disappointment; he's thankful to have finally told his tale, but also devastated that this story doesn't have a definite ending. Bradley also doesn't know where to go from here.

Then, he feels a gentle hand on top of his and when he looks up, he sees his sister. She's smiling at him and it's something Bradley has wished to see again.

'So, that's where you've been, all this time?' Nora says, her eyes begin to fill up with tears. 'I thought you'd left because we drifted apart…'

'I've been everywhere, for so many years.' Bradley clings onto Nora's hand, as if he could lose her at any moment. 'But we could never drift apart, Nora. Nothing could ever separate us, no matter what. While I love my family, you've been there since the day we were born. I'm so sorry, Nora… I shouldn't have left you without explaining.'

'It's ok, Bradley. In fact, I'm sorry for the years of neglect, towards you.' Nora hangs her head in shame. 'I was just so angry because I'd lost so much. But I could never erase you from my memories, even though I tried. I may have burnt the letters you sent me but your presence was still in The Author's Library. It's where we've always belonged. I'll never forgive myself, for the way I treated you.'

'You had your heart broken, it's understandable,' Bradley reassures her. 'But I'll forgive you if you can forgive the both of us?'

'We may have lost some important people, in our family,' Nora admits, 'but I don't want to forget you anymore, Bradley.'

Memories Reunited

Throughout the week, Nora begins to accept her brother's return. Even though they didn't decide it amongst themselves, the Figment twins came to the bookshop every day and spent it together. Penny would catch them wandering in-between the bookcases. There'd be an awkward silence between them, while pointing out their favourite books, every so often. Or they would sit silently in armchairs and share and pot of tea.

Neither of them know what to say to each other. At first, Nora was still suspicious of Bradley's return. When she looks at her brother after years apart, she's reminded of the hurt she endured and it strikes deep and painfully into her heart. But if she can forgive her brother after everything's he's done, maybe she won't lose him again. Even though she's already lost him, once before. Over time, the anger and betrayal that Nora felt became a core part of her, destroying her from the inside-out.

When she opens her mouth to speak, she stops herself, before she can reminisce anything. The thought of being reunited with Bradley and only to lose him again, makes her heart ache more than it ever did before.

'Don't do this to yourself.' Nora thinks one day, as she and Bradley share a pot of tea in silence. She watches him gaze up at all the adventure books. 'But it's Bradley and he came back… He used to be my only family. I can't lose him again…'

'Do you remember the time when you rescued me?' Bradley says, suddenly interrupting her thoughts.

'I beg your pardon?'

Bradley chuckles. 'When we first came to the bookshop, when we were children. A group of schoolboy-bullies chased me up one of the bookcases. But just before they could point and laugh, you came storming up to them. Even though they were older than us, you scared them away by being so ferocious with your words. When I still didn't want to come down, you came up and joined me. We watched over the bookshop until the sun set.'

Nora gasps. 'Yes, I remember that, now. Why are you mentioning this?'

'It's because when we were children, we always stuck by each other. Especially when we only ever had each other…'

Bradley swiftly stops talking, when Nora looks away from him. She has tears in her eyes but doesn't want to embarrass herself.

'Nora?'

She looks back at her brother. Tears are now falling down her face but she doesn't feel ashamed. She's feels a warmth in the pit of her stomach, when Bradley gently places his hand over hers.

'I'm so sorry,' Bradley begins to say. 'For all the pain I caused, when I left you.'

'Will you leave me again?' Nora whispers.

'No, not this time. I'll be right by your side.' Nora closes her eyes and takes a deep breath. 'I'm sorry, Bradley,' she tells him, as she exhales.

He furrows his brow, in confusion. 'What for?'

She wraps her arms around him and he does the same. Tears stream down her face and splash onto his shirt.

'I tried to forget you and pretend you didn't exist.' Nora sobs. Whenever you approached me, I drove you away. If only I'd just listened to you, all those years ago. You could've known Emily, your niece. The mystery of Robert Figment could've... Oh, God. Ruth and Father must be so disappointed in me...'

Bradley holds his sister out at arm's length, his hands planted firmly on her shoulders and then he looks directly at her.

'Nora. You could never disappoint anyone.' Bradley's tone softens and although Nora keeps sobbing, there's a smile on her face. 'It may have taken us so long to reunite but that's what our story has become. We can't change that. I'm just so grateful that I could see you again and explain everything.'

Slowly and with smiles on their faces, the two of them sink into their armchairs and Nora pours them another cup of tea. Only this time, it feels a lot more comforting.

'What a dramatic world we've lived in,' Nora admits, as she sips her tea.

'Yet, we're stronger than ever before.'

The Figment twins watch Penny emerge from behind the bookcase, before bounding towards them with a wide grin on her face. When Penny and Nora catch a glance at each other, she silently signals to her granddaughter that a broken-heart is beginning to heal.

'Penny, thank you.' Nora says. 'For reuniting me with my brother.'

'I'm glad I did.'

'Did Penny show you what she found in the basement?' Bradley asks his sister.

'No?'

He reaches into his satchel and begins to show Nora all the sketches and books that they once adored. Nora gasps, as she takes each one in turn. She holds them in her trembling hands and studies everything she can see.

'You're such a clever girl,' Bradley says to Penny, making her blush. 'You should be so proud of yourself.'

'I am, actually,' Penny admits.

'You went down here with Emily, the first time,' Nora says, looking up at Penny. 'Didn't you?'

'Err… Yeah, we did. She would've loved to have figured it all out with me.'

Nora smiles at her. 'Don't worry about that, Penny.

I think she's always been with you, along the way.'

'I just have one more question,' Penny says. 'What about everything behind the locked door? Was it meant to be hidden away?'

Nora sighs and rests the books in her lap. But this time, she isn't scared to admit anything. 'When everything happened, in such a short amount of time, I was so angry and broken. I didn't want to remember anything about the basement, because all the good memories had turned sour. At first, I wanted to burn it all: every book, sketch and note. That way, no one would ever know. My shame would burn along with it. But when I went to the basement, one last time, I just couldn't bring myself to do it. Those moments were too precious to me. So when I found the door behind the bookcase, I hid it all away. I was so flustered to forget it all, I didn't even think about anyone finding it, again. So when I locked the door and hid it with the curtain, I never looked back. Although, I always wanted to. Now, I'm glad I have.'

'I loved the mural.' Penny pipes up.

'Aah, my favourite piece of work.' Bradley says, proudly. 'I'd love to go down there and finish it, one day.'

'Tell me everything about it.'

But while Bradley tells Penny the tale, Nora doesn't listen to a word of it. Instead, she flicks through the pages of Michael's old notebooks. She always loved his handwriting and his words were so intellectual. Then, she flicks through all her Greek tragedies and reads all her notes around the text. When she looks at the back page of *Medea,* Nora's heart drops at what she'd written on the bottom:

Let it be known that I have fallen in love with Michael Marblelight.

I love you, Nora Figment.

She remembers the night it was written. It was towards the end of 1955 where joy had reached its peak, before it all came crashing down. Tears start to fall down Nora's face, again. She thinks back to a time where she honestly thought that Michael Marblelight had loved her back.

'What's the matter, Grandma?' Penny entwines her fingers with Nora's. Bradley offers his sister a handkerchief to wipe away her tears.

'I was so naïve, back then.' Nora sobs. 'I always tried to act older than I was but I never know any better. So, when I was alone, all I could do was look to the future. Dedicate my life to Emily because back then, she was all I had. I was always going to be by her side.'

'At least there are no more secrets in the family,' Bradley reminds them.

'Almost,' Nora mutters. She picks up her handbag and hobbles into the depths of The Author's Library, leaving Penny and Bradley very confused.

Nora follows the twists and turns of all the bookcases, disappearing behind one and then emerging from another. She knows exactly where to go and when she amongst the ancient Greek literature, she waits for him.

'He'll always be here,' she thinks.

For the first time since 1956, Nora wants to own up to everything. But she hasn't got a clue what's going to happen. There's a part of her that wants to open her heart to Michael and maybe he could love her back, after all these years. Then again, she wants to scream at him like a bacchus.

Nora sighs. It wouldn't be sensible to do any of those things. But all she's ever wanted from this is closure. She felt as if she'd blinked and all of a sudden, she was left alone. Everyone she loved had left her, with no explanation. Even though it broke her, all Nora could do was move forward. Now, she wanted answers.

Thankfully, she doesn't have to wait long. When Michael Marblelight turns the corner and sees Nora, it's almost as if he's been looking for her.

'Hello, Michael.' Nora looks up at the tragedies, trying to stand tall and sound as confident as possible. Although, she clasps her hands around her walking stick to stop them from trembling.

'Nora.'

Michael stands next to her and looks up, as well.

Neither of them says anything for a few moments, but simultaneously take in the books that surround them.

'Have you seen Penny yet?' Nora asks him.

'Not yet. But I hope so. I love spending time with her; she really is a lovely girl.'

'She really is,' Nora thinks and smiles to herself.

'Are you here to see your granddaughter today?' Michael asks.

'Actually, I came here to see you.'

'Me?'

When Nora looks over to him, she can see the twinkle in his eyes and how perfect his lips are, when he gasps in astonishment. He's still so beautiful that she can't help but place a gentle hand on his bicep.

'Even after all these years, you're still so beautiful.' she whispers.

'I could say the same thing about you.'

'Is there something you want to say to me?'

With lips slightly parted, Nora edges towards him. She closes her eyes and breathes in his familiar scent of rum and cigars. She can almost imagine being back in the basement, where everything was wonderful.

'You know, there's so much I want to say to you.' Michael rests his fingers underneath her chin and gently lifts her gaze to meet his. 'But will you run away from me, again?'

'That sounds like something I should ask you.'

Nora closes her eyes and rests her head on Michael's chest as he wraps an arm around her.

'I've always loved you,' Michael tells her.

'I've always loved you, too.'

With her hands clasped to her heart, Nora gently presses her lips against Michael's. He responds by tentatively placing his hands over hers. When one draws back, the other brings them in closer. They have a connection that no one else can break. As the two of them slowly break apart, they stay close to each other.

'I hate that we've been apart for so long,' Michael says.

'Really?'

'Don't you feel the same way?'

'A part of me does. But you left me, Michael and I want to know why...'

'I can explain everything...'

'But before you do,' Nora places her finger over Michael's lips, to stop him from saying anything else, 'there's two other people that need to know.'

Nora takes him by the land and begins to retrace her steps. Back to Penny and Bradley.

'Is that Michael Marblelight?' Bradley whispers to Penny, his mouth gaping open as they walk towards them.

'Yep.'

Bradley gasps when Michael stands by his side. 'It

is you.'

'Bradley Figment?' Michael asks, his eyes widen in astonishment. Then, he chuckles. 'It's been so long.'

Michael goes to shake Bradley's hand but Bradley ignores this. Instead, he stands up and gives him a hug.

'It's good to see you again, old friend,' Bradley mutters.

'I've missed you,' Michael admits.

'When was the last time the three of us were all together?' Bradley asks, as everyone begins to get comfortable. Penny brings a third armchair for Michael and she sits at the trio's feet.

'The Twelfth of December nineteen fifty-five.' Nora replies, instantly.

'Oh, yes. I remember now,' Michael says. 'It didn't feel like the last time…'

'It all ended so suddenly,' Nora says, quickly. 'We all thought it would last forever.'

'So what happened after that?' Penny asks Michael. Her eyes widen with excitement.

'I definitely need to explain myself,' Michael mutters, looking down at his shoes.

'I'm listening.' Nora tells him.

Michael takes a deep breath and when he exhales, he begins to tell his story. He never takes his eyes off Nora.

'Even though I left, I never forgot about you, Nora,' Michael begins to say. 'You always had a place in my heart and I've always loved you. I cherished those moments we spent together, back in 1955.'

'I always thought you left because I wasn't good enough for you,' Nora admits, slightly blushing.

'You were always good enough, Nora. But you knew that back then, I was engaged to another woman,' Michael continues to say.

'I remember,' Nora replies.

'Wait, what?' Penny cries with her mouth hanging open. 'There was nothing about that in the basement.'

'I didn't know anything about this,' Bradley adds.

Michael sighs. 'That's why I wanted to keep our romantic affair a secret. It's why I came to the basement every night, to escape my own life for a few hours. My parents never knew where I went, so I always had an excuse for them. Either that, or I would sneak out. They wanted me to be more like them: disciplined but empty inside. My parents planned for me to join the family business and marry a woman they approved of. But it's not what I wanted. I wanted to fall in love with Nora and live in The Author's Library, for the rest of my life.'

'I wanted that too,' Nora tells him.

Michael sighs and rests his head in his hands. 'My fiancée never wanted me to be happy. She always said that she only intended to marry me for the money and nothing else. But on the last night we were all together, she found a way into the bookshop and spied on me. Then, she told my parents everything. I remember they were furious with me and gave me a choice: To either marry the woman they chose and work for them or be with Nora and be cut off from the family.'

'So, that's why you left?' Nora whispers, with angry tears in her eyes. 'You chose money over love? Did you even fight for me?'

Michael lowers his head, in shame. 'I should've fought harder. It was a coward's choice and I should've chosen you, all along. I regretted that decision from the moment I made it. But I was living in fear of my parents and, soon enough, I was living in fear of her. If I could make that decision again, I would always choose you. It's always been you, Nora. I missed being here so much.'

'So when did you come back?' Penny asks.

'When I was married, I couldn't go back to the bookshop because my parents forbade it. Disownment always hung over my head, like a storm-cloud. My wife was a nasty woman, who abused me and had so many affairs. But I couldn't do anything else about it; she knew I was scared and that I wouldn't run away. But after three decades of misery, I couldn't do it anymore and I finally had the courage to leave it all behind. Coming back to the bookshop was the first place I could think of. It was all I could think about, when I'd lost all hope in everything else. I never forgot about you, Nora. But when I came back, you weren't there. Emily had taken over the responsibility and Penny was just a little girl.'

'I've know you all my life,' Penny mutters.

'That's why I've always come back. To make up for lost time and the hope to see you again.' Michael interlinks his fingers with Nora's. She lets him and watches the tears roll down his face. 'Will you ever forgive me?'

Nora looks away from them all and gazes into the old bookshop. 'Now I know it all.' she mutters. 'I never loved anyone else, Michael. When I became pregnant with Emily, all I ever wanted was to give her the best life imaginable…'

Penny stops listening to her grandma and begins to piece the story together, in her head. There's still one question that's always been unanswered and Penny never thought twice about it. But now, everything slowly became connected. Surely, it wasn't true?

'Grandma?' Penny's heart begins to pound beneath her shirt. 'If you never loved anyone else, after Mr. Marblelight… Then, is Emily's dad…'

Nora says nothing else, but she closes her eyes and slowly nods her head. Mr. Marblelight gasps and Penny notices that he's suddenly gone incredibly pale. Bradley awkwardly looks at his shoes.

'Despite your disappearance, you left me with the

most precious thing in the world,' Nora tells him. 'You gave me Emily.'

Michael's speechless, and so is Penny. Even though her mind is exploding with more questions, she can't seem to focus on anything else.

'He's my grandad,' Penny thinks, keeping her eyes on Mr. Marblelight.

Family Reunion I

No one says anything, for several minutes. Michael rests his head in his hands and stares into the distance. Nora sits up tall and doesn't dare look at him; she doesn't even want to know what he's thinking. A part of her can't really believe it, herself. From the moment Emily was born, Nora swore that she would never tell anyone who the father was and it soon became her biggest secret.

'Were you ever going to tell me?' Michael asks her. When Nora looks at him, he still keeps his gaze distant. 'That I was Emily's father?'

'I thought you knew,' Nora whispers. Her heart weighs as heavy as an anchor, but she has enough strength to carry on. 'But you married her and didn't want to commit to me.'

'What do you mean? I never knew anything about this,' Michael replies, running his hands all over his head.

'When I knew you weren't going to come back, I had to do it all alone,' Nora tells him. 'I couldn't wait around for you anymore, Michael. Emily became my priority and for the longest time, we were all the family we ever needed.'

'So what did you say when Emily asked about who her dad was?' Penny asks.

'She only ever asked me once, when she was younger,' Nora replies. 'I told her that I loved her father, once. But he made a choice to not be a part of our lives. I told her the truth…'

'But if I'd known, I would've loved to have been a father,' Michael says. His voice is loud and clear and he has tears in his eyes. 'I didn't even know that you were pregnant.'

'What?' Nora asks. 'I tried every way to tell you. I rang you on numbers that never worked and wrote you letters which I sent out on the same day. But I never got a response, so I always thought you knew. I couldn't understand how you choose her over me, marrying someone you didn't truly love.'

'What letters, Nora?' Michael asks. 'I didn't receive any calls or anything from you.'

'But I did.'

'She's telling the truth, Michael,' Bradley adds, giving Nora and comforting nod. 'I saw it all. She drove herself insane, trying to contact you. But she didn't tell me, either.'

'I was so scared, at first,' Nora admits. 'I had to let the truth sink in, before I told anyone else.'

'But how could I miss all of this?' Michael asks. 'It doesn't make any sense.'

Nora keeps her eyes on Michael. When Emily was growing up, there were times where Nora thought about what would've happened if Michael had chosen her. Maybe he could've married her, instead. They'd raise Emily together and maybe have another child, down the line. The two of them would work in

The Author's Library and they'd be happy. Nora would finally know what it would feel like to be good enough. But she always knew that these were just stories in her head. Instead, she had to make do with what she had and gave herself the confidence to go on. It was all she could ever do.

'I even told your fiancée, when she visited me in the bookshop,' Nora tells him.

'Did you?' Michael asks.

'Yes, I did…'

'Listen, you poor little bookseller.' Michael's fiancée was tall enough that she could patronisingly bend down to Nora's level, eye-to-eye. Her facial features were sharp enough to look as if she were always judging you. 'Stop trying to talk to Michael, he's mine, now. We're getting married and there's nothing you can do about it.'

Nora's heart pounded beneath her blouse, as she looked closely at Michael's fiancée. 'He doesn't love you.' She told her, as she stood tall with hands on her hips. 'Michael loves me. He said…'

'If you think he loves you, then why has he chosen to marry me?' The fiancée taunted and waved an expensive engagement ring in Nora's face. 'You would never be good enough for him.'

Although her eyes were filled with tears, Nora refused to cry in front of his woman. Instead, she placed a hand over her stomach and hardened her glare.

'Well, you can give him a message from me,' Nora told her, sternly. 'I'm pregnant and he's the father. Why don't you tell him that and he can make a decision, then? He has *a right to know.'*

Unexpectedly, she stood up straight and gave Nora a wide, patronising smile. Then, she grabbed her cheek and pinched it between her sharp fingers. 'Of course I can, darling. Congratulations, you little bitch.' Her voice went from sweet to snarled, before she sauntered out of the bookshop.

Michael slowly sinks back into his chair and rests his head in the palm of his hand. He can't believe it. All this time, he never knew: When he came back to The Author's Library and saw Emily, she was his daughter all along. How could one poor decision affect a lifetime of happiness? Michael always knew he'd made the wrong decision; he would dream about being with Nora and one day starting a family, together. Now, it seemed like they already had but it was too late.

'She never told me you were pregnant,' Michael admits. 'In fact, she told me that you wanted nothing to do with me, because I had chosen to marry her.'

'Of course, I was angry, Michael.' Nora cries. 'But I never stopped loving you. Even when I wanted to forget everything.'

'If I'd known you were pregnant with my child, I would've dropped everything and come back to you.' Tears now start to roll down Michael's face. 'I should've taken control of my life and not lived under the rule of my parents or my horrid ex-wife. She only ever had the intention to make me miserable. I could've been the father that Emily deserved.'

'I wished for that too,' Nora admits.

'But when you saw me, again. Why didn't you tell me then?' Michael asks, leaning forward and looking at his silver shoes. His voice begins to tremble. 'All this time, I could've known?'

'I never knew how to tell you because I didn't think I'd ever speak to you again. When I first spoke to you after so long, it took me by surprise.'

'I wish you'd told me, Nora,' Michael says, solemnly. 'Even if she's not here anymore.'

'Emily's always here.' She corrects him. Then, she gives Michael an apologetic look. 'But you're right. I shouldn't make excuses, anymore. I'm sorry, Michael. You always had a right to know.'

'I told myself that I was going to come back, even if it was going to take a century,' Michael tells her.

'I always thought you fell out of love with me.' Nora looks down with her cheeks flushing red and begins to sob.

'How could I ever fall out of love with you, Nora Figment?' Michael moves in closer and plants a soft kiss on her cheek. 'I made some foolish decisions, in my life. But at least I once knew my daughter and I'm honoured to have been a part of her life.'

'We may have spent so much time apart, but I'm glad we're back together,' Nora says, smiling at him.

'But why did you keep this from me?' Penny asks,

suddenly.

Up until now, Penny's been keeping quiet and trying to process everything. But it's almost as if she's faded into the background. For the longest time, Penny had a grandad that she saw almost every day and she never knew. If Penny hadn't discovered everything else, she never would've made that connection. If anything, it begins to make her blood boil. All this time, Penny had more family than she could've ever imagined. Emily never knew her dad, when she could've for so long.

'I know I kept a lot of secrets from you, Penny.' Nora gives her granddaughter a hopeful smile. Penny's expression remains blank. 'I just couldn't tell you or Emily, because remembering everything was always so painful.'

'You kept so many secrets throughout your life…' Penny whispers, with furious tears in her eyes. She digs her fingernails into her knees. 'For the past two years, you've been my only family but you knew that wasn't true. If it wasn't for Emily who discovered the basement, none of this would've ever happened in the first place.'

'Penny, I…'

But Penny doesn't want to hear this, anymore. It's too much information to for her to bare, so she jumps onto her feet and runs away into the depths of The Author's Library. Just wanting to be on her own for a few moments and lose herself in yet another story.

When Penny thinks she's far enough, she grabs *The Lion, The Witch and The Wardrobe* off the shelf and sinks to the floor. She opens the front cover and sinks her nose into the pages. She doesn't even notice Mr. Marblelight emerge from the behind the bookcase. She looks up when she hears him chuckle.

'You found me, then?' Penny asks.

'I knew exactly where you'd be,' he tells her, calmly. 'I remember the day I bought a copy of that book, from you.'

'You told me you used to hide it from your parents, when you were younger.'

'They always thought they could have control over everything I did. But they could never control my thoughts.'

'Mum told me that, once. She learnt it from *1984*.'

'Fancy taking a stroll with me?'

'Maybe for a bit.'

Penny still has *The Chronicles of Narnia* tucked under one arm and she and Mr. Marblelight take a slow wander throughout the bookshop. At first, they don't say anything to each other.

'On the day you bought this book, I thought you were maybe a wizard in a past life,' Penny says. 'I probably would've believed it more, than knowing that you're my grandad.'

'I probably would've believed it too.' Michael chuckles. 'But I want you to know that I'm so proud to call you my granddaughter. Even though I never knew it, I watched you grow into being this wonderful person. Your curiosity is remarkable. You remind me so much of your mum, sometimes.'

'I'm not good enough to be like Emily.'

'You are always good enough, never forget that.' He reassures her. When he puts an arm around Penny, it really feels like a comforting hug from her grandad. 'You brought your family together, without even knowing it. Everything would've remained a mystery, if it wasn't for you.'

'I had a little help,' Penny admits. Although, when she thinks of Christopher, Millie and Dexter, it makes her heart ache.

'But you led the way towards that discovery.'

The two of them stop walking and Penny gives him a hug. Michael responds and holds onto his granddaughter.

'Emily would've loved to have known about all of this,' Penny mutters.

'I think she knows. Emily knew the exact same moment that you did.'

'I miss her.'

'Of course you do, so do I. So does Nora.'

'Are you angry at Grandma for keeping this all a secret from you?'

'I'll always wish that I'd chosen Nora in the first place,' Michael says. 'But we've both made mistakes in our decisions. That's just how our stories were written.'

'I still can't believe Grandma would keep this from me, though...'

'I understand why you feel this way.' Michael reassures her. They break away from their hug but his hands are firmly planted on Penny's shoulders.

'I always had a hunch that my grandma had something to do with the basement,' Penny tells him. 'I just never thought she would be keeping secrets this big, for such a long time.'

'You have to remember, Penny, that Nora was broken-hearted for a long time. She had to focus on her family. You and Emily. Sometimes, when your spirit is cracked, you just want to forget all about it.'

'I guess it runs in the family,' Penny mutters.

'But we are a family,' Michael reminds her. 'No matter what. While life can write us a story that we never could imagine, your family is always by your side. You can never be rid of it.'

'I'll never be forgiven,' Nora says with a lot of regret in her voice. Nora and Bradley have been sitting in an uncomfortable silence, for several minutes.

'You don't know that.' Bradley reassures her.

'But I was the one who told Penny not to go looking for trouble. I was terrified that she would stumble across my secrets.'

'But aren't you glad that she did?'

'I guess... I guess I may have been wrong,' Nora grumbles.

Bradley laughs. 'I know how much you hate being wrong.'

'Only because I'm not, usually.'

'But it makes you a human being, to admit it. People screw up. I think we've all learnt that amongst us, we've all made mistakes. Michael and I left you with no explanation and you've been keeping life-changing secrets for most of your life. I know you better than most, Nora. You've always strived for perfection and never wanted to show that you were wrong…'

'I just wanted to make father proud,' Nora says. 'I always wanted to be good enough because I never believed it in myself.'

'He was always proud of you,' Bradley tells her. He gives her a hug and Nora clings on tightly to her brother. 'That's why he left you in charge of the bookshop.'

'If I remember correctly, I used to be the one who always calmed you down, from a panic,' Nora says, with a smile growing on her face.

'You did more than enough to help me. Now it's my turn.'

When Penny and Michael appear from behind the bookcase, Nora holds her breath and looks at her brother, in apprehension. But when Bradley gives her a smile and a comforting nod, it gives Nora enough confidence to go on.

'Penny. Michael,' Nora mutters, when Michael sits

back down in the armchair and her granddaughter sits at their feet. Thankfully, Penny isn't glaring at her this time. 'I know that I should've told you the truth a long time ago. I'm sorry, to everyone. I let my anger and broken-heart take control over me and I never should've allowed it.'

'It's ok, Nora,' Michael tells her. 'We're sorry too.'

Nora keeps her gaze on Penny. When her granddaughter became that curious and determined, it really reminded Nora of Emily. 'I'm not angry anymore, Penny. If anything, I'm so proud of everything you've achieved. Will you ever forgive me?'

Nora lowers her head and begins to silently sob. But she's taken by surprise when Penny jumps onto her feet and gives her a big hug. It's warm and comforting for the both of them.

'It's ok, Grandma,' Penny tells her, softly. 'I forgive you.'

'At least our family's all together now,' Nora announces. That alone, sends a smile on everyone's face.

The Madness of Penny Figment

The next day, Nora, Bradley and Michael come back to The Author's Library, from the moment it opens. They all sit in armchairs amongst the ancient Greek literature, sharing a pot of tea between them.

'It's almost like how it used to be.' Nora says, the first one to break the silence. She pours them all a strong brew in matching teacups and saucers. 'Although I've always preferred a cup of tea to a thimble of rum.'

Michael chuckles. 'I haven't drunk it in years. So why don't we cheers to old friends, reunited?'

Gently, the three of them clink their teacups with their pinkies out. Then when they've drunk their tea, Nora slips her hand into Michael and Bradley's, creating a bond that can never be broken.

'Do you remember how happy we used to be?' Nora asks.

'We were such different people, back then,' Bradley pipes up.

'What do you mean?' Nora asks.

'Looking back, I think we all thought that we were once the wisest we could possibly be. But we were much younger. We didn't have a clue what we were doing. When we were down in the basement, the three of us could forget that we were unconfident, foolish in love, and we kept putting off big decisions. We used to read the books we adored but didn't always understand.'

'Bradley, what are you getting at?' Michael asks.

'Just letting out some thoughts,' Bradley replies. 'Over the years, we've changed so much. We're older and wiser. We've made mistakes that we can learn from. Now we're back together, I have a new-found appreciation for you both.'

Nora bows her head and closes her eyes, thinking back to the times gone by. 'I've missed you both so much...'

Michael gently wipes away her tears and holds her face in his hands. 'Nora? Will we ever...'

Nora stops him from finishing his sentence, by gently pressing her lips against his. They gently kiss and stay close to one another, for several moments.

'Yes,' she tells him. 'I love you.'

'I love you, too.' Michael whispers. Even when they break apart, they can't keep their eyes off each other.

'Nora, there's something I need to tell you.' Bradley says, his cheeks flushing scarlet.

'What is it?' she asks, smiling back at her brother.

'When I was uncovering the mystery of Robert Figment, I grew a lot in confidence,' Bradley begins to say. 'But there was always something within me, that I wanted to accept but I didn't know how the world would react.'

'Which was what?' Michael asks.

Bradley looks at him and gives Michael a nod. 'I remember saying how I felt about you, back in '55. Even to this day, I think you're so beautiful.'

'Aah, yes. I remember, now.' Michael chuckles. 'You flatter me, Bradley.'

'I don't understand?' Nora says.

'It wasn't until I met my husband, that I was able to fully embrace who I was,' Bradley says, with a beaming smile on his face.

'Bradley?' she gasps. 'Are you telling me…'

'I'm gay, Nora. I suppose I always knew it, in myself. But even though it took me so long to accept it, I'm so happily in love.'

'I'm really happy for you, Bradley,' she says, smiling back at him. 'But why didn't you tell me, back then?'

'I could barely admit it to myself. I was scared that you might treat me differently, if you knew…'

'Bradley Figment, you fool!' Nora cries. 'I would've never treated you differently. It's a part of who you are.'

'I would love for the two of you to meet my husband, Edgar.' Bradley sways in his seat at the mention of his husband. 'He has a particular fascination for ancient Greek masks…'

'It seems that Penny has more family than she ever knew.' Michael chuckles.

Nora sighs and clasps her hands in her lap. 'She's so loyal to this family. But I know that deep down, she's lonely too. She hasn't been the same ever since Emily…' Nora can't bear to say anything else.

'I saw Penny with a group of people, not long ago.' Michael reassures her. 'They were running throughout the bookshop, laughing like lunatics. They seemed like a bunch of lovely people. She looked happy.'

Nora, Bradley and Michael eventually leave together. Meanwhile on the other side of the bookcase, Penny slowly sinks to the floor and drops a small stack of books to the side. With her back against the shelves, she hugs her knees to her chest and slowly lowers her head, holding it in her hands. She allows her hair to fall in front of her eyes, surrounding herself with darkness. There are tears in her eyes, but she screws up her face and refuses to let herself cry.

'Why am I not happier?' she thinks. 'After everything's that's happened. No more secrets...'

But despite this, there's still a sense of guilt and loneliness that sits in the pit of Penny's stomach. Even though she tried to distract herself with family mysteries, it just wasn't enough. Penny hasn't spoken to Christopher, Millie and Dexter in over a week. They were so good to her but she ran away, before giving the friendship a chance. Even when they called or texted her, Penny never responded. When they tried to search for her, Penny would always hide from them; she'd scamper up her bookcases and watch them, from above. She'd convinced herself that if she stayed with them for long enough, she'd scare them away, for being too weird. She knows she'll never be good enough to keep friends in her life. That's usually what's happened, before.

Yet, the only person who could ever pick Penny up when she was down, was Emily. But Penny's mum wasn't here this time...

When Emily grew too weak to work in The Author's Library, it wasn't long before she could barely leave her bed. But she refused to be locked upstairs, so her final wish was spent surrounded by her family in the bookshop. Emily's bed was moved downstairs and the bookshop was closed, temporarily. Penny, Nora and Ivy took it in turns to watch over Emily, day and night. They were good company and kept her away from sadness. They fed her and watched her sleep; reassuring Emily when she woke up, sobbing from constant nightmares about death. They tried to distract her with laughter, something they all needed.

'Will you keep an eye on Penny? You know… once I'm gone?' Emily asked Ivy, her voice barely louder than a murmur.

'Of course.' Gently, Ivy kissed her friend on the top of her head. 'We're all family, after all.'

'I know she's old enough to look after herself,' Emily added. 'But I know what she's like. She'll want to be on her own, or she'll believe it'll be better for her to do so. But she needs to remember that her family will always be by her side, no matter what. Penny's had her heart broken, before. She's put her trust in friendships that hadn't ended well. But this time, I won't be there to protect her…'

When Emily began to sob, Ivy wrapped her arms around her. 'I'll be there, for her. You can rely on me.'

'We've always relied on each other.'

'I depended on you to get us into trouble.' Ivy teases.

'Do you remember back in '78? When we sat in the middle of the bookshop and sang songs until our voices were sore?' Emily had just enough energy to stifle a small giggle.

'I played the guitar and you bashed the tambourine? Neither of us could sing, but everyone sat down with us and joined in.'

'Mum hated the noise. She told me that the bookshop was a quiet place and it was only the stories that could loudly...'

'The Author's Library was never quiet, when you're around.' The two of them chuckle, as they reminisce.

But from the other side of the bookcase, Penny sunk to the floor and began to silently sob into her hands. The books on their shelves weren't as comforting as they usually were; as if all the stories had lost their colour and they became nothing more than words on the page. When she sat with her mum, Penny reassured Emily that everything was going to be ok. But that was all Penny could ever think about: Making her mum happy, right until the very end. Penny didn't even want to think about a life without Emily in it. The bookshop soon became a very lonely place...

The next day, is a quiet day in The Author's Library. Penny sinks into her armchair, remembering sitting at her mum's bedside. When Emily could barely focus for more than a few moments, Penny would read her some of her favourite books, from cover to cover. Emily would fall asleep to her daughter's soothing voice and she awoke to her still reading, aloud. Penny wished every night that that the two of them could fall into the world of fiction and never come back to reality...

'Emily, you must eat something.' Defeated, Nora put down a full bowl of hot soup and sighed.

'I'm not hungry,' Emily muttered, miserably. She

gently leaned back and shut her eyes. 'I can feed myself, Mum.'

'You cannot convince me, Emily. Yesterday, you could barely hold a glass of water.'

'I just bloody hate being stuck in this bed!' Emily's heart quickly began to ache when she opened her eyes and watched her mum blinking furiously, fighting back the tears that still roll down her delicate face.

'Oh, Mum. I'm sorry...' When Emily tried to sit up to comfort her, she winced in tremendous pain.

Nora quickly lay her daughter back down and kissed her sweat-soaked forehead. 'No, don't apologise. I've looked after you since the day you were born and now I'll do so until the end. I just wish I had the power to take away your pain...'

'You raised me by yourself. That was all the power I ever needed.' Emily gently wrapped her arms around her mum. The two of them held each other for a long time.

'Hiya.' When Nora and Emily break apart, they watched Ivy appear from behind the bookcase and sit by Emily's side.

'I thought you were coming to visit me tomorrow?' Emily asked her.

'Penny told me to come, tonight,' Ivy replied. 'She says she has something planned.'

At the mention of her name, Penny soon appeared in front of her family. With one hand behind her back, she dragged a make-shift spaceship and was wearing an astronaut's helmet on her head (both made from tin foil and numerous cereal boxes).

'Penny, what is all of this nonsense?' Nora demanded.

'What's all of this?' Emily asked.

Penny cleared her voice, but her cheeks were blushing pink. 'I just thought, if we can't take Mum on any adventures, we could bring the adventure to her. Ta-Da!'

Swiftly, Penny revealed a puppet of Emily Figment from behind her back. With a lucky-purple-scrunchie in her hair, dungarees and a tattoo of a jigsaw-puzzle drawn on her wrist.

'Is that supposed to be me?' Emily chuckled. 'Looks nothing like me.'

'You get the idea,' Penny said. Then she looked at puppet-Emily. 'So, what adventure are we having tonight?' she asked.

'We're going to the moon,' Penny replied as puppet-Emily, doing her best impression of her mum.

'I also sound nothing like that…' Emily muttered, as she stifled her giggles.

'Comment ignored,' Penny immediately replied, as she clambered into her spaceship. It was barely big enough to fit Penny and the puppet and her feet stuck out in front. 'Ready? Then, let's go!'

The evening commenced with a dramatic story of Penny and Emily's trip into space. Soon enough, imagination and laughter had filled 'The Author's Library'. The story was disjointed and made no sense; at one point, Penny and puppet-Emily forgot that they were time-travelling, too. But it was the happiest that anyone had been, for a long time. Emily would even come up with suggestions, of what could happen next. But eventually, the story had a happy ending, with Penny and puppet-Emily landing safely back to earth, after defeating the evil aliens who wanted to invade their planet. By the time her family had applauded Penny and she had taken a bow, it was gone midnight.

'I'll watch over you, tonight,' Penny said to her mum. When Nora and Ivy said goodnight, Penny sat beside her. She handed her the puppet, which Emily tucked underneath her arm.

'I can't believe you took me on an adventure,' Emily whispered.

'Next time, we could travel back in time to Ancient Egypt and discover the tomb of Tutankhamun...'

'It doesn't matter where we go,' Emily replied. 'So long as we're always together.'

'We always will.' Penny reassured her, as she held her mum close.

'Everything's going to be ok, Penny.'

'How do you know that?'

'Because I'm always right.'

Penny quickly broke away from her mum and burst out laughing. 'Sod off! I can think of countless times where you were wrong...'

'You could, but I'd rather you didn't,' Emily said. 'But I want you to know that you'll never be alone. Our family is strong and it always has been. We're by each other's side, always. Just promise me that you'll always try to surround yourself with joy and laughter. There's no need to be scared.'

'I will,' Penny said. She sat back in her armchair and watched her mum fall asleep, before doing the same.

Emily Figment died as dawn broke through The Author's Library...

But Penny didn't stick to her promise, after her mum had died. On the day she died, Nora and Ivy couldn't stop crying even though Emily specifically told them not to. But all Penny could do was wander continuously throughout her bookshop, with her head in daze, trying to come to terms with it all. She didn't want to believe in a life without Emily.

On the night of Emily's funeral, Penny told herself that it's better for her to be alone; therefore, nobody can ever hurt you. Even though it became a lonely life to live, Penny always thought she was protecting herself from any emotional harm. But there were some days, where putting one step in front of the other was tiresome; as if she were pushing a boulder up a hill, only for it to roll back down when she got to the top. Nothing seemed fun, anymore. Whenever Penny stroked the tattoo on her collarbone, she felt there was a part of her that was missing. Which is why she tried to escape into every book she read, forgetting the pain in her past and filling the emptiness with imagination. Books were magical and there was always a story to jump into. So that's how it was, for the next two years.

Penny sinks off the armchair and onto the floor, hiding her head in her hands. She just wanted to hide from the world but didn't have the energy to do so. Suddenly, she feels familiar and comforting arms wrapped around her shoulders. When Penny looks up, it's Ivy holding onto her.

'Oh, Penny,' Ivy whispers. She lightly kisses the top of Penny's head. 'I miss Emily, too.'

'How do you know what I'm thinking about?'

'I could hear you muttering her name. But it's good that you're letting it all out...'

'I wasn't crying,' Penny says, quickly wiping away

her tears.

'It's ok, if you were…'

'I'm fine!'

Leaving Ivy startled, Penny jumps onto her feet and sprints into the depths of her bookshop which seems to be getting darker and overwhelmingly bigger, almost as if Penny's shrinking. But it's the middle of the day and everything in the bookshop is exactly how it always is. All Penny wants to do is run away from it all. But when she turns around every bookcase, she's reminded of working in the bookshop with Emily, falling in love with Christopher and laughing with Millie and Dexter.

Her mind becomes foggy and her heart is pounding through her ribcage. In an instant, Penny crouches onto the floor and screws her face up tight, hiding her head in her hands.

'I'm sorry for disappointing you,' she mutters, her thoughts tumbling out of her mouth. 'I told you that everything was going to be fine… but I'm so empty, even after discovering everything else… There's so much I want to tell you…'

All her anxieties and emotions are ready to explode, no matter how hard Penny tries to supress them. All she wants to do is disappear into another world but when she looks up, she's still in her bookshop. Customers stare at her, but she doesn't care. Deluded, she stumbles through her bookshop. She bumps into bookcases, letting paperbacks rain down on her. Penny groans and frantically runs her hands through her hair, telling herself to forget everything. Grabbing books off the shelf, she flicks through the pages, but she can't connect to the story.

But when she reaches the door to the basement, she's stands frozen in front of it for a few minutes. She can still hear Ivy calling out her name. With all her might, Penny rips the curtain away and flings open the door. But before she sprints down the stairs, she stares into its depths. She remembers uncovering all the mysteries with her friends; the basement wouldn't have been discovered in the first place, if it weren't for Emily. She wouldn't have continued, if it weren't for her friends.

'Penny?'

She knows that familiar, female voice. It's someone Penny's has wanted to hear from for so long, even though she's convinced herself, otherwise. When Penny turns around, she sees Millie emerge from behind the bookcase. Christopher and Dexter soon follow behind her.

'We've found you. Finally,' Christopher says. It's almost as if he's relieved to see her.

When the three of them move closer towards her, Penny stays frozen, to the spot. Her eyes are so wide, it's as if they might pop out of their sockets. Her face is drained of its colour and she can feel a chill creeping over her arms, giving goose-bumps. She pinches herself, to make sure she's not imagining anything.

'Penny? Are you ok?' Dexter asks.

'Will you talk to us? Please?' Millie asks, running her fingers through her hair. 'We've been so worried about you…'

Penny opens her mouth but doesn't know what to say. But when she takes a step back, it's a step too far. She forgets that the steps to the basement are behind her. She falls backwards, letting out a piecing scream and plummets into the darkness.

Stay With Me

The further down she falls, the more it feels as if she's falling into Wonderland. Penny's limbs feel heavy like an anchor but her body feels as light as a feather. Darkness is all that surrounds her, with no end in sight. There are moments where Penny doesn't feel like falling. Maybe she's floating? But amidst the darkness, come flashes of memories that Penny has tried so hard to forget. They play over and over again, in black and white, like old movies. It feels like a nightmare: Of secondary-school bullies, who Penny thought were her friends; they ripped her confidence to pieces, whenever she tried to build it up. They called her weird and made her feel ashamed. She remembers hanging out with Echo and trying so desperately to get him to like her. All Penny ever wanted was someone to call a friend. But it was always Emily who picked up Penny's broken pieces. They pinkie-swore that they would always remain the best of friends.

But when Penny stood over her mum's grave, she didn't want to believe that Emily Figment was truly gone. Maybe there was always a part of her that never wanted to believe it. At first, she told herself that it was just a nightmare that she would soon wake up from. But when Penny was standing alone in The Author's Library, all she could do was embrace the loneliness.

Eventually, Penny begins to stir but she continues to mumble in her sleep.

'Stay with me… Please don't leave me…'

As her memories begin to fade, she can hear three familiar voices.

'She's waking up,' a female voice, announces. 'Go and make her a cup of tea.'

'You've assumed this five times, already,' a male voice grumbles.

'I know I'm right this time.' Penny can feel gentle fingers being run through her hair, which is quite soothing. 'Poor darling. I hope she hasn't hurt herself…'

'She fell down a flight of stairs. I'm surprised if she ever wakes up.'

'She's been out-cold, for ages.' another male voice, softly adds. 'I wonder what's going on inside her head. What else could we do to wake her up?'

'I don't know, Prince Charming. Do you want a dragon to fight?' the first man replies, sarcastically. 'All we can do is wait…'

'Hey!' The woman squeals. 'She's waking up.'

Cautiously, Penny opens her eyes. Her head is resting on Millie's lap and there's a blanket wrapped around her legs. When she reaches for her glasses, they're bent and lopsided but at least they're not broken. She gently shakes her arms and legs and at least they're still working. Although, Penny's got a feeling that a few bruises will appear over the next few days.

But the first thing Penny sees are the kind faces of Christopher, Millie and Dexter. They watch over her, hesitantly.

'Did I hear something about a cup of tea?' Penny mutters.

Millie sharply turns her head to Dexter and silently orders him to do so. When he comes back with a steaming mug of tea, Penny slowly sits up and feels the comforting warmth of the brew beneath her fingers.

'I won't run away again, I promise,' Penny reassures them, breaking the silence. The others all look as if they're about to pounce on her, if she tried to move.

'How're you feeling?' Christopher asks. When he puts his arm around her, she snuggles into him and it feels nice.

'A little bit light-headed, but I'm ok,' Penny mutters. 'What happened?'

They tell her the story. From the moment Penny fell, Christopher and Dexter charged after her and caught her by the hand just before she thumped to the floor. However, her body hit most of the stairs along the way and she still banged the back of her head. While the boys carried Penny back up the stairs, Millie cleared all the customers out and closed up the bookshop. Then, the three of them laid her down, padded with all the pillows and blankets they could find and stayed with her until she woke up, doing everything they could to keep her comfortable.

'You guys looked after me?' Penny asks, almost speechless.

'Did you think we were going to leave you alone in your bookshop? Christopher teases. 'Of course, we were going to help you.'

'I… I don't know what to say,' Penny admits.

'Oh, Penny,' Millie says, tearfully. She throws her arms around Penny, which she happily accepts.

'Careful, Mills,' Dexter says, softly. 'You don't want to knock her out, again.'

But Penny clings onto Millie and she gets teary, too. 'I'm so sorry.'

'Why are you apologising?' Christopher asks.

'For running away and trying to avoid you guys. I never wanted to.' Penny's cheeks flush a deep shade of red. 'I probably sound ridiculous…'

'No, you don't.' Christopher reassures her.

'But why did you?' Dexter asks. 'We were all so worried about you. We thought we'd done something to upset you.'

Penny breaks away from Millie and sits cross-legged on the floor, surrounded by her friends. 'You guys have done nothing at all. You've all been so wonderful to me…'

Penny begins to sob and burrows her face in her hands. There's still a part of her that wants to disappear from the world. But that feeling instantly evaporates when Christopher, Millie and Dexter huddle around her; keeping her safe and protected. The ache in her heart slowly begins to fade away.

'I couldn't do it to myself again. I told myself, I wouldn't,' Penny whispers.

'If you want to talk about it, we're here for you,' Christopher tells her.

'But only if you want to,' Millie says.

'We'll always be by your side,' Dexter adds.

'I want to talk about it,' Penny says. 'It's something I've needed to talk about, for a while.'

'We're all listening,' Christopher says.

The four of them break apart, but still remain close. Penny wipes the tears from her eyes, takes a deep breath and relaxes every muscle in her body.

'I've never been good at making friends,' Penny announces. She strokes her tattoo, for moral support. 'I guess I was always too odd for people to handle, so they'd eventually run away. When I was younger, I wanted to be normal.'

'Why would you ever want to be like that?' Dexter asks. 'Normal is boring.'

'I know that now,' Christopher mutters.

Penny giggles. 'That's what Emily used to tell me. When I was in secondary school, I had a group of friends, but I felt like the odd one out. I tried so hard to get them to accept me. So, I worshipped the ground they walked on, because they were always so confident and clever. I used to think I was scum, compared to them… which sounds ridiculous, when I say it out loud.'

'Babe, we've all been there,' Millie mutters, giving Penny and reassuring smile.

'They told me I was stupid and I believed them, for a long time. It soon became really toxic, me versus them. They started having sleepovers and hanging out without me.'

'Did you tell anyone about this?' Christopher asks.

'I told my mum,' Penny replies, instantly. 'I could never keep anything from her. I remember it all so well. She went mad…'

With the phone pressed against her ear, her other hand was trembling in fury. Emily stormed all throughout The Author's Library, with red cheeks and tears in her eyes. Meanwhile, Nora followed close behind her, trying to calm her down.

'What are you going to do about it?' Emily thundered down the phone to Penny's school. Her voice echoed throughout the whole bookshop.

'Emily, you need to calm down,' Nora said. 'We don't need Penny to hear all of this…'

'…My daughter is being bullied in your school,' Emily told them, sharply and ignored her mum. 'There's a group of kids in her class, who have been calling her names and pretending she doesn't exist. Today, she came home crying because they told her that she's too stupid to make a good life for herself. Who comes up with something like that? This is just unacceptable…'

Meanwhile, twelve-year-old Penny was sitting on top of one of the bookcases, with her legs swinging on either side. She hid her head in her hands and hoped that if she couldn't see anything, all her problems would go away. They were supposed to be her friends and Penny thought that if she tried hard enough, she could be good enough for them. She almost fell off her bookcase, when she heard her mum suddenly roar like a Bacchus.

'Are you calling my daughter a liar!' Emily grabbed the first book she could find and launched it furiously into the depths of the bookshop. 'No, they're not "nice children, who would never do anything like that." They're nasty and my daughter should not be treated that way.'

The argument continued over the phone for a while. Even when Emily told them to go to hell and eventually hung up, she didn't stop moving.

'I'm going to have to go down to that school and sort this out myself,' she grumbled, as she stormed throughout the bookshop.

'No, Emily,' Nora cried, sternly. Only then, Emily stopped to face her mum. 'Don't be ridiculous. You're going to make matters worse…'

'I can't send Penny back to that school.' Tears of rage began to fall down Emily's face. 'It breaks my heart knowing that she's being treated like that.'

'Emily, look at me.' Nora firmly planted her hands on Emily's shoulders. 'Penny will always have her family, no matter what. We can teach her to be a good person and she'll grow stronger from this. She'll work hard and then prove to everyone else that she can make a good life for

herself...'

Eventually, as the evening crept by, Emily clambered up the bookcase and sat opposite Penny.

'Did you hear all of that?' Emily asked.

'Yep.'

As Emily wrapped her arms around her daughter, Penny clung on tight. Tears began to roll down Penny's face.

'Sshh... You're going to be ok, Penny.' Emily whispered, as she gently rocked her back and forth, soothing her sobs.

'I don't want to go back, Mum.' Penny muttered. 'I'm too weird and no one wants to be my friend...'

'Hey, hey.' Emily let go of Penny, but the two of them still kept their eyes on each other. 'What's wrong with being a bit weird? It's much more fun. Just get through school and I'll always be here to make you happy.'

Penny giggled through her tears. 'I guess... Thanks, Mum.'

Emily kissed the top of her daughter's head. 'Sleepover in the bookshop, tonight?'

'But, it's a school night.'

'So, what? Don't tell your grandma. I'll get the blankets and pillows. You make the hot chocolate and choose the movie.'

Penny smiled. 'Sounds good.'

'Kids can be so cruel,' Millie says, clenching her fists. 'I'm so sorry, Penny.'

'Going to school every day was like wandering into a witch's lair,' Penny admits. 'But I wasn't afraid because I always had my mum to come back to. She wanted me to forget everything and focus on having fun. No matter what, I always had my mum. But it was still hard, you know? There was a part of me that wanted friends, my own age. But when I tried, they always ran away…' Penny stops and looks around at her friends. 'You guys haven't run away, yet.'

'If anything, we're chasing after you,' Christopher replies.

'You can't scare us off, that easily,' Dexter teases.

'It's an odd feeling, to have friends who won't run away. That's what scared me,' Penny admits. 'But there was only ever one person before, who I thought I could trust and thought to be a good friend. His name was Echo Kingsley and I thought he really understood me. We met in the bookshop, when I was tormented by a gang of young men, after I left school. When he scared them away for me, I thought he was my hero. Echo was a moody kind of guy. I don't think I ever saw him smile. He hardly said a word but he also didn't have any friends, like me. So, we stuck together and I thought it was perfect. Well, I stayed by him. I used to think he was like a brother to me. But I don't think he saw me the same way.'

'What happened to him?' Millie asks.

'We only ever hung out in the bookshop and nothing else. I was always the one who called or texted him and I'd be lucky if I ever got a response.

When we were together, I'd ramble to him for hours and convinced myself that he was listening. At the time, I thought I was happy because I'd found someone I could call a friend.'

'He's sounds like an idiot,' Dexter says.

'Dexter,' Millie hisses, prodding her husband in the arm.

'No, you're right,' Penny says, calmly. 'He was shit. Emily even tried to tell me, but I didn't want to listen…'

'Why can't you just be happy for me?'

Penny stormed away from her mum and didn't care where she was going. She pushed her badly-dyed, navy hair out of her eyes and tripped over her platform-heels which were way too big for her. Penny didn't like the way she looked, but she didn't want to admit it. She felt like a demon who was about to hit the runway.

'I don't know if he's good for you,' Emily said, when she caught up with her daughter. She grabbed Penny by the hand and spun her around to face her. 'Is he really a good friend to you?'

'Of course, he is,' Penny cried, defensively. 'Otherwise, I wouldn't be friends with him. Echo understands me…'

'He's a bit weird,' Emily muttered.

'I'm weird.'

'Not that weird.'

'Echo's my best friend. He's my hero. He saved me from those bullies…'

'Once. Three years ago,' Emily reminded her.

'No one has bullied me, since.'

'But you don't do anything. I think you're just kidding yourself.'

'We hang out, sometimes.'

'Is that all?'

'That's what you do with Ivy. All the time.'

'I've known Ivy for over thirty years. She's like family to us. She's always been there for me...'

'Echo's there when I need him,' Penny said, sounding flustered. Although, she'd really been trying to convince herself of that.

'Oh, really?' Emily asked, unconvinced. 'To me, it looks like you put all the effort in. You're the one who asks when he's free, it's you who takes an interest in his miserable life...'

'Echo's life isn't miserable! He's misunderstood...'

'The boy doesn't speak. You're even dressing like him. When was the last time you wore any other colour, other than black?'

'I like the way I look.' But Penny and Emily both knew that was a lie.

When Emily drew her daughter in for a hug, she accepted.

'I know you call him your friend and you tell me that you're happy. I want you to be happy, I really do,' Emily told her. 'I just don't want to see you disheartened...'

'I'm know, Mum.' Penny replied, clinging on harder. 'Echo's the first friend who hasn't run away...'

'Penny, you shouldn't be scared of your friends running away from you.' Christopher reassures her.

'It's only because I'd heard it all before. I've made

those friendship promises and I've watched them disappear, without a trace. When your friends run away, you have no one else to blame but yourself.'

'If they're good friends then they won't run away,' Millie tells her.

'That's true,' Penny replies. 'But it was such a lonely time, even with Emily by my side. I was constantly living with that feeling where I never thought I was good enough. So that's why I was so excited to have Echo as my friend. Someone actually wanted to hang out with me. But a few years later, he found a new group of people to hang out with…'

'Uh-oh,' Christopher mutters.

'They were just like him: Moody, intimidating and unfriendly. But he was the happiest that I had ever seen him, so I tried to tag along.'

'They sound like a fun bunch,' Dexter mutters, sarcastically.

'You guys are so much more fun,' Penny replies. 'Hanging out with them consisted of lurking down alleyways and feeling sorry for yourself. Besides, they didn't like me, anyway. I was too colourful for someone who tried to be like them, so they cut me out as soon as possible.'

'Bastards,' Millie grumbles.

'You're much better than them, Penny,' Christopher says.

'I know that, now.' Penny smiles at all her friends. 'I wanted Echo to be happy, but I also wanted to keep him as my friend. So I did whatever I could to keep him in my life. That's when he only ever called me because he wanted something: When he ran out of money, I always lent it to him and he never paid me back. When he was in trouble, I let him stay in the bookshop and kept him safe. I was always his shoulder to cry on and all I wanted in return, was for him to be my friend.'

'I'm guessing that changed, too?' Dexter asks.

'Yep. At first, Echo spent the whole time on his phone, messaging his new friends. This time, I knew he wasn't listening to me. Then one day, he simply got bored of me. Echo stopped replying and when I arranged for us to hang out, he never turned up. I remember waiting for hours…'

It was Penny and Emily's day off. But when Penny waited by the front door for three hours, Emily joined her with a tea and coffee in each hand. Penny accepted the tea; there was still an awkward silence between them. They had hardly spoken to each other for weeks. Penny had been so busy trying to impress Echo and his friends that she had forgotten about her responsibility to The Author's Library.

'Is Echo going to turn up?' Emily asked

'He will, this time. He promised.' There were tears in Penny's eyes, but she refused to give up and cry.

'Ok.'

The two of them sat in silence for another half an hour and waited for Echo.

'He's not coming,' Penny admitted, as the sun began to

set. She suddenly dropped her head into her hands and sobbed.

'Hey, there.' Emily wrapped her arms around her daughter and held her tight, just like when she was younger. 'Talk to me?'

'A part of me knew he wasn't going to come.' Penny said, through muffled sobs. 'But he promised that we would hang out and I suggested today.'

'You deserve better than this, Penny.' Emily kissed the top of her daughter's head and nuzzled her face into her hair.

'I never hear from him, unless I call first,' Penny said, as she kept her gaze to the floor. 'But now he's disappeared, it's as if he never existed. What did I do wrong? Am I not good enough?'

'You've done nothing wrong,' Emily told her. 'You're too good for him and never forget it. If he were truly your friend, he wouldn't do something like this. It wouldn't matter how you dressed or how you act. It's his loss.'

Slowly, Penny looked up at her mum and gave her a lipstick-stained smile. 'Thanks for waiting with me Mum. I really appreciate it…'

But Emily had suddenly erupted into an inappropriate fit of the giggles, when she saw her daughter's face. Penny was covered in a pale foundation, with heavy, black eye-makeup that had run down to her chin and dark lipstick was smudged up to her cheekbones.

'What's so funny?' Penny asked.

'I'm sorry…' Emily said, in-between giggles. 'I know this is meant to be a precious moment between the two of us… but you look ridiculous.'

'Sod off.' Penny swiftly pushed her mum over and began to tickle her. Soon enough, the bookshop was filled with laughter.

'You look like a sad clown at a kid's birthday,' Emily shrieked.

'Shut up. I've seen old photos of you. You've dressed worse than this.'

'Well, who else is going to make fun of you?'

'True.'

When the two of them were out of breath, they helped each other back onto their feet. With their arms around each other, they walked into the depths of The Author's Library.

'Do you want to hang out tonight?' Emily asked.

Penny stopped to look back at the front door. 'Maybe I should still wait for him…'

'You can, if you want. But maybe wait while you're having fun? You'll get cold, if you keep waiting by the front door?'

'Ok. So what do you want to do?'

'First of all, let's wash your face and dye your hair back to its original colour,' Emily suggested. 'Then, we'll get into our pyjamas and build a blanket-fort.'

'Are you ever going to let me forget about this?' But Penny already knew the answer.

'Never.'

'In the end, Emily was my true hero,' Penny says. 'When I knew that Echo wasn't going to come back, it was the lowest I'd felt in a long time. I thought I'd scared another one away. But I always had my mum by my side. Throughout it all, she's always been my best friend. Emily was my shoulder to cry on and when I cried all night, she was there. When I was having a down day, she refused to open the bookshop and we'd listen to sad songs and watch sad movies...'

Penny stops talking because thinking about how much her mum was there for her, makes her heart ache. She begins to cry but this time, she doesn't feel ashamed.

'If you don't want to talk about it anymore, then you don't have to,' Christopher reassures her. 'But just know, that we're always here for you.'

'Thanks guys,' Penny says, smiling through her tears. 'Emily was always there for me. But while I was so fixated on wanting to be Echo's friend, I didn't worry about anything else. Over time, Mum grew weaker and more ill but she didn't tell anyone about it. I should've noticed it, all along...'

'You can't blame yourself, for that,' Millie reassures her, giving Penny a hug. 'You didn't know.'

'Mum would have her own bad days where she was really sick but she told everyone that she was fine. She pushed her own needs aside, to look after me when I needed it. But she was dying and when she told me, nothing else mattered anymore. Emily said that she always wanted to make me happy and she didn't want to cause me anymore misery. But Mum was my first and only priority and I wanted to make her happy. I was by her side, until the day she died.'

'I'm so sorry, Penny,' Christopher says, gently. 'No wonder you didn't want to tell anyone this.'

'Losing my mum was the worst thing ever.' Penny admits, while Millie wipes away her tears. 'I'd also lost a best friend, who always stood by my side. It was as if a part of me was missing and when I tried to get back to my life, it wasn't the same. The bookshop felt bigger and emptier, without her. There were times when I didn't want to exist, without her. I wanted to fall asleep and disappear into thin air, as if the world never knew Penny Figment. I didn't want to go on and I don't think I would've, if it wasn't for my grandma. For the first few months after Mum's funeral, Grandma looked after me and helped me out in the bookshop. But she was too old to do it all again. So, it's been just me since then.'

'It must've been lonely at times,' Dexter says.

'It was. But I could never bring myself to try and make new friends. Not without Emily this time. So I told myself that it was be better to be on my own, and nobody could hurt me.'

'So that's why you ran away from us?' Christopher asks.

'It's why I wanted to lose myself in every book I read,' Penny admits. 'I wanted to escape reality and forget all the pain.'

'Sometimes, we all do.' Christopher reminds her.

'But then I met you guys…' Penny says, thinking aloud. 'You always came back…'

'Of course we did,' Dexter says.

'Maybe I am good enough to have friend, after all,' Penny mutters.

'Of course you are,' Millie cries, throwing her arms in the air.

Penny stares at her friends and a warm sensation of comfort rushes over her entire body. From telling her story, she suddenly felt lighter. If anything, Penny's allowing herself to be happy. She has friends who make her laugh and look after her, even when she didn't think she needed it. They love Penny for who she truly is. They were just as curious as her and always just as fun. This time, Penny doesn't want to run away.

'Is there anything we can do, Penny?' Millie asks.

A grin begins to grow across Penny's face. 'Right now? Stay with me.'

Christopher wraps his arms around Penny and holds her close. Millie slides over to her, hugging her brother and dragging Dexter behind her to do the same. The four of them hold each other close.

It's been a long time since Penny's felt all warm and fuzzy inside; that feeling that gives you goose-bumps and you embrace the butterflies that flutter in your tummy, when the love is shared. Whilst there were those who had left her before, there were those who had stayed. This time, Penny knows that her friends will never leave her. They will be by her side, just like Emily.

Family Reunion II

It's the end of another day in The Author's Library. After a steady day of book selling, Penny sits at the window-sill, watching the sunset with a steaming cup of tea in her hand. As well as wearing her pyjamas, she snuggles under the warmth of her duvet.

Even though she worked alone in the bookshop today, it didn't bother her and loneliness doesn't follow her around like a miserable companion. Penny knows that her family and friends are always there for her. For once, she doesn't try to lose herself in another story and the books on their shelves were treated like old friends. She clambered up the bookcases and watched from above. She rode on the back of her book trolley, weaving in-between the bookcases and picking up speed with her feet, letting the adrenaline run through her skin and hair. When she's reminded of the memories she shared with Emily, she smiles rather than trying not cry. She knows that her mum is smiling back at her.

It's been a month since Penny opened up to her friends and life has begun to get easier. Penny told them everything she found out about her family: What happened in the basement, who Bradley Figment was, the mystery of Robert Figment and Penny's grandad. Her friends were amazed that she'd managed to uncover it all.

Christopher decided to cut back on his hours of writing and helps Penny out on busy days. He's tall enough to reach the higher shelves and knows what books to recommend to customers; most are stories that Penny's pretended to have read. Even though she loves having Christopher around, she still doesn't know what to say to him. Sometimes, they'd give each other an awkward smile and there were awkward moments where they were in each other's way. Penny would sometimes watch him, as he studied the books on the shelf; she still thought he was gorgeous, after all. But Penny wasn't sure if Christopher still felt the same way about her and neither of them had spoken about it. She didn't want to be the first one to say anything.

Millie and Dexter still visited Penny on most evenings. They'd either watch a bad movie on a Friday night, sing karaoke or tell ghost stories until the early hours of the morning. On bad days, when Penny was overwhelmed with her anxiety and loneliness Millie would be there with a kind smile, a flask of hot-chocolate and a tin of baked goods at hand. Penny would cry on her shoulder and Millie would hold onto her best friend, until everything was alright.

Penny also started having regular catch-ups with Ivy. Over the past month, she hasn't been afraid to talk about her mum and if anything, it actually makes her smile, when she thinks about her. The first time Penny saw her godmother, she ran up to her and gave her a big hug. She almost knocked Ivy off her feet.

'What's all this for?' Ivy asked her, hugging her back.

'I wanted to thank you, for always watching over me.'

'I wasn't going to let my only goddaughter get herself into trouble, now was I?'

'Cup of tea?'

'Yes please.'

Nowadays, Penny always makes tea for Ivy, when she comes to visit. They always have a cup of tea and think back to happy moments with Emily. Sometimes, Ivy even helps Penny out in the shop.

Bradley still comes to visit Penny and introduced her to his husband, Edgar. Over time, they slowly got to know each other better. On one Saturday evening, they taught Penny how to paint. It was a very serene evening, even if Penny wasn't very good at it.

Of course, Nora still sees Penny every Sunday, arriving two minutes earlier as always. Only this time, she has Penny's grandfather on her arm and a pot of tea is always set for three. Nora always makes a fuss of her granddaughter and Michael reassures Nora that Penny's questionable fashion taste and curious ramblings are a reminder of Emily's spirit.

Last night, Penny hosted a gathering for all her friends and family. She summoned them to the centre of The Author's Library and laid out armchairs in a circle for everyone. Mr. Marblelight poured everyone a thimble of dark rum and cheers to the night ahead. Even though Penny despised the taste, she didn't care. She had warm, fuzzy feelings in her tummy just from being surrounded by her loved ones. Everyone was getting to know one another, almost as if they were one, big family.

'Hey, everyone,' Penny announced later on in the night, standing on her armchair and clinking her glass with her glasses.

'Goodness, Penny… That's going to collapse,' Nora cried, still smiling.

'I've got something to say,' Penny replies.

'Speech! Speech!' Millie and Dexter cried, in unison.

Penny cleared her throat, before speaking. 'When Mum died, I'd never thought I find happiness again. Emily used to say that two of us fit together like two pieces of jigsaw-puzzle, but without her I felt like a jigsaw-puzzle with a missing piece.

'Oh, Penny,' Ivy whispered, with tears in her eyes.

'But when I found my family, everything seemed to be ok. At first, it was scary but I'm so grateful to have you all here. I want to thank you for everything you've done for me. I've got more family than ever, even beyond being a Figment. Even when I pushed you and ran away and I'm sorry.'

'It's ok, Penny,' Mr. Marblelight said. 'We

understand.'

'I finally allowed myself to be happy, because I didn't want to be alone, anymore,' Penny said. 'I don't want my past to affect what will happen in the future. But I couldn't have done it without knowing you all.'

Millie threw her arms around Penny's legs, lifting her off the table and swinging her around, with tears in their eyes.

'We love you, Penny. Never forget that.' Millie muttered.

'I love you too.' When Millie puts her down, the two of them smiled at each other and giggled.

'Now that all the emotions are out of the way, shall we continue the party?' Christopher asked.

'Cheers!' Bradley said, raising his drink.

The rest of the night was filled with joy and laughter. Even when it came to an end, the fuzzy feeling in Penny's tummy stayed with her all throughout the next day and into the following evening.

So when Penny watches the sunset, she watches the burning colours of the sun disappear behind the hills. The sky begins to darken, welcoming the arrival of the early evening. Throughout everything, it has been a while since Penny took the time to watch the sunset. She forgot how beautiful it was until you watched it like a hawk.

'Penny?'

Christopher emerges from behind the bookcase, but Penny doesn't hear him and keeps her gaze on the evening sky. He calls out her name again, as he walks towards her, but Penny's mind is lost in the sunset.

'Penny?' Christopher asks, for the final time. He places a gentle hand on her shoulder.

'Yaah!'

Penny immediately jumps out of her trance. But before she realises that it's Christopher, she hurls herself around and holds out her empty mug, as a weapon.

'It's only me,' Christopher cries, jumping a foot back. 'You can put the mug down.'

As if it never happened, Penny drops the mug to the floor and huddles back into her blanket, hiding her blushing-red cheeks.

'Hi,' Penny mumbles. 'I didn't know you were here.'

Christopher chuckles and joins her opposite the window-sill. 'We thought we'd pop over and see you. I hope that's alright?'

There's a twinge of awkwardness, in his voice. Christopher looks down at his shoes and blushes beneath his beard.

'Of course it is,' Penny says, with a grin on her face. Christopher sighs with relief. 'Where are the others?'

'They'll be here, soon. I lost them amongst the

fantasy books. Dexter's trying to get Millie to actually read *Game of Thrones* this time.'

'How did you find me?' Penny asks.

'I knew exactly where to look. This was where I properly got to know you. When you told me all about your family mysteries. Where all the madness began.'

'It seems like it was so long ago. I can't believe I dragged you guys with me.'

'We wanted to come with you. It's how we all came together,' Christopher reminds her. 'You would've sent yourself mad, if you did it all by yourself. Which, almost happened…'

'Oh, God. Please don't remind me,' Penny mumbles, covering her face with her hands to hide the embarrassment.

But Christopher takes her hands into his own and gives them a reassuring squeeze. Penny giggles nervously, and her heart starts to flutter. Then, the smile drops off her face and looks out of the window.

'What's the matter?' Christopher asks, with concern.

'You guys have been so good to me,' Penny says. 'I just hope that I'm good enough for you…'

'Hey,' Christopher interrupts. His voice is soft but firm. 'Don't ever think that you're not good enough for anyone.'

'It's just when friends left, I always blamed myself. I always thought it was because I wasn't enough. But

Mum told me that they weren't good enough for me.'

'She's right, Penny. You've been my light at the end of a dark tunnel. You allowed me to let go and have fun. Before I met you, I was too wrapped up in the mistakes I'd made in the past. But when I was with you, I didn't need to feel ashamed. It was all down to you...'

'Well... If you want, you could stay here?' Penny says. She nervously plays with her hair and tries to avoid Christopher's gaze.

'Really?'

'Only if you want to. Stay here with me.'

Without saying anything else, Christopher tucks a strand of Penny's hair behind her ear. When she looks up at him, he cups her small face with his hands. He gradually draws her in closer and gently presses his lips against hers. Simultaneously, the two of them close their eyes and cling onto each other; living in the moment and never wanting it to end. In-between kisses, Penny smiles from ear-to-ear, with butterflies fluttering and fireworks exploding in her tummy.

'...The moody intellectual falls in love with the humble bookseller...' Penny mutters, not realising that she's speaking out loud.

'Wait, what?' Christopher asks, tilting his head in confusion.

Penny snaps her eyes open, wide. 'Nothing.'

'You are so strange.' Christopher chuckles.

'Thank you.'

'Ooohh!'

Just before they kiss again, Penny and Christopher break apart at the sound of Millie's squeals.

'It's happening, Dexter.' Millie flings her arms around her husband and shakes him up and down, almost lifting him off his feet. 'It's a magical moment.'

Penny and Christopher awkwardly giggle, before looking back at Millie and Dexter.

'I can see it for myself, Mills,' Dexter replies, holding onto her for dear life. 'But, please put me down. I'm going to be sick.'

'You found us, then?' Christopher asks, when Millie and Dexter join them, sitting cross-legged on the floor. He gives Dexter a confident smile.

'Don't think you can get rid of us, that easily,' Dexter teases.

'You guys are so cute together,' Millie announces to Penny and Christopher. She clasps her hands to her heart and sighs. 'It's almost like I predicted this…'

'Are you ever going to let us forget it?' Penny asks.

'Never.'

'But don't think that just because you're all lovey-dovey, your world's only big enough for the two of you,' Dexter tells them, pointing to himself and Millie. 'If you're gonna run away into the sunset, you're taking us with you.'

'Of course,' Penny replies. 'Wherever I go, I want you guys to come with me.'

'I don't have a choice in the matter,' Christopher grumbles, although he's still smiling.

'I love you, guys,' Penny says, confidently. 'You're more than friends, to me. You're the family I've chosen for myself.'

'Oh, Penny.' Millie gasps, wrapping her arms around her best friend. 'Love you, too,' she mutters.

'I'm not crying.' Dexter sniffles, quickly rubbing his eyes before shoving his glasses back on.

'Are you sure about that, Dex?' Christopher teases, looking at him up close. 'The only time I've ever seen you cry, was when we watched *Revenge of the Sith.*'

'For the last time, I've never cried during *Star Wars,*' Dexter says, playfully pushing Christopher away. 'I… I had something in my eye, that day…'

'Sure, you did…' Christopher mutters, sarcastically.

'Why don't we build a blanket fort?' Penny suggests, suddenly. 'That'll stop us from getting emotional.'

'Yes, yes, yes.' Millie squeals, as the two girls high-five.

'I was not getting emotional.' Dexter grumbles, but he nods.

'I haven't made a blanket fort in years,' Christopher admits, stroking his beard intently.

'We haven't built one for years because you always

took them too seriously,' Millie tells him.

'Mum and I used to make blanket-forts all the time,' Penny tells them. 'We'd have competitions and battles to see who could gain the most land. As well as who had the better-looking fort...'

'Building a blanket-fort is an art that should be taken seriously,' Millie announces. She jumps onto her feet and begins to pace up and down, with her hands behind her back.

'Blanket-forts are Millie's specialty,' Dexter mutters to Penny. 'She likes to be in charge and you never interrupt her.'

'We'll need a couple of duvets and lots of throws,' Millie mutters, under her breath. 'As well as many pillows and an army of teddy bears to protect us...'

'I can do that,' Penny cries, marching over to Millie and linking arms with her.

'The only problem is Mr. Analytical, over there.' Dexter points to Christopher.

'Me?' Christopher gives Dexter a confused look.

'Chris, please don't make this boring,' Millie groans.

'What have I done?'

'You always try to make every blanket-fort historically accurate,' Dexter reminds him, as he stands up and links arms with Penny.

'Oh, God,' Penny groans, disgusted but still smitten. 'Please don't over-analyse this.'

Christopher marches over to his sister and links

arms with her. 'Well, it made sense to include authentic medieval battlements, with realistic structure. It makes it more believable...'

'Here he goes again,' Millie grumbles.

'It's a good job you're pretty,' Dexter mutters, to him.

'Let's go!' Penny declares, leading her gang into the depths of The Author's Library.

Soon enough, the group stand in the middle of the bookshop, with as many blankets and pillows that they could carry down from Penny's flat. For two hours, they mark out the territory of their blanket-fort, stretching it out as far as possible and as high as they could reach.

Penny hangs several blankets across the bookcases, holding them in place with the heaviest hardbacks that she could find. She places multi-coloured sofa cushions at all the exits of blanket-fort, to prevent any monsters from invading. Christopher helps by making sure the blanket-fort is as high as possible. But just before he can secure it into place, he and Penny secretly kiss again, the moment just as magical as the last. As he goes to hold her in his arms, the blanket falls on top of them.

'Shit,' Christopher mumbles. His cheeks flush red. 'I forgot I was holding that up...'

'It doesn't matter,' Penny says, softly.

They try to kiss again, but jump into the air when they hear Millie's orders shrieking in the distance.

Penny giggles and takes the blanket off the both of them, watching Millie pad out the floor and crying demands. All while Dexter vertically drapes more blankets, to build up the walls.

'Don't be ridiculous, Dexter,' Millie shrieks, playfully hitting him with a cushion. 'That's going to fall down! Hang it up, there…'

'It's a good job I love you… You know that, right?' Dexter reminds her, sarcastically. The two of them giggle and have a quick kiss, before getting back to work.

Eventually, the four of them stand proudly at the entrance of their blanket-fort. They all high-five each other, and clamber inside; crawling through their fortifications before sitting in a huddle, in the centre of it all.

'Can we stay here forever?' Millie asks, with a triumphant sigh.

'That would be amazing,' Christopher says, lying down with his hands behind his head.

'I don't think I would've done it without you,' Penny admits, resting her head in Millie's lap.

The four of them are so exhausted that they all fall asleep pretty quickly. Penny falls asleep on Millie's lap and eventually, Millie lays down with her limbs sprawled out. Meanwhile, Christopher gently shuts his eyes and falls asleep, with Dexter sleeping at his feet, hugging Christopher's knees without realising.

They sleep peacefully, until the early morning. But

when Christopher slowly rolls over in his sleep, he accidentally drags the blanket-fort down with him. Instantly, everyone wakes up startled as their fortress of pillows and blankets topple over them.

'Aagh!' Penny wrestles a blanket off her face. 'Good morning.'

'Our blanket-fort clearly wasn't strong enough,' Christopher grumbles, slowly sitting up with a case of serious bedhead. When he looks at Penny, he kisses the top of her head. 'Good morning.'

'How did you sleep?'

'As well as I could, in the middle of a blanket-fort.'

Penny gives him a kiss on the cheek and Christopher puts his arms around her. As she snuggles into his arms, he pushes her unruly hair out of her face, revealing her blushing cheeks. They quickly kiss each other, before Millie and Dexter can catch them.

'Good morning,' Dexter grumbles, as he slowly emerges from a sea of blankets. 'What happened here?'

'Who destroyed our fortress?' Millie objects, sitting up and crossing her arms in frustration. 'Come on, own up. Who was it?'

'Not me,' Penny says.

'Me neither,' Dexter states.

'Err…I don't think it was me,' Christopher replies.

'It might be one of the ghosts,' Penny says. 'Maybe they didn't want us staying in our blanket-fort forever…'

'No more ghost stories, please,' Dexter cries, sticking his fingers in his ears.

Eventually, the four of them dismantle the blanket-fort and Penny makes them a cup of tea, as they sit by the window.

'Are you going to open the bookshop today?' Christopher asks.

'I probably should…' Penny replies, dreamily. 'But I'm having so much fun with you guys…'

'Have you ever thought to go exploring?' Millie asks. 'See what lies beyond your bookshop?'

Penny looks out at the rolling hills and the forests that lie for miles beyond The Author's Library. It's the perfect weather for going on an adventure; there's a slight sunshine poking through the clouds and a light breeze that wafts through the trees. She notices that the tress gently sway in different directions and the leaves are the same colour as a phoenix's wings; every branch leaning towards the sun, almost inviting her outside.

'I don't know,' Penny finally admits.

'Have you ever wanted to find out?' Dexter asks.

'Mum and I had always wanted to have our own adventure outside the bookshop.' Penny sighs and leans back against the bookcase. 'But that never happened.'

'Why don't we find out?' Christopher asks.

Penny looks at her, utterly speechless. 'For the last

two years, I never wanted to venture out. I always wanted to stay in my bookshop, where the stories are.'

'But there's a whole world to explore, out there,' Christopher tells her. 'More stories to discover.'

With high amounts of confidence, Penny grabs hold of Christopher's hand and gives him a triumphant look. 'Let's do it.'

'Someone's going to have to look after Christopher, though,' Dexter says

'I'll look after Penny if you look after him,' Millie suggests.

'I don't need looking after!' Penny and Christopher say, simultaneously. They look each other and then burst out laughing.

In the space of ten minutes, Christopher, Millie and Dexter stand at the front door, ready to leave.

'Hurry up, Penny,' Millie calls out.

'Do you think she's gotten lost?' Dexter asks.

'Penny wouldn't get lost in her own bookshop, Dex,' Christopher replies.

She eventually emerges from behind the bookcase, clutching a large flask of hot chocolate. Penny's dressed in a blue-spotted raincoat, purple and yellow striped wellies and a rainbow bobble hat. She has a wide grin on her face, as she looks at her confused friends.

'What?' Penny asks them.

'What are you wearing?' Christopher asks.

'What's wrong with what I'm wearing?'

'You don't leave the bookshop much, do you?' Dexter asks.

'Not really, why?'

'We're going for a walk in the English countryside. Not trekking through the jungle through monsoon season...'

'I love your wellies,' Millie giggles.

'Where's your sense of adventure?' Penny asks Christopher and Dexter. 'You don't know what we could encounter...'

'You might scare away a few squirrels with your questionable fashion sense...' Dexter mumbles.

'Can we get going?' Millie taps her foot impatiently.

Before they set off, Penny opens the door and Tiny-Dancer saunters in. He clambers up the bookshelf, before jumping onto Penny's shoulders.

'The cat's coming too,' she declares.

'Of course he is,' Dexter grumbles, sarcastically.

But just before they step outside, they're suddenly greeted by Nora, Bradley and Mr. Marblelight.

'What's happening here?' Nora asks, as they hobble inside.

'We're going exploring, Grandma.' Penny tells them, proudly.

'I'll keep her safe,' Millie reassures them.

'Someone has to, sometimes,' Mr. Marblelight mutters.

'You're going to leave the bookshop, unattended?' Nora says.

'I'm not opening the shop at all, today,' Penny admits.

'I beg your pardon?' Nora scoffs. 'You've been closing the bookshop an awful lot, recently...'

'I'm seeking the cry for adventure.'

'You're dressed so loudly, you could be seen from a mile away,' Nora says, stifling her laughter.

'Well, why don't you guys looks after the bookshop today?' Penny asks her grandparents and Bradley.

'So you can get yourself into trouble?' Nora says.

'We're only going for a walk in the countryside,' Christopher says.

'I haven't worked in The Author's Library, for years,' Bradley says, with a sigh in his voice. 'Why don't we spend the day here?'

'Only if you're up for the job?' Penny asks her grandma, swinging the keys around her fingers.

'Penny, I've been working in this bookshop for much longer than you.' Nora quickly grabs the keys from her granddaughter, but still flashes her a grin. 'Go on and have fun on your unruly adventure.'

'Bye!' Millie heads out of the door, dragging Dexter behind her and soon followed by Christopher. Nora, Mr. Marblelight and Bradley slowly venture into their beloved bookshop.

However, Penny stops, just before she walks out of

the door. She looks back one last time

'I'll be back.' She thinks. 'I'll always come back. There's always a story if you know where to look.'

The End.

Acknowledgements

Writing *The Author's Library* was one of the biggest challenges I've ever faced, but I'm so happy to finally share it with you all. I have so many people to thank:

First of all, I want to thank my family for always being so supportive and giving me a push in the right direction. They have always known my love for writing and I would never have finished my book if it wasn't for their encouragement.

I also want to thank my friends, who have always stuck by me, through it all. The importance of family and friendship was what inspired me to write *The Author's Library,* in the first place.

A massive thank you to my partner, Zach. He has been my rock for a long time and has heard me ramble on about this book for so long! I would read chapters to him down the phone and he helped me correct anything that was historically inaccurate.

Thank you to Sarah Barton (@theartybarty) for creating such an amazing book cover! I absolutely love what you've produced and you were also a wonderful illustrator to work with.

Also, a thank you to my editor, Deborah Blake. You are incredible to work with and for providing an excellent editing service, especially for a first-time author, like me!

I'd also like to thank all my BETA readers who took the time to read the beginning of *The Author's Library.* It might have been a long time ago, but it gave me the confidence to keep writing.

A thanks to John Hemmings and Ashley Hickson-Lovence for giving me advice on writing. Much appreciated!

Thank you, Amazon KDP for giving me the platform to self-publish my book.

I also want to express my love for every bookshop I've ever been to. There's something magical about stepping inside a bookshop and years spent buying books was definitely an inspiration for me to write *The Author's Library*.

Finally, dear reader. Thank you, for taking the time to read *The Author's Library*. I hope you enjoyed reading this book as much as I enjoyed writing it.

Love Carrie.

About the Author

Growing up, Carrie was always coming up with stories and her love for books has never changed. She has a degree in Classical Studies from UWTSD Lampeter, focusing on Greek mythology and ancient Greek literature. During her final year, she loved to write stories and began writing *The Author's Library* after she graduated.

Nowadays, you can usually find her snuggled up with a good book and a cup of tea. She's also been blogging since 2015 about books, musings of life and anything that she finds curious. Carrie also loves to travel the world when she can and is always seeking the next adventure.

Carrie Duggan currently lives in London. This is her first book.

Instagram: carriedugganwriter

Blog: weareallmadhere97.wordpress.com

Printed in Great Britain
by Amazon

65901659R00187